# THE DEAD SPY'S GUIDE TO ESPIONAGE

DAVE SINCLAIR

# EVA DESTRUCTION RETURNS!

Forget James Bond.

Forget Jason Bourne.

When the world's on the brink of a second Cold War, the only
person to call is Eva Destruction.

After a bombing in a Russian embassy, the murder of a CIA agent
in Budapest, and an attack on MI6 itself, Eva assembles a team of
Cold War veterans and puts the pedal to the metal in a race to
prevent chaos on a global scale.

With twists at every turn, she'll do almost anything to bring down
those responsible—except drink instant coffee.

*The Dead Spy's Guide to Espionage* is a globetrotting, fast-paced
thriller that will keep you turning pages well into the night.

Note to the reader: Although the Eva Destruction novels can be read in any order, *The Dead Spy's Guide to Espionage* follows on directly from the end of *The Amnesiac's Guide to Espionage*.

*For Kristi*

# CHAPTER ONE

Strolling down leafy Bayswater Road, home to London's embassies and upmarket eateries, Eva Destruction finally felt her head clearing after her last mission. Although she still bore the scars and bruises, her body was healing. But her mind had some serious catching up to do.

She pulled out her phone, but before she could make the call, it rang. The caller's number was blocked. Reluctantly, she answered.

"Hello?"

"Hello, Eva."

She knew the voice. Intimately. She was too shocked to answer.

"Miss me?"

"No." Her voice was a block of ice.

The man who had put her through so much. The man who had tormented her dreams for years. The man who had bought her a castle.

"How can you be so calm when your pants are on fire?" he asked.

Eva ground her teeth. This man was the last person she wanted to speak to. He had manipulated governments and corporations and tried to reshape the world as he saw fit.

"Aren't you meant to be in a deep hole somewhere, Harry?"

"Me? No, you must have me confused with someone else." The casual tone grated on her.

"What do you want, Harry?"

"To hear you say you miss me too."

"Not going to happen."

"Then I'm upset."

"Diddums."

Just as she managed a measured breath, the Russian embassy exploded, engulfed in a giant fireball. The orange and black of the explosion was in direct contrast to the stark blue sky. A second explosion blew away a section of the front wall. Billowing black clouds belched from the huge building.

Eva staggered towards the chaos, phone pressed against her ear. Harry was still on the line. When he spoke, his voice was flat and emotionless.

"We need to talk."

The acrid smoke stung Eva's lungs. As she stumbled down the road, the serene street was rocked by more blasts from the embassy. She grabbed a lamppost, pausing to catch her breath as she tried to make sense of the chaos. Flaming debris surged skyward as dense smoke descended over the exclusive neighbourhood like a dark hood. Another explosion blew out the gothic windows and fractured the massive building's façade. Black clouds billowed from the embassy.

A cacophony of screams and car alarms assaulted Eva's ears. The wave of heat carried with it the stench of singed paper, carbonised chemicals and burnt flesh. Panic-stricken people darted in all directions, either blaring orders or hysterically screaming. The magnitude of destruction was massive, the devastation wrought on human life would be far worse.

There would be many dead. Some would be dying at that very moment. Screams of pain were gurgled and silenced soon after. From the front entrance a charred human form staggered out, still smoking and barely human. It collapsed on the front lawn with a thud. It didn't move. A nearby woman screamed.

Barely able to hear the person yelling on the phone she realised she held to her ear.

"Eva! Are you there? Eva?"

She hung up.

Eva didn't need to talk. She needed to act. She ran towards the chaos, ready to help the injured. This was not her first crisis. Far from it. In fact, it seemed to be her life now.

A young Asian couple were huddled in front of a pram. Their baby screamed as they scrambled to undo the straps.

Eva skidded beside them. "Is your child okay?"

The man lifted the child and carefully patted him, checking for injuries, then sighed with relief. "Yes, just a little shocked, I think."

The child's mother shook her head, staring at the unfolding chaos. "Who would do such a thing?"

That was a good question for another time. Right now, Eva needed to move. Distant sirens sounded – help was coming. Without another word, Eva ran towards an elderly couple a few metres away. The woman had a cut above her eye, but was still standing. Eva used tissues to stem the bleeding, and the woman's companion gave Eva a dazed but thankful smile.

With her hand still on the woman's forehead, Eva took in the damage. One whole side of the building had been blown away. The front façade seemed to have been ripped from the structure.

Charred paper floated lazily in the smoke-choked air. Figures lay unmoving on the gravel driveway, pools of blood spreading beneath their prone bodies. Eva knew she couldn't go inside. Contrary to popular belief, embassies aren't the sovereign territory of the represented state, but the Russian Federation still wouldn't take kindly to outsiders rushing in, even in an emergency. Especially if they knew Eva worked for MI6. Besides, she couldn't do anything to help those motionless bodies.

But that wasn't the most disturbing thing.

Harry had called right before the explosion. She'd told him never to contact her again, and he shouldn't have been able to. The maximum security prison he was locked away in did not allow outside phone calls.

Worse, Harry hadn't seemed at all fazed when the explosions occurred. In fact, it had almost seemed like he expected them.

"We can hire you out to disrupt foreign governments—we'll make a fortune."

"Not funny, Paul."

Eva sat in Paul Cavendish's office at the SIS Building at Vauxhall Cross. He was dressed in his usual three-piece Tom Ford suit. Paul was Eva's MI6 handler, and also one of her very best friends. He was the first person Eva had called after the embassy bombing. Now they sat on opposite sides of his large mahogany desk eating Jaffa Cakes, the only food he had in his office. He could be so British sometimes.

"You're a trouble magnet, Evie. If we could just figure out a way to monetise it, we'd be as rich as Croesus."

Paul wasn't being crass, he was trying to cheer Eva up. For once, it wasn't working. The horrors she'd seen made cheering up an impossibility. Images of the dead, the charred and the screaming would haunt her for a very long time.

There was one piece of information Eva hadn't shared with Paul yet.

"There was a phone call."

"A what now?" Paul asked, taking another bite of his biscuit.

"Harry." Eva took a deep breath. "Harry called me. Right before the explosions."

Paul calmly placed the uneaten portion of Jaffa Cake back on the plate. "You're going to have to repeat that, Evie, and slowly."

Eva recounted the brief conversation in detail. She had been walking through Hyde Park clearing her head after her last mission. He hadn't said his name, but he hadn't had to—she'd known immediately who it was.

"You're sure?" Paul asked, his face now bereft of his previous good humour. "The explosion came first, and then he said you needed to talk? He didn't ask what the noise was?"

"No, that's what made me suspicious. Any sane person would have been mid-convo, heard an explosion and asked, 'oi, what was that?' But he just ploughed on. In fact, he may have... never mind."

"No, tell me."

Eva traced a pattern on the armchair. "It's nothing, really."

"Evie, you have the best instincts of any agent I've ever known. Spill."

She sighed. "I think he actually waited for the explosion before saying we needed to talk. Like it would add gravitas or something. He always had a flair for the dramatic."

"That's all?"

"Yeah. I hung up after that."

Paul nodded, then picked up the phone and called His Majesty's Principal Secretary of State for Justice. It was the importance Paul's position held. He asked the cabinet minister to personally look into Horatio Lancing's whereabouts. Only Eva knew him as Harry. The Principal Secretary asked for a few minutes.

While they waited, the pair sat in silence, drinking tea and munching on biscuits.

Eva's ex was once the most dangerous man on the planet. As far as most of the world was concerned, the head of the Lancing Corporation had simply vanished. His disappearance had become legend, right up there with Jimmy Hoffa, Harold Holt and Amelia Earhart. There was a time when Harry, the richest man in the world, had threatened that every government on Earth must care for their citizens or he'd unleash all their dirty little secrets. That stunt put him on every news service in the world. Some hailed him as a saviour, a man of the people; others regarded him as a Machiavellian villain of the highest order. Then suddenly, before anyone had made up their minds ... nothing. Harry disappeared.

The disappearance of Horatio Lancing had launched countless conspiracy theories. Only a few people knew his exact whereabouts. Eva was one of them. She was the one who'd brought him in.

What made the memory of Harry so painful was she'd loved

him like no other man before or since. She'd always had a weakness for bad boys, and she'd fallen for the baddest of them all. The emotional scars still ached.

Before Eva could throw herself a fully-fledged pity party, Paul broke the silence. "He didn't say anything directly about the explosions?"

"No, not directly."

"Or suggest that what he wanted to talk about had anything to do with them, or Russia, or anything of the sort?"

Eva saw where this was going. "No. I know it's a hunch, Paul, nothing more."

Paul nodded and took another bite of his biscuit. "I'm not dismissing it, Evie. Your hunches are better than most people's facts, but right now we have nothing else to go on, so let's keep it under our bowlers unless something else turns up."

They descended into silence once more. The phone startled them both. Paul answered. "Uh huh," he muttered into the mouthpiece, then hung up.

"The Principal Secretary states unequivocally that Lancing is still in high-security custody and has no access to any telephone or internet connection. She's unequivocal about it, Evie. Lancing is locked up tighter than a platypus' pocket, as you Australians say."

"We never say that," Eva said with a smile, which soon disappeared. "Then how did he—"

"I don't know. A question for another time, maybe."

Eva frowned. She couldn't accept this. Not fully. She knew Harry's voice. It haunted her dreams. He had definitely phoned her. Not only that, he'd done it at the exact moment a major diplomatic furore erupted. That wasn't a coincidence. But like Paul said, that would have to wait. There was work to be done.

"There's something going on, Evie. This is the second major incident targeting a former superpower in two days. It's beginning to smell fishier than a hatful of badgers."

"Wait, the second?"

"Two days ago a US diplomatic attaché, we suspect CIA, called Mark Field was found dead in suspicious circumstances in

Budapest. Police arrested a known GRU operative working out of the Russian Consulate. If this escalates any further, the West will be on the brink of another Cold War."

Eva let out a low whistle. "I take it our priority is to find out what happened to the Russian embassy?"

"Like I said, Evie, you have great instincts."

"What's next, boss?"

Paul tugged his vest down and adjusted his Windsor knot. "We figure out who's behind the bombing and punch them in the taint."

"Sounds like fun."

Eva spent the next several hours charging from one MI6 department to another. Paul was briefing the new Chief of the Secret Intelligence Service and bringing her up to speed. He'd asked Eva to liaise with the appropriate teams before the interdepartmental briefing. She spoke to departmental assistants and a few department heads from every single group, except Sanitation. Which was a shame—the people in that group had more insight than some of the department heads she spoke to.

Normally after an assignment like Eva's last one, she would be prescribed a mandatory leave of absence. But in the aftermath of the bombing, MI6 offered no such luxury. The organisation was on the highest alert since 9/11, and the second highest since the end of the Cold War. Ministers were baying for blood, and the opposition was screaming at a government not yet fully formed after the ramifications of Eva's last mission. The country was teetering, and someone was trying to push it over the edge. Eva wasn't going to let that happen.

The UK government wasn't the only one in crisis. Russia was still destabilised after its small civil war a few years back. Eva knew all about it, mainly because of her ex, Harry, had engineered it. It was only thanks to Eva that the entire world hadn't suffered a similar fate. Harry was the reason she'd become an MI6 agent in the first place. It always seemed to come back to Harry. One day she would step out of his shadow. She hoped.

Eva returned to Paul's office and sauntered in without knocking. She flopped into the overstuffed leather chair and put her feet up on his desk. To anyone else, this would have been an affront to protocol and a gross violation of the chain of command. To Eva it was a Tuesday.

Paul strolled over to his wet bar and poured two cups of Earl Grey. He handed one to Eva without asking, and nodded for her to report.

"After an exhaustive survey of all department heads, I can categorically say that the collective knowledge the Secret Service has on this could be placed in a particularly small thimble. And there'd still be plenty of room left. Nobody knows a thing. Not a single MI6 department, not MI5, not a foreign agency—donuts. Although Florence the sandwich lady reckons it was, and I quote, 'The fucking Krauts', but I think she's on the sauce again."

"There's no sandwich lady called Florence," Paul said, stony-faced.

"But it would be sweet if there was, right?" Eva smirked.

Her friend simpered, appearing pleased with himself. "Only if she had an eyepatch and called everyone Fruit Gum. And her name was Doris."

"Damn, Doris would have been better."

Paul winked and asked for a detailed rundown of Eva's discussions. After being brought up to speed, he stood and said, "Come on then."

He hadn't touched his tea.

"Come on where?"

"The interdepartmental briefing," he stated matter-of-factly.

"Me?" Eva glanced down at her clothes. She hadn't changed since the explosion, and was hardly dressed for such a high-level briefing. "Shouldn't I change?"

"Don't you ever change, Evie. Come on."

If Eva was given to daunt, the meeting would have been daunting. The head of every department at MI6, several governmental lackeys and the brand-new Chief of SIS were all crammed into the largest briefing room MI6 had. There were far too many blue ties for Eva's liking. Fortunately, the smaller number of women present held their own, and added extra intelligence to the robust discussion. Unfortunately, the main gist of the meeting was as per Eva's briefing to Paul—nobody knew anything.

What Eva did learn from the meeting was that people were rattled. The experts in the intelligence community were worried. And in Eva's experience, when the smartest people were anxious, everyone else should be, too.

Forensic investigations were still ongoing, and the Russians were cooperating, to an extent. The new Chief commented wryly that the Russians would rebuild the embassy but seemed determined to have enough material left over to restore the iron curtain.

Paul's input was brief but insightful, due in no small part to Eva's information-gathering exercise. As he spoke, it became evident why he'd sent Eva out to talk to all those departments. There were good reasons he held the position he did. Paul never entered a meeting if he didn't already have all the answers. He may never have been a field agent, but that was only because his skills lay elsewhere.

Throughout the meeting, Eva kept her mouth closed, which was a rarity in itself. The fact she that was there at all was surprising. She'd never been involved in such a high-level discussion. Was Paul grooming her for greater things? Was she destined to be more than just a field agent? Eva was never arrogant enough to be too ambitious. She knew her intellect could be used in different areas, but she was smart enough to know she had a lot to learn.

The meeting concluded with the promise of further briefings. Paul nodded, indicating that they were done, and Eva gathered their notes. From behind them, a polite cough caught their attention. Eva turned to see the grinning face of her fellow field operative, Bishop.

The suave new arrival leaned over and said, "How did you enjoy the little get-together?"

Bishop was smoking. Well, not actually smoking, but he was always so debonair he *looked* like he had a cigarette in his hand, like an old-time movie star. He looked like Cary Grant, with Frank Sinatra's swagger. Three-piece suit, tailored to perfection, chiselled jaw, blonde cropped hair and an incandescent smile. Who was Eva kidding? Bishop was smoking hot.

"If you want, we can have our own private get-together later on." Bishop's Cheshire-cat grin was luminous. "I'm thinking candlelight, a nice violin concerto and I've just procured quite a reasonable deal on some industrial-strength massage oil."

Eva let out an annoyed sigh. Unfortunately, while Bishop had a nice arse, he also was one.

"Bishop, your hebetude is surpassed only by your vaingloriousness."

Bishop scowled. "You're in so much trouble when I get my hands on a dictionary."

Paul sighed and shook his head. "You two can flirt in your own time." He pointed to the front of the rapidly clearing room. "The Chief wants a quick word. I'll meet you in ten minutes, if you can keep your hands off each other for that long."

"I can do ten minutes," Bishop said with a hopeful raise of his eyebrows.

Eva frowned. "You know that's nothing to brag about, right?"

She motioned for Bishop to follow her out. The two had been partnered on several missions together, and worked exceptionally well as a team. They'd saved each other's lives more times than Eva could count. He may have been an arrogant sexist, but he was *her* arrogant sexist. Bishop was all talk, at least when it came to Eva. He knew his boundaries, even if she did have to remind him every so often.

As they walked down the sterile halls of MI6, Bishop's attention remained on Eva. Normally, his gaze darted between everything in a skirt like a kid with ADHD in a toy store who'd been given a truckload of sugar and a Red Bull. But not today. In fact, it had been some time since he'd mentioned a conquest. Perhaps he was maturing. Maybe he just wasn't telling Eva. For some unknown reason she suspected it was the former. An even crazier thought was that he was doing it for her. Freud would call that Projection.

Leaning towards Eva, Bishop inhaled deeply. "You smell good."

"Thanks, I use both nostrils." She groaned. "Is there something I can help you with, Bishop, or is it my turn to bring you up on a sexual harassment charge this week?"

"Unfortunately, it's all business." He straightened his perfectly straight tie. "Trev asked me to finger you."

"I'm sure he didn't use those exact words."

Bishop's eyebrows seemed to dance off his head. It was like they had a mind of their own. Eva was sure they weren't the only part of Bishop that had a mind of its own.

"When does he want to see me?"

"Now."

Trev was like the photographic negative of Bishop. Not what you'd call handsome, but he was polite, respectful, and wouldn't know flirtation if it wore a stripper's outfit and slid down a pole in front of him.

Deep inside his IT cavern, he was hunkered down in a dark underbelly of Vauxhall Cross. Trev had recently been promoted, following his key role in Eva's last assignment, but his change in rank hadn't affected his workspace cleanliness. Large headphones on, he was surrounded by four screens, endless computers in various stages of disassembly, and dozens of discarded disposable coffee cups. A few of the cups were from Eva's coffee shop, Kanga Brew.

"You know, you should really buy a re-usable cup, dude," Eva said playfully. "There's an entire forest here."

"Eva!"

Trev spun his chair in surprise, but as he shot out of his seat to greet her, his head was yanked back by the cord on his headphones and he went sprawling to the floor. Eva raced to help him while Bishop leaned against the doorjamb and shook his head.

Collapsing into his chair, Trev turned as red as a sunburnt tomato. He spluttered a series of frantic apologies.

"No worries, Trev, seriously." The poor kid had a crush on Eva and must have been deeply embarrassed. Eva moved on to save him further humiliation. "Bishop said you wanted to see me?"

"Oh yes." Trev bounced in his chair and reached for a Lancing computer pad. He traced his finger about the screen. "I came across something while I was running a program. The station chief in Saint Petersburg asked me to run a decryption program on a cipher he received about an hour ago."

"Cipher?"

"A typed letter was sent directly to the station chief. Hand delivered by a clueless courier. Signals knew I'd been working on a cipher program, so asked me to have a look."

"Typed?" Bishop asked. "As in… typed?"

"On a typewriter, yeah." Trev's face lit up. "Totally retro."

Bishop frowned. "Why would Signals send it your way?"

"They've been a bit miffed because I've been working on my own decoder program. We went head to head." Trev's face lit up. "I cracked it before they did. The lads in Signals owe me a six pack of Guinness's finest." His grin enveloped his entire face. "It was a way old Soviet VIC cipher used in the 50s. Apparently uncrackable back in the day. It's only recently that some boffins worked out the enciphering algorithm. Because, like, you have to know the algorithm to crack the cipher, yeah? My program has this one, and thousands more. It cracked this code in, like, ten minutes."

"That's all fine and good, Trev," Eva said, "but what does a typed letter in Saint Petersburg have to do with me?"

Trev tilted his head and scratched his elbow. "Well, it was addressed to you."

"What was?"

"The cipher. The message."

"Me?"

"Yeah, check it."

Trev held up his pad. The screen was split in two. On the left was a typed letter using Russian Cyrillic script; on the right was the translation. The message greeted Eva formally by name and proceeded to advise her that the author of the letter had critical information regarding the bombing of the Russian embassy in London.

"What's this bit?" Eva asked, pointing to the screen. "It says that in exchange for the information, they want to defect."

Bishop stepped forward and scooped up the pad. "They what? Nobody defects anymore."

Trev spun on his chair while staring at the ceiling. "Well, whoever wrote this wants to."

Eva shook her head. "Do they want smoking for the whole family, radioactive toothpaste and a ride on Sputnik, too?"

Trev shrugged. "Don't know. But you can ask them when you see them."

Eva stared at him blankly. "What?"

"Down the bottom. They ask for you to meet them personally. Even tells you where, when and a secret phrase and everything. Totally the most spy thing I've ever seen."

"Why ask for me?"

Trevor shrugged. "You'll have to ask them. I'm nothing but a lowly IT desk monkey."

With a grin, Eva said, "That's what you say now, but don't forget I owe you a night on the town. That could all change."

Trev went red all over again.

Bishop frowned. "A date?" There was a distinct hint of jealousy in his tone.

"Totally not a date, but I promised Trev I'd treat him to a night out to thank him for his stellar work," Eva said, beaming. "As a woman of her word, I fully intend for our friend here to have a night that will blow his mind."

For Trev, that could mean two shots in a bar and a sideways glance from a pretty girl.

"Glad you're all working hard."

All heads turned to Paul, who loomed in the doorway.

"How did you find us?" Eva asked.

"The Chief advised me of the message. It took all my deductive reasoning and years of training to figure young Trevor here would be keen to pass the information on."

If Trev could have sunk any further into his seat he would have descended all the way through to New Zealand. There was no malice in Paul's voice, merely a statement of fact, but poor Trev didn't know Paul was messing with him.

"So when do I head to Saint Petersburg, boss?"

"You're on the first flight out tomorrow."

"And if they genuinely want to defect in return for information about the bombing?"

"Then we give them tea and crumpets and their choice of rooms at Buck Palace."

# CHAPTER TWO

---

"Gandalf the beige?" Eva shouted, holding up an almond milk flat white.

In the tight confines of Eva's café, a tall bearded banker type wearing an ill-fitting taupe suit, ten years out of fashion, stepped forward. With a smile as sincere as a real estate agent's Christmas card, he took the coffee and left. The afternoon crowd at Kanga Brew was beginning to thin and Eva wiped her coffee-stained hands on her apron. Business was good, and she was in her element. Her place. Her people. Well, except for that banker guy.

A few stuffed shirts at MI6 had initially protested at the idea of an agent operating a side business. That was until Li Wei fell in their laps. Li was a recently promoted envoy from the Cultural Attaché division of Cultural Affairs for the People's Republic of China. He was also spying for the United Kingdom. He passed on state secrets to Eva via her café. As far as anyone looking on could tell, half an hour earlier Li had purchased a coffee, just like every other worker in central London. Nobody had seen the two trade reusable coffee cups with USB sticks hidden inside.

Never privy to the information being passed back and forth, Eva was content knowing her café played a central role in obtaining top-secret information from the emerging superpower. Plus, she could still make kickarse coffee. Win/win.

Her offsider and now part-owner, Anchor, the big Swedish Goth/skateboarder, was on a date with an "up-and-coming" (read: unemployed) West End actor. She wished him well, but given Anchor's dating history, it was probably doomed to fail. She hoped this one would work out. Anchor was one of Eva's favourite humans.

"Oi, coffee wench, don't be a ghoul and make me one of ye flat whites, ya big eejit!"

Eva laughed. The newcomer was a short Irish firecracker, and on the very top of Eva's list of favourite humans. Nancy was her best friend in the world. She had once referred to Eva's coffee as "God's semen". Eva still wasn't sure how she felt about that one.

The two women embraced, and Eva's recent stresses faded away. Nancy knew her better than any other person alive. She'd witnessed her previous dating disasters, and even seen a few up close and was still probably emotionally scarred. Like the time Eva went on a second date with a guy and made it a double-date with Nancy and her husband. All was fine until they noticed the guy was stealing all the cutlery. Later, he claimed he had a phone call and went outside to take it. He never came back. They later they realised it was Nancy's phone he'd taken.

Nancy and Eva had recently had a big misunderstanding, but thankfully the two had patched up their quarrel. Now they were back to looking out for one another, exchanging low-level abuse and sharing each other's lives—to a point.

Eva was happy to have some time with Nancy, something she'd sorely missed in recent weeks. Together, they closed the café and cleaned up, then sat down with a well-earned coffee and chatted like only old friends could.

"You'll never believe what my arsehat of a husband has done now."

Eva snorted. "Did he accidentally buy a pedigree greyhound that turned out to be five hamsters in a dog suit?"

"Close. The fecken eejit got a," Nancy used air quotes, "'great deal' on Russian caviar, despite the fact that neither of us had even tasted it. It arrived yesterday."

Eva winced, guessing what was coming. "Was it Russian?"

"Russian? Feck. It wasn't even caviar. Best I can make out, he spent a hundred quid on shit. Literally. Fish shit."

Eva laughed until it hurt. She loved Nancy's stories about her hopeless husband. It was a side she didn't get to see every day. While the two were as close as best friends could be, there were two things Nancy didn't know. The first was that Eva was a spy for MI6. The second, and probably more difficult, thing was that Nancy's feckless husband was Eva's boss, Paul. Nancy probably still thought Paul worked for the Treasury. That said, Nancy was extremely smart and may well have figured out that Paul's sleepless nights weren't related to the UK's trade deficit.

"Given the problems with Russia at the moment," Eva said, "it's probably best you didn't get the real deal in the end." As soon as she'd said it, she wanted to move on. Catching up with Nancy was meant to take her mind off work, not remind her of it.

"Bah," Nancy replied. "Some twat lit a gas stove wrong at the embassy and people are talking like it's the Cuban Missile Crisis. This will blow over by tomorrow."

Eva's mind was flooded with images of the explosions and dead bodies littering the embassy grounds. As a spy, she'd been working on her poker face, but her best friend must have seen a change

"What?" Nancy's face turned sombre as she saw Eva's face. "I was only joshing. I know it's serious." She patted Eva's hand. "London's seen bombings before, love, we'll be right."

Eva nodded, and did her best impersonation of a cheery disposition. "How's work?"

Nancy was an administrator at HSBC. She swayed between having a love/hate relationship with her role and a hate/hate one.

Nancy sneered. "Ugh, a nightmare as usual. Sometimes I just wanna…" She mimed holding a hand grenade, taking the pin out with her teeth and tossing it, "… into Steve's office and walkin' away, ya know?"

Eva nodded, only half listening, still haunted by lingering images of the bombing. "Except you'd probably lose all your teeth."

"What?"

"The grenade. Pulling the pin with your teeth would most likely lead to your teeth being pulled out completely. Modern grenade pins are designed to be difficult to pull out, to avoid accidents, so you'd have to pull really hard with your teeth to get it out of the grenade."

Nancy stared at her for a moment. "How on Earth would you know that?"

Jolted back to the present, Eva realised what she'd said. "Ah, I read a lot."

Nancy frowned. "Yeah, I know, but I didn't think Kafka covered modern weaponry."

"I don't know. Some of the passages in *The Trail* were the bomb."

Her friend laughed politely at the feeble joke, but Eva saw cogs working in the back of her friend's brain. She'd have to be more careful if she was going to keep her friend away from her dangerous profession.

Thankfully, Nancy moved on. "So, who's the new one?"

Tilting her head in confusion, Eva asked, "New what?"

"New bloke," Nancy said with a smirk. "You've always got some pleb lined up to break your heart and/or clear out your bank balance. I swear to god they could do a study on you. It could be called 'suicidal dating rituals'."

Eva sipped her coffee. Nancy really did know her better than anyone else.

Eager to change the subject, Eva changed the subject. "So, it's still stressing you out? Work, I mean?"

It was Nancy's turn to lose her joyous demeanour. "Yeah, doesn't seem to be letting up. Bloody need a holiday. Want to head somewhere exotic with me?"

Eva could have laughed out loud. In just a few hours she'd be heading off to Saint Petersburg to find the author of the message.

That was pretty exotic, but not exactly the boozy girls' getaway Nancy was angling for. Eva was pretty certain Paul wouldn't agree to send his wife along on a mission that reeked of Cold War espionage.

For the first time, Eva wondered how the old Russian cipher had affected Paul. He had an unpleasant family history with Cold War spies. His father had been executed by the KGB in Warsaw in 1982. It was one of the biggest scandals of the Cold War. One MI6 operative killed, another disappeared—some say defected. The whole thing had been named after the missing agent: the Amanda Bourke Affair. The scandal was never resolved, and had led to wild speculation over the years. Did Amanda Bourke defect? Was she killed? Had MI6 or the CIA staged the whole thing?

One thing Eva knew for certain was that Paul had become a spy even though his father had lost his life to the Service. That said a lot about him. He never spoke of it, but Eva knew he still railed against the ghost of his father. The extra dedication, having to know everything before he stepped into briefings, the ridiculously long hours—Paul's commitment wasn't just because his position demanded it. The spectre of his lineage hung over him like a shroud, and he was determined to be more than the son of a dead agent. Paul wanted to forge his own destiny. It was a struggle Nancy knew nothing of.

"I wish. I'm pretty damn stressed at the moment, myself," Eva said.

Her friend looked at her curiously. Eva hesitated, eyeing her friend cautiously, then jiggled her empty cup. "Can I get you another?"

Pulkovo Airport was more modern than Eva had envisaged. She shouldn't have been surprised. After all, this wasn't the USSR; Saint Petersburg was a major tourist destination, and had once been the home of Russian royalty. It was a city of art, opera and culture. The modern architecture of the airport terminal was vast and striking, with plenty of high-end shops, if only Eva had time to be distracted. She didn't.

Having passed through immigration, she hustled down the concourse, eager to make her rendezvous. Bishop lagged behind, playing her hopeless partner, for anyone who happened to be observing. He'd insisted that their cover be a married couple. Eva's compromise was that they'd been married for years, so wouldn't need to be fawning over one another, much to Bishop's disappointment.

They wore matching outfits: puffy black hiking vests, black fleece jackets and cargo pants. Even their luggage matched. If anyone was watching they'd assume they were a couple of tourists ready to take in the sights. But that was the thing: if anyone was watching. Eva still had her doubts. What did a sixty-year-old cipher in Saint Petersburg have to do with the bombing in London? And why not pick up the phone? Send an email? Post something on social media? Hell, even SIS had a Facebook page now.

To Eva it felt like a wild goose chase. If the mission was a wash, she'd take a few days to soak in the city and enjoy the small break she definitely needed. She could clear her mind with a stroll or two down the many rivers and canals the city had to offer. Or pay a visit to the stunning Winter Palace, where Catherine the Great used to hang out to recharge her depleted batteries. But that was only if the whole thing turned out to be a waste of time, which was a big *if*. Someone had gone to a lot of trouble to reach out to her. Eva had to be alert and ready. Spies never fully relaxed.

She checked the time on her phone. "I think the car rentals are this way."

"Oh, so we're talking now," Bishop replied. "That's good." His voice dripped with sarcasm.

On the flight over she'd completely ignored Bishop. She'd popped in her earphones almost the moment they'd been seated. It had been a deliberate choice. Some might even call it self-preservation. Eva's chat with Nancy had reminded her to keep away from men who were no good for her. Bishop was a New York cheesecake with caramel fudge sauce and Oreo crumb topping. Delicious, sure, but the last thing she needed. Eva chose to focus on important things, things that made her happy. Like dresses with pockets.

"Lyle," Eva started, using Bishop's alias for the mission. She'd chosen it herself. "We have a lot going on at the moment, so let's focus on the task at hand."

Bishop nodded, but his face showed that he was far from convinced. "Fine, but I think we need to talk. Although I'm not sure what we need to talk about."

He was right. They really did need to talk. It was just that Eva didn't want to. Not now. She nodded in reply, but remained mute.

After a few moments of walking, Lyle/Bishop rolled their luggage to a stop. "I need to spend a rouble."

Without waiting for a reply, he proceeded to the men's toilets. Eva stood next to a mature couple with the exact same luggage that she and Bishop had. She gave them a weak smile and placed her bag to the right of theirs. The couple didn't return her greeting. Eva checked her phone again. They still had time to make their appointment, but couldn't dawdle.

After a few minutes, Bishop emerged. Eva picked up the bag on the left and headed towards the car hire desks, the subtle exchange completed. They now had their weapons and surveillance pack.

Several minutes of stilted English later, Eva had the keys to a BMW. She was thankful it wasn't a Lada; they wanted to make their meeting. The BMW was the highest performance vehicle the company had, and you never knew when you'd need the horsepower.

Using the GPS as their guide, they made their way towards the city centre. Saint Petersburg felt like the imperial capital Eva had expected. It was a city of monuments and palaces. It was also a city of death. Nearly two million people had died in the battle for the city during World War II. The mid-morning sun reflected off Saint Isaacs' golden dome, but under the bright sunshine and wide welcoming streets, blood soaked the city's very foundations.

She also knew it was a strategic city, mainly due to the year-round access to the Baltic Sea. Russia's first warships had been built there. The country's kings and queens were buried nearby. As Eva drove, she lamented the fact that she couldn't spend more time in this fascinating city, built from the imaginings of Peter the Great.

She soon realised that she had even less time to admire the sights than she'd thought. She checked the rear-view mirror again to confirm she wasn't imagining it.

*Womble spunktrumpets.*

"We've got company."

Eva grinned at the cliché. She used to use that phrase back in her home town of Melbourne in her youth, as a joke to liven up boring drives. Back when she broke the law instead of defending it. In those days she didn't hire cars, she stole them. That was where she'd gained her killer driving skills. She suspected she was about to need them.

Bishop was suddenly alert, checking his own mirrors. Behind them, a darkly-tinted black Lexus sedan sat low on its tyres, meaning it was either carrying a lot of passengers or was heavily armoured. Possibly both. It had been trailing them for about five kilometres, being careful to stay exactly three cars behind, no matter how much Eva sped up or slowed down. She'd taken an alternative road just to be sure, but the Lexus stuck with her. They definitely had a tail.

Bishop pulled out his phone. "I'll call it in." He quickly contacted the local station chief and advised her of the situation and their location, then hung up and kept his eye on the shadowing vehicle.

The five lanes of Moskovsky Avenue provided plenty of space, but the heavy traffic limited manoeuvrability. The tram line and strip of grass dividing the traffic gave the street a picture-postcard feel, but limited sudden changes in direction, and their lack of knowledge about the city's streets put them at a disadvantage.

Sitting straighter in her seat, Eva didn't take her eyes off the mirror as she asked, "Do you have the weapons pack?"

"Yes."

"Good."

"It's in the boot," Bishop said, gesturing towards the rear of the car.

Eva spared a second to glance at Bishop. "That's handy."

"Isn't it?" Bishop reached into his jacket. "I do have this." He held up a pistol.

"That won't do much."

"You'd be amazed what I can do with the right equipment in a tight spot."

Eva gave him a sideways glance. "No, I wouldn't be surprised at all."

They shared a sly smirk, but their expressions soon became sombre.

"What's the play?" Bishop asked, his seriousness matching Eva's.

"We make sure we don't get our bond back on the car."

"Do it."

"Hold onto your cocks, people."

She dropped down a gear and the engine howled in protest. Eva ignored it; she needed the extra torque. She wished rental companies offered manual cars, they gave far better control, but she'd work with what she had.

Taking her foot off the accelerator, Eva yanked the wheel hard to the right, crossing two lanes of traffic, and threaded past a taxi and a Mercedes. With centimetres to spare, Eva guided the BMW through a gap in the trees then straightened out on the unoccupied tram lane. She stamped on the accelerator, and the car lurched forward with a roar.

The gap behind them widened as the Lexus fought to mirror Eva's radical manoeuvres, but it was only a few moments before they too were on the tram lane and gathering speed.

Bishop tapped his window with his gun. "Should I take a shot?"

"You don't strike me as one to discharge first, Bishop."

He grinned his lady-killer smile. "You're right, of course. I always like the other party to release first."

"Good boy." Fast approaching a tram, Eva kept the car's pace and readied herself to make the next move. "Plus, we don't know if they're friend or foe."

"Friends usually say hi first." He held his pistol at the ready. "And I don't know about your friends, but mine don't usually engage in high-speed pursuits without asking politely."

"You need better friends, dude." Eva glanced at the clock.

Their meeting was in less than twenty minutes; they didn't have time to waste. With no way to communicate with whoever had sent the message, if they missed this window there would never be a second chance. It was unlikely that whoever sent the message was behind the tail. Why send goons to chase them through the streets when they already knew their final destination? But whoever their pursuers were, they had to lose them.

Tamping the accelerator, Eva surged the BMW forward and around the tram. Sliding back into its lane, she slowed to match the tram's speed, staying only a metre in front of it. The tram driver frantically rang the bell in distress, gesturing wildly with his hands. Eva gave him a friendly wave.

She'd lost sight of the vehicle pursuing them, just as she'd intended. The driver of the Lexus couldn't know Eva's intentions. Was she going to stay on the tram line or whip the car right to re-join the traffic? If he bet wrong, he'd lose her for sure.

The snarl of the Lexus could be heard over the clang of the tram's bell. It was coming on the left, and fast.

"Gun," Bishop yelled.

Eva saw it too, a silhouette on the passenger side. That sealed it. She hit the accelerator just as the Lexus came into her peripheral vision. It sped up to match. Eva couldn't see the driver's face through the tinted glass, but she was sure they weren't happy with her. That wasn't about to change.

As the Lexus drew level with the BMW, Eva tapped the brakes. The tram driver doubled his frantic bell ringing and slowed hard. The Lexus pulled ahead. As its rear wheels aligned with the BMW's front ones, Eva yanked the steering wheel and gently tapped the Lexus's side, steering into it. She stamped the accelerator to make sure the Lexus' bumper didn't slide off. Its rear tyres lost traction and skidded on the grass embankment. Eva decelerated to give it space as the driver of the other vehicle fought for control. He lost. The car spun, fishtailing wildly. It clipped a tree and savagely flipped several times before sliding on its roof between the two sets of tracks.

Eva hit the brakes and she and Bishop exited the BMW. Bishop covered the wreckage, aiming his weapon at the smoking Lexus, while Eva lost precious seconds scrambling to the rear of the car to extract a snub-nosed submachine gun. The MI6 agents approached silently. No orders were issued; the two moved as seamlessly as lovers, covering each other while keeping their weapons trained on the threat.

They needn't have bothered. The Lexus contained only two occupants: a burly driver and passenger. Both were unconscious, but alive. The tram kept well back, but Eva had no doubt the driver would have called it in. They didn't have much time.

A screech of tyres caused Eva to glance up. A brown Volvo pulled up on the roadside beside them, causing the cars behind to honk in protest. The two occupants exited the vehicle. It was the couple they had traded luggage with at the airport. They exchanged nods, but no words, then all four MI6 operatives carried the two unconscious bodies to the Volvo, where they were unceremoniously thrown into the back seat.

The older man slammed the car door shut, then gave a bow. Their captives were secure.

"The safe house is nearby," he said with a Midlands accent. "We'll let you know what they have to say."

Eva patted the man's shoulder in way of thanks and ran back towards the BMW. She didn't have time to think about how they were going to extract the information. She had a rendezvous to make.

The cipher had stated that the meet was at the Church of the

Saviour on Spilled Blood—because why meet at the Tea Rooms of Friendship and Hugs? The church was as ominous as its name. A mishmash of baroque and neoclassical styles, if the architects had been aiming for creepy and imposing, they'd hit the mark. As Eva walked along the Griboyedov Canal towards the imposing façade, she checked her communications gear.

"Testing, testing, flamingo, foxtrot, Winnebago, frotting, over."

Bishop sighed. "Flamingo and foxtrot start with the same letter."

A storm was approaching from the east, and the streets were relatively empty, save for the occasional tourist taking photos of the church against the rapidly darkening sky.

The entrance to the church was dominated by a pedestrian square. Eva walked briskly, carefully eyeing every individual in the piazza.

Smiling, she said, "And frotting, don't forget frotting."

"I don't even know what that means."

"Best to look it up at your next family gathering."

Bishop seemed keen to get on with the mission, but after the car chase through the city, Eva needed a little distraction. Their pursuers had unnerved her. What else was going on that she didn't know about?

Bishop had suggested calling off the meet, but Eva refused. She was built of stronger stuff. The men in the car may or may not have been there because of the message, but Eva doubted they were the ones behind it. Within moments, she hoped to find out who was.

Eying the imposing towers and intricate religious decoration, Eva couldn't help being impressed. Subtle it wasn't, but it was striking. Eva's mind wandered. She still had a fair distance to cover. Maybe one more little distraction.

"There's something we need to talk about..." Eva began.

If Eva was honest with herself, the car chase had rattled her. Time was precious. She didn't want to waste the limited time she had left on this planet. Which was probably *very* limited, given her profession.

"Can it wait?" Bishop asked. "We need to focus."

"This helps me focus. So," Eva gulped. Why was it easier to talk over a securely encoded link than face to face? "Look, I've been thinking. A lot. There are certain things you said during the last mission that got me thinking…"

"It's *this* mission you should be thinking about. Three o'clock, nun alert."

In a hushed voice, Eva asked, "Did you just say 'nun alert'?"

Over her shoulder a gaggle of nuns approached surprisingly fast. What was the collective noun for a bunch of nuns? A habit? Murmur? Prey? Eva vaguely remembered something about super-fluity. She vowed to look it up when she had the chance.

There was no need to explain to Bishop why she'd gone silent as she walked towards the church; he was watching her through binoculars in the car. He'd have an eye on her every step of the way. Once she was inside the church, he'd stay in contact, and proceed into the church only when necessary. The other operatives, the older couple, were meant to have been in the church already, but now that they were tasked with the interrogation, Eva was on her own.

"You're now live with Ops, Eva," Bishop said in her ear.

So much for her intimate chat with Bishop. Eva imagined a room full of blue-suited middle-aged men sipping tea and listening to her every word with disdain. It probably wasn't far from the truth.

Striding up to the church, Eva wondered if she needed to cross herself or something. Was that what people did for this kind of church? She should have researched it. Eva half suspected she'd burst into flames. Given her history, it was a distinct possibility. She and God had parted ways many years before. He never wrote.

As Eva crossed the threshold into the church, all flippancy was erased. The church itself was quite literally breathtaking. The incredibly high ceilings were decorated in conversely minute detail on a grandiose scale.

The church had been given its feelgood name because it was

built on the site where Alexander II was assassinated. Thinking about that failed to ease Eva's unsettled mood.

A deep exhale focused her mind. She was here on a mission. Game on.

As instructed, Eva made her way past the altar. Thankfully, the weather had seen to it that there were few tourists about.

The roof was dominated by mosaic icons with images of the patron saint of the Romanov family. It was striking. Eva walked past the rows of candles and took a seat on the front pew. There was a smattering of worshippers among the pews, but only one in the first row; an elderly priest, hunched with age. His features were worn, his back stooped, and he swayed back and forth, praying. He fumbled for a large hanky and wiped his grey-whiskered face. Eva was reasonably certain this wasn't her contact. He wasn't exactly Russia's James Bond.

Eva waited patiently for five minutes, eying off anyone who approached. But no one sat in the front pew. Checking the time on her phone, Eva feared she'd missed the meeting. Cursing herself, she stood to leave.

But she didn't. She glanced at the old priest to her right, and sat back down. There was a grandfatherly vibe about him. His features were plain—even when he was younger, he would have been quite unremarkable. His face was so unmemorable it seemed to slip from your brain, as if made from Teflon.

In other words, he was the perfect spy.

Eva leaned over and asked the man in English, "Do you know if this church was used for worship?"

The old man let out a dry cough. Once he recovered, he said, "It was, once, but was long time in past."

His accent was thick. Very Russian.

Eva recounted her next line. "A shame. People seem to have forgotten the old ways. There is much to learn from the past."

The man glanced at her for the first time. His bright blue eyes were in stark contrast to his weathered winkled face. "There is Russian proverb, past is for God, future for Tsars."

Their code having been exchanged, Eva knew she was now face

to face with the person who had brought her to Saint Petersburg. The man who supposedly had information about the London bombing. Not having expected to get this far, Eva was lost as to what to do next.

She leaned over to the man and said, "Brezhnev had some awesome eyebrows."

He shook his head in slight confusion. "That is not part of code phrase."

"I know, I was just making an observation."

An amused grin further creased his already crinkly face. "This is funny, I think."

Eva tried to imagine what the man would have looked like in his younger days. He would never have been handsome, always destined to be nondescript and as plain as a bag of flour. Unlike Bishop, who could stand out in a crowd by standing still.

Eva shifted closer to the man, but faced the altar as she spoke. "So, you're real."

"Da."

"You asked for me to come to Saint Petersburg, I came. You're up."

The old man coughed again and stared into space. Eva didn't know if he was choosing his words carefully or creating a dramatic pause.

"Is he miming his answer?" Bishop asked in her earpiece.

She ignored him.

"I am ex-KGB." He paused and frowned. "Well, I guess everyone is ex-KGB these days, da?"

Eva let him talk.

"You want my name, yes? That is way of things. I am Alaksiej Barinov." He turned to face Eva. "My friends, if any were left, called me Alexie."

The sound of typing came through Eva's earpiece, followed by a loud sigh. "MI6 have no Alaksiej Barinov on file."

As if in reply, Barinov tilted his head and pointed a stumpy, calloused finger to his ear. "Tell little buzzy voice in ear to search under 'deceased'. If does not work, tell them look for codename

Englishmen gave me. They called me …" There was a pause again, but Eva sensed this was due to embarrassment, rather than for dramatic effect. "Red Scorpion."

Eva frowned approvingly. "It's a better codename than Fluffy McCuddles."

"I did not choose name. It is childish machismo name, I think, da?"

Choosing not to answer, a hush fell over them while Eva waited.

"Holy—" Bishop began, then proceeded to supply a series of grunts, which didn't help Eva in the slightest. She waited for actual words. "Eva, if this was thirty years ago I would be yelling at you to run, but that'd be kind of redundant because you'd already be dead. This guy," he let out a low whistle, "if he did half of things attributed to his codename he was one dangerous son of a bitch. Assassinations, sabotage, stealing state secrets, engineering Marxist revolts in South Africa, Red Scorpion did it all. Christ, Eva. MI6 were after him for years. We had him passing away in Prague in '91. Guess the record needs an update."

So the old man was less grandfatherly than he appeared. Unless your grandfather was Carlos the Jackal.

Silence swirled around them as Eva reassessed the apparently deadly man beside her.

"Thank you for coming to Leningrad, Miss Destruction."

"Leningrad? That's a bit old school, isn't it?"

The elderly man shrugged. "Is Russia, everything is old school."

"If you want old, why not call it Saint Petersburg?"

Alexie shrugged. "Why not Petrograd? You see, my city has had many identities, it is unsure of its true identity. The city and I are very alike, I think."

"Ask him why he wants to defect," an unfamiliar voice asked over the earpiece.

Eva wanted to nod, even though there was no one to nod to. "Tell me, Alexie, if you love your city then why ask to defect? You know that's not really a thing these days, right?"

A glint in his eye shone as brightly as the light hitting his gold tooth. "I am an old man. I wish to die somewhere not depressing, not where old women dress like tractor."

Eva chuckled, but didn't interrupt him.

He went on. "But I have lived this long by knowing when threats are real, and when they are imagined. The threats are real. This bombs in London, and you know of killing in Budapest? This is just start. More bloodshed is coming. We can stop. In exchange, I live somewhere nice, with ducks."

Eva was surprised he knew about the CIA agent who'd been murdered in Budapest. It hadn't been reported on any news service. She had to stop being so surprised by this man.

"You seem well informed for an ex-KGB agent."

"I have ear to grindstone."

"I think you'll find the saying is 'ear to the ground'."

"I know. Is joke."

Was he deliberately trying to keep her off balance? Probably. He'd been in the spy business before she was a drunken twinkle in her father's eye. Eva must have seemed like she was in kindergarten to him.

"Eva Destruction, it is long time since I have done right thing. Is time I did."

"Is that the only reason?"

"No." He leaned forward. "I wish to spend rest of days with plump English lady who cooks me sausages and calls me 'Dumpling'."

Eva had no idea if he was being serious or not. He had a killer poker face.

"Alexie, do you know anything about a tail we had from the airport?"

"You were followed?" Alarm crossed his features. "We must act quickly. If they know we are talking, none of us are safe." He looked ready to run.

"The two goons are on ice for now, but before we go anywhere, we need some information. First things first." Eva scratched her shoulder. "Why me? Why not just tell the embassy what you have to say?"

Tilting his head, Alexie squinted at Eva. "You do not know? This is interesting to me I think. You are the person to tell, Miss Destruction. It is all connected."

"What is connected?"

"The events. They are all linked."

"To what?" Eva asked, not wanting to hear the answer.

He leaned forward. "To you."

"I don't understand."

Alexie rubbed his grey-stubbled face. "No. I expect you do not. But like lady on first date, you do not give everything up at once, no? I am same."

With a clenched fist, Eva tried to keep her emotions in check. This man was equal parts charming and frustrating. But Eva also sensed an underlying danger to him. There was something about him that made her hope she never got on his wrong side.

As if sensing her mood, Bishop whispered over the link, "Take your time. We'll get to the bottom of it."

"Fine," Eva said, not hiding her irritation. "How about you let me know how you know who I am?"

"Do you have saying, once spy, always spy?"

"We have something similar, yes."

He said nothing further, but threw up his hands as if to say, *there you are.* Eva couldn't decide if he was being cagey or if she was being played. How was this old man so well informed? Why the cloak and dagger routine? How did this supposedly dead KGB agent know about the bombing and murder in Budapest when even her agency was in the dark? There was far more going on than Eva knew.

"So, you can supply these things I ask? You will bring me back with you?" He waved at Eva's ear. "What does little man in ear say? Have agreement?"

As if on cue, the unfamiliar voice from before said, "You are approved to proceed, operative Destruction. We authorise you to extract him. As long as he gives us a name."

"My superiors are willing to make a deal," Eva said as she raised a finger, "but only if you tell us who is behind this. You give us the name, we take you back with us. Not the other way around, you understand?"

"Da. I understand. I might be old to your eyes, Eva Destruction, but I am not senile. I have mind like steel sieve." He tapped his temple. Upon seeing Eva's confused face, he said, "Is another joke."

"Uh huh."

"But you want name. Is fair. I will tell you. But first you tell superiors I would like Lakes District. It very nice. I only need small cottage. Near a lake, with ducks. I am simple man. You tell them this."

He'd obviously thought this through. Eva nodded. "You just did."

"Da. This is good." The old man rubbed his face again. For the first time, Eva saw hesitation in his features. Why come this far only to hesitate?

"The man who blew up embassy, he wants to start new Cold War. We need to stop him."

"Who? Who is it, Alexie?"

For the first time she sensed fear in the man. He glanced about the church nervously, then leaned forward.

In a hushed tone, he said, "His name is…"

# CHAPTER THREE

"Harry Lancing," Eva said in the calmest voice she could manage.

The guard stared at her, stony faced. "Could you repeat that, please?"

They stood in the 'Supermax' maximum security wing of Wakefield Prison in West Yorkshire. Eva thought that was redundant. If the prison was maximum security, how could you have more maximum? What was more than maximum? The tautology had obviously made sense to someone.

Before her was, ironically, a Lancing computer pad with a flashing cursor asking for the inmate she wished to see. Eva had tried "Harry Lancing'" and "Horatio Lancing", but neither had shown any results, which was why she'd asked the guard.

"What makes you think we got Lancing here, Love?" He scoffed, then snapped his fingers. "Wait on, my mistake. I think I saw 'im in the parade ground this morning. Yeah, yeah, I totally did. 'e was playing marbles with Al Capone and Lord Voldemort." He shook his head. "Is this a prank? Did Terry put you up to it? Is this because of the sandwich thing?"

"That will be all, thank you Justin."

They both turned to a seasoned, grey-haired man standing

rigidly straight in the doorway. His eyes were as dark as his skin. He wore no uniform, but a crisp suit and tie. Eva assumed he was the warden.

"If you could issue the lady with a pass, I will take care of it."

The guard shrugged, as if to say *I just work here*. His fingers hovered over the keyboard and he glared at her. "Name?"

"Eva Destruction."

The guard peered over his glasses and groaned. "Now I know someone's winding me up. You can tell Terry I never touched his bloody sandwich, and if he thinks he can—"

"Just process it, thank you Justin," the warden said in a tired, even voice.

With a grunt, the guard did as requested and practically flung the lanyard at Eva. The warden jerked his head towards the door and Eva followed. As they walked down the stark white hallway he said, "I'm Warden Wooley. I apologise for my man back there. Mr Lancing's incarceration has not been widely disclosed, for obvious reasons."

Wakefield Prison was nicknamed "Monster Mansion" due to the large number of murderers and other undesirables who resided there. It was Western Europe's largest prison, and had a reputation for being harsh and unforgiving. The abundance of wings must have been the reason Harry had been imprisoned there. Placing him in a smaller, less secure prison might have aroused suspicion. The man was still officially MIA. In Wakefield, Harry could be hidden among the cracks, at the mercy of the large prison machine. If Eva didn't know what he'd done to end up here she might feel sorry for him. She knew, and she only had slight pangs of guilt. Or that might have been the airport burrito she had for lunch.

As soon as Alexie uttered the words "Horatio Lancing", Eva's world turned end over end. Yet again, Harry had asserted his influence on her life. Would she ever be free of him?

There was a time, a brief, glorious time, when Eva loved Harry Lancing. The thought of it made her ache, not from regret, but from knowing what she'd once had and lost. She suspected few people experienced that sort of intense love—a blinding, all-encompassing passion that devours the soul whole. Harry had been her life. The fact that he was the richest man in the world was irrelevant. She would have followed him into the jaws of hell even if he was a penniless pauper.

But things had soured when Harry began to change. Eva didn't know why at the time, but it was the beginning of the end when she found out about his clandestine schemes. No longer the loving man Eva had known, he became secretive and distant. She'd been the one to walk away, but it hadn't ended there.

There was the stalking, and sending armed men into her apartment if she dared take a man home. You could only put up with so many terrified naked men before it crimped her already shaky love life. Then of course there were the worldwide stratagems to manipulate every government on earth to bend to his will. Harry had genuinely believed he was helping the world, although the world leaders begged to differ. In the end, while Eva could understand why he was doing what he did, she'd chosen to stop him.

Two years ago Eva had been recruited by MI6 to find her ex-lover. Few believed she'd succeed. That he was locked up now was proof that you should never underestimate Eva Destruction. She'd thought it was all done with. That was until Harry's phone call, and Alaksiej Barinov.

The information Alexie claimed to have was enough for the higher-ups at MI6 to authorise extraction. The former KGB agent said it was only the beginning. It had justifiably scared enough senior officials to grease the wheels of officialdom. How he knew Harry was behind the bombing, what specific evidence he held and how he had come to be in possession of those facts were details that Alexie would supply only when MI6 had upheld their end of the bargain.

Eva wanted more information, but she was overruled. Alexie had been rushed to the British consulate and issued with a fake passport. He, Eva and Bishop took the first flight out of Saint Petersburg. Upon landing, Alexie was immediately whisked off to a safe location and Eva had been driven straight to Monster

Mansion. Bishop had wanted to go with her, but she'd refused. This was something Eva had to face alone.

The two brutes who had pursued them through the streets of Saint Petersburg turned out to be little more than goons-for-hire. They apparently had no idea who had hired them or why. All they had been tasked with was to tail Eva and Bishop at all costs. They were aiding MI6 in trying to trace the payments, but nobody believed it would amount to much.

There were still numerous questions, many of them about the man Eva was here to see. How had Harry manipulated events while in prison? If he hadn't, then how did he know to call Eva at the exact moment the embassy was about to blow up? Had he organised the murder of a CIA agent? If so, how? And if he was behind it all, the biggest question was why? To what end? Also, how had Alexie come across information about Harry, and more importantly, what was it? Eva's head spun at the sheer volume of uncertainties. She needed answers. She needed to see Harry.

The warden halted at what appeared to be more of a bank vault than a door, it was so heavy and secured. On the keypad he typed in a ten-digit code, leaned forward and scanned his retina. Finally, he breathed on a small receptacle, then a tiny green light buzzed and a series of loud clicking sounds emanated from deep within the fortified door. Eva was surprised the door didn't take a DNA swab and insert a rectal thermomotor. With a heave, the warden opened it, and motioned for Eva to follow.

The next corridor was saturated with cameras and sensors of all descriptions. Heavily armed guards were posted every thirty metres. Security was tighter than a backup dancer's pants. How had someone managed to slip Harry a phone under this sort of surveillance? It would be impossible to hide one without being discovered in three seconds flat.

Finally, Eva was shown to a single white door. She expected the warden to follow, but he remained by the desk, standing to attention. He assessed Eva up and down, and did not appear to like what he saw.

"I don't know what sort of connections you have," he sighed, "but I would appreciate it if you could inform the Principal Secretary I run a tight ship and don't need to be second-guessed by anyone."

Offering no reply, Eva opened the door and entered. The room was dimly lit. Before her was a single wooden chair, and in front of that, a window. On the other side of the window was a vacant chair. With nothing else to do, Eva sat and waited.

What was she going to say? Would she be able to make any sound at all? What could she say to the man who had once been her everything? Could she interrogate someone she'd once loved so completely? Eva knew Harry had a way about him, a way of twisting her thoughts until everything he said made all the sense in the world. Had she grown enough since they were last together to withstand his charm?

Eva jumped when the door on the other side of the window creaked open and a lone inmate walked in. He was obscured by the gloomy light. The figure was thinner than when Eva had last seen him, but had the familiar foppish hair and childlike grin. He sat before her and smiled.

"Hello Eva."

Eva stared at him for the longest time. Her lips snapped shut, unable to say a word. She stood and pivoted on the spot, then without explanation, she yanked the door open and left.

The warden straightened his back and appeared startled when she appeared. Ignoring him, Eva marched past the security desk and back the way she had come. The warden scrambled after her.

"What are you doing? You came all this way, went through all the checkpoints..."

Eva took out her phone and found the contact she needed. Reaching a heavy security door, she clicked her fingers at the warden to open it while she waited for the other party to answer.

When they finally did, Eva simply said, "Paul, we have a problem."

They certainly did. The man Eva had seen through the secure glass, the man who had gazed into her eyes and said only two words: it wasn't Harry Lancing.

~

"You're sure?" Paul asked.

Eva wished he could see her sarcastic expression over the phone. Of course she was sure. The man she'd gazed lovingly at thousands of times was not the same man who had stared back at her from behind the prison glass. It was a damn good replica, Eva had to admit. Presumably some poor bastard had been paid a ridiculous amount of money to undergo surgery and become Horatio Lancing 2.0, but Eva had seen through it in less than a second.

In Harry's favour was the fact that he had once been a recluse, an enigmatic figure who had run an empire yet avoided the public's gaze. There had been only a few press conferences and the occasional interview, so there weren't many images of Horatio Lancing floating about. That must have made installing a doppelganger that much easier.

As the government car raced through traffic to London, Eva fumed.

"So who's the fellow in his place?" Paul asked.

"Don't know. Gary from Accounts? No fucking idea. The point is, he escaped, Paul. We don't know how long ago, but he's out. Alexie said Harry was behind it all, and the fact that he's not in prison, that he called me when he did…"

Eva couldn't finish the thought. It was too much. In an ideal world, the memories she had of her ex would be pleasant ones. The time spent with him had been the happiest of her life. She wished she could focus on the good, remember how empowered she'd felt when she moved on and left. But unfortunately, Harry Lancing had a way of ensuring that life was never simple. She'd been caught by Harry's gravity and pulled into his orbit once again.

Watching the landscape speed past, Eva asked, "What now?"

"I wrangle some things to assign you to this case. You found Lancing once, I have no doubt you can do it again, Evie. That is, if…" Paul let the question hang, unuttered.

"Do it, Paul. I'm ready. Don't you dare put another operative on this. I'm fine. Whatever's going on, Harry's up to his neck in it. I know him better than he knows himself. I'm fine."

Eva was so convincing, she almost believed herself.

"Very well," Paul said. "While I get the ball rolling on that, there are a few things I need from you. Li Wei has signalled that he's ready for another drop. This one's a priority, apparently, so I'll need you in the café in an hour. While you're there, we have Alexie staying at Buckingham Gate…"

"Fancy," Eva interrupted, thankful for the change in topic.

"…and need you to escort him into Vauxhall Cross."

Eva grinned for the first time. "You want me to bring a KGB agent into MI6 headquarters?" She whistled. "There are a few old spies who would be spinning in their graves right about now."

"Ex-KGB. In light of the Lancing thing, the number of interested parties has increased exponentially. Barinov is the hottest ticket in town. Makes sense to bring Mohamed to the mountain."

Not entirely sure that was the correct idiom to use, Eva let it go. Alexie did seem to be the key to the whole thing. Without him, MI6 would still be in the dark about the embassy bombing, the government would be under the impression Harry Lancing was still locked up, and the governor of Wakefield Prison would still have a job. They had to find out what Alexie knew and how.

More importantly, at least as far as Eva was concerned, she needed to find Harry Lancing and end his influence for once and for all.

"I thought English drink tea?"

Eva chuckled as Alexie strolled into her café. "Ah that was before they tasted my coffee."

A perplexed expression crossed his face, and only multiplied when Eva walked around the counter, put on an apron and started making coffees as if she owned the place.

Looming next to him was a ridiculously over-muscled

weightlifter in a suit. He was Alexie's MI6 escort, who had delivered the former KGB agent from his hotel to Eva. It was as if someone had overstuffed a cheap suit with tennis balls. The big brute nodded to her, and in reply she bowed her head, acknowledging that the exchange of Alexie had taken place. Without a word, the escort turned and left, apparently under the impression words were overrated. Either that or the steroids had locked his jaw.

Alexie still wore the same shabby suit he'd worn on their flight out of Saint Petersburg. He carried an old tattered briefcase under his arm; the only luggage he'd brought with him. Eva assumed there was some sentimental attachment, because it appeared ready to fall apart at any moment, held together by electrical tape and stubbornness.

She was thankful she'd been tasked with taking Alexie on his final leg into MI6. The thinking was that he would feel more comfortable entering the belly of the beast if he had a friendly face by his side. Besides, she was warming to the gruff former KGB agent.

Watching Eva expertly manipulate her beloved La Marzocco, Alexie tilted his head and asked, "You work in shop?"

"I own shop." Tilting her head in Anchor's direction, she added, "Well, part own".

Eva introduced Alexie to her business partner as an old family friend. The sweet Swedish skater was clearly confused when the "family friend" spoke with a thick Russian accent and not an Australian one, but had the good manners to not to mention it.

While Alexie sipped on his coffee in the corner of the café, Eva caught a glimpse of Li. When he reached the front of the line he ordered a coffee like everyone else, and handed over his re-usable coffee cup. Feigning it slipping from her hand, Eva swapped the cup for another, completing the switch. She made his coffee just like she would for any other customer, and handed it back to him without fanfare.

After serving another dozen or so customers, Eva made herself a latte and took off her apron. She sat down next to Alexie.

"I have two question," he said. "First, how did you learn to make such good drink?"

"I grew up in Melbourne." Eva was thankful for the compliment. "We obsess about caffeine more than we do about sport, and that's saying something. You either live coffee or you're banished to the decaffeinated badlands."

Alexie nodded as if Eva's response made any sense. "Second question. How long has British government traded secrets with Chinese man?"

Actively struggling to keep her face from morphing into shock, Eva hefted an eyebrow and took another sip of coffee, ignoring the question. The cup exchange had been faultless, or so she'd thought. She hoped the Chinese secret service wasn't as astute as the old KGB agent.

"Are you alright to walk to the office from here? It's about three blocks."

"I am old, not invalid," Alexie said dismissively. "We walk."

The sky was thankfully clear for an early London afternoon. Mindful not to discuss anything pertinent until they were safely within the confines of MI6, Eva wanted to keep their talk general.

"So what was it like to be a spy back then?" she asked. "During the Cold War?"

Alexie contemplated the question for a moment, seemingly rolling it around his brain. Finally, a rare grin creased the old man's lips. "Was fun."

"That's not the answer I expected."

"You expect maybe terrifying? Was also that, many times. Often I thought I would die, or someone I care about die. Many times. There were missions which still haunt me, very dangerous, where you could be exposed at any moment if someone betray you. But when not those times, was fun. I have seen West spy films. USSR always very cold, big fur hats, always snow and sadness. Sometimes that, yes, but not what you think." His face fell into a theatrical frown. "Not depressing." His face brightened again. "There was much sunshine. People are people. There was much partying, laughter, pretty girls and fucking."

Eva let out a little giggle. "Was there a lot of that?"

"Fucking? Oh yes. I was spy." He beat his chest proudly. "I was like rock star."

Once again, Eva wasn't sure if Alexie was serious or not.

Thinking back over her own espionage career, Eva had to acknowledge she'd done things she regretted, and that she had to admit, in retrospect, could have been avoided. Eva wondered if it was the way of a spy.

"Do you have regrets? Things you would have changed?"

"Da. Many many things." His face clouded over, as if he was going through them one by one. "We all did back then. All of us. Both sides."

"Like what?"

A sly smile crossed Alexie's lips. "You want me to say classified, don't you? Everything we did would still be classified."

"Anything that's not?"

"Frivolous things, I guess. Things that seem deathly earnest at time, but now are silly."

"Like?"

His face morphed into reluctant amusement. "You heard of Perfume Assassin?"

Eva shook her head.

He scoffed, at himself, it seemed. "Perfume Assassin." A shake of his head. "Dramatic, da?" He grimaced. "I had comrade who went by this name. Was arrogance of youth. Stupidity." A sigh. "If enemy agent who was causing problem, Perfume Assassin would send them bullet soaked in ladies' perfume. Sometimes would make them to do something rash, da? It panicked them because knew time was up. They would soon be dead."

Again, Eva was reminded that the man who strolled beside her was not some lovable old grandfather. He had once associated with killers like the Perfume Assassin and he himself was once the cold-blooded killer known as Red Scorpion. It would serve her well to remember.

"Did you believe in what you were doing? In communism?"

"Of course! It was West who were attacking us, preventing

inevitable. Communism spread across world so fast because the people wanted, da? It was the ideology of intellect, of Marx, of Lenin. We would prevail because we were right. Why would West stop this progress? Because greed. You capitalists were illogical, *you* were backwards." His face clouded over. "I saw much death. Too much I think. And for what?" He shrugged. "It was all meaningless in end. When wall fell, so did our beliefs. Hammer and sickle gave way to blue jeans and David Hasselhoff. Men like me were no longer needed, obsolete. We were to expire like that poem, go gentle into good night. You know this poem?"

"'Don't succumb to the peaceful release of death, old age should burn and rave at close of day, rage, rage against the dying of the light'. Dylan Thomas. One of my favourites."

"Is good poem. He writes like Russian."

They ambled silently for a time, each lost in their own thoughts.

As they passed Riverside Walk Gardens they saw a father chasing his squealing daughter, pretending to be a dinosaur, much to her delight. A young couple stopped their stroll to kiss before walking on.

Alexie watched this unfold and casually asked, "How long have you and this Bishop been sleeping together?"

Eva half wished she'd been sipping on coffee so she'd have an excuse to do a spit take.

"What?"

Alexie shrugged and watched a passing double-decker bus. "Is plain as Moldovan pinup. You two have hots for one another. Do people say 'hots' still? I remember this word."

Eva didn't want to get into that conversation, for so many reasons. Partly because this wasn't something she wanted to discuss with Alexie. But mainly because she didn't know how she felt about the topic. After the end of her previous relationship, which was... complex, to say the least, she had discovered her long-suppressed feelings for Bishop. She was yet to determine whether she wanted to continue suppressing them.

Bishop was bad for her, that was obvious. Eva should know;

she had a long long history of choosing men who were bad for her. He could be casually sexist, egotistical and arrogant. And yet... and yet she felt an increasingly strong attraction to the man. He cared deeply for her, and had saved her life many times. They'd had fun nights, like the time she'd introduced him to Bond films. Was that enough for an ongoing relationship? Eva had no idea.

If their attraction was obvious enough for Alexie to see it, was Eva in more trouble than she thought? Bishop knew something was up, too. That's what she'd been trying to discuss over the link in Saint Petersburg.

Stepping onto Vauxhall Bridge, Eva shook her head, trying to dislodge the thoughts. She had to focus. Across the river, SIS head-quarters shone in the early afternoon sun. It had once been London's worst-kept secret, supposedly protected by the Official Secrets Act, known only to every taxi driver, tour guide and KGB agent. And here was Eva, escorting one right through the front gates.

They continued walking in silence.

"I knew this man in Moscow," Alexie said, facing forward.

Amused at the randomness of the statement, Eva replied, "Okay."

"He was known as Alexander the Great."

"Pretty sure he was before your time."

Alexie turned to her and frowned. "No, different Alexander. Maybe one time he was called Alexander the Mediocre, I do not know." He faced forward again. "He ran nightclub. Best nightclub in Moscow. Very popular. Very exclusive. Same time as Studio 54 in New York City, but this better. Alexander had alchemy with people. He could get group of different people, who did not know each other, and they would have best night of lives. He was master. He just knew people. It was amazing. This, unfortunately was his downfall also. Party officials, they wanted in on amazing nights, da? But he would say nyet, only let in people he knew would be part of his alchemy, part of his scheme yes? He did not want boring old party man to ruin his talent." He waved his finger in the air theatrically. "He was artist!"

"I take it this story doesn't end well for Alexander?"

"Not so much." Alexie shook his head. "One day men in black car come for him. He is sent to prison for dissent. There he stayed for long time. Then one day, was stabbed in ribs and died. Very sad."

Unsure whether to smile or grimace, Eva asked, "Why did you tell me this story?"

"Because no matter how good you are, someone always there to stab you in ribs."

Again, Eva didn't know if Alexie was completely serious or not. Why had he told her this story? "Seems rather merciless."

"I am Russian. This is way of life."

Still trying to process Alexie's little story, Eva walked on. The closer they came, the more imposing the SIS headquarters appeared. Fortified gates, razor wire and security cameras all screamed *not welcome*. Inside, however, it was much like any office building, albeit with less junk food.

As they ambled towards their goal, Eva noticed two hunched figures by the south gate. Arms overhanging the bridge railing, they seemed to be assessing the MI6 building intently. That in itself wasn't unusual; it was a well-known landmark. What made them stand out to Eva were their long coats, which didn't make sense on such a warm day. The unsightly bulges protruding from beneath the coats also made the figures appear far more menacing. They could have had hockey sticks under there, but Eva doubted it.

The men's close-cropped hair made them appear more skin-head than terrorist. Regardless, Eva's suspicions were aroused. Ever since the MI6 building had been hit by a rogue RPG years ago, everyone was hyperaware of potential threats. And now, given the recent attack on the Russian embassy, even more so.

Walking as fast as she could without leaving Alexie behind, Eva bounded towards the first security checkpoint. Showing her pass and advising Alexie's status, she hurried through a large metal barrier into a well-fortified second security area. This internal area had an x-ray machine and metal detector checkpoint. A line of six people waited patiently in line to traverse the checkpoint and proceed through the security gate to a bank of elevators beyond.

Eva quickly turned to her companion. "Alexie, I need to alert security. Those men on the bridge…"

"I saw them. Go."

Racing past the line, Eva drew the attention of the security chief on duty. She did this by waving her arms beyond the glass security barrier and yelling, "Oi fucker!"

Early on in her time at MI6, the Security Chief, Callahan, had stopped Eva from entering the building due to, in his words, "too many tats, not enough decorum". From anyone else, she would have taken it as a compliment. Since then, the two had developed a deep and abiding mutual loathing.

"Callahan, there are two blokes on the bridge, highly sus, big coats…"

"We've seen them," he said, nodding to the bank of monitors on his side of the partition. "We see the likes of them every other day, mate. You tryin' to jump the queue again?"

"That was once." Eva paused, then added, "Okay, twice." She pointed to the monitors. "Look closer. They both have bulges under the coats. Left side. Isn't it a bit balmy for that sort of kit? Also, see how the coats flare at the bottom? There's something long and straight under there, and we'd be kidding ourselves to assume they're that well-endowed. I'd say it's roughly the dimensions of an RPG-18 or RPG-22."

Callahan leaned down to the monitors, hoisted up the glasses that hung around his neck on a chain. He squinted, and after clicking a few buttons he muttered, "Huh."

The cogs were whirring in his skull. His demeanour showed that although he desperately wanted to tell her to go to hell, he could see she had a point. With a nod, more to himself than to Eva, he raised his voice and said, "McMahon, alert the bobbies we have a 2-10 on the south of the bridge. Call a yellow alert, but isolate to security areas for now. And let's clear this area, we don't need the entrance crowded."

"Yes sir!" McMahon shouted in reply. Eva was surprised he didn't click his heels and salute.

Callahan gave Eva the most respectful expression he'd ever given her. Which is to say, it contained the least amount of loathing.

Turning to Alexie, she said, "Sorry, I need to leave you here. I'm going back out there, but it's probably best if you stay here…"

The Russian waved his hand dismissively and halted Eva's apology with a cheeky grin. "I am spy, not hero." He looked around. "Do I stay here or go to meeting room?"

Clicking her fingers to gain Callahan's attention, Eva gestured to Alexie. "He needs to be escorted to conference room D, level nine."

"I'll see to it, Miss." There was hesitation in his manner, which was uncommon for the big man. "Miss Destruction?"

"Yes, Callahan?"

"Good spotting."

She couldn't help but smile. "You're welcome."

Jogging towards the entrance, Eva wondered why she felt compelled to watch the takedown of the two punks. If they were attached in any way to the attack on the embassy, she wanted to know what they knew. MI6 had scant intelligence to say the least, and they'd have even less without Alexie, so this could help. But she knew she was clutching at straws.

Rounding the security barrier, she hung back in the shadows to watch the scene unfold. It didn't take long. Four uniformed officers congregated across the road, seemingly having a casual chat, not facing their target at all. Two plain-clothed police officers exited the far side of SIS headquarters and circled around the pair, pretending to be tourists. One stood on one side of the suspects, supposedly posing for a photo in front of the Thames. His offsider stood on the other side, taking the photo. Eva was impressed with their approach. They knew what they were doing.

The two punks seemed oblivious to what was going down. Eva had always found it easy to spot a Plain Clothes. It had become somewhat of a sixth sense back when her activities were less than legitimate.

One moment the two punks were surrounded by random individuals, the next they'd been descended upon en masse. The whole thing unfolded so quickly and seamlessly the two kids had no time to react. Within seconds they were on the ground, writhing under the steady knee of a shouting police officer. One of the cops flipped up the side of one punk's coat.

*Holy fucking snatchtrumpets.*

They really did have RPGs under there.

The shouting intensified. More security arrived on the scene, and Eva walked quickly towards the growing melee. As she grew closer, alarm bells began ringing in her mind. Something about the whole scene didn't add up. It took roughly ten metres for an RPG motor to kick in. The punks were about twenty metres from the outer fence of MI6. They would certainly hit the building from that range, but then what would they do? Run back across the bridge? In front of all those cameras? RPGs had a range of over five hundred metres, so why get close enough to MI6 to rub up against it inappropriately?

Something smelt fishier than an overworked fishmonger's jockstrap. As Eva pulled out her phone to call Paul, something caught her eye. Across the river, two white trails of smoke streaked from the opposite bank.

Words stuck in her throat as the rocket-propelled grenades struck the upper floors of the SIS building with a booming *thwump*. The explosions blew out windows and hurled debris outward. All around her were screams and cries of fear.

MI6 was under attack.

# CHAPTER FOUR

"You can't punch them."

Eva stared at Paul, unsure if he was joking.

"I know that," she replied evenly.

"Not even a little."

"I know."

"I have met you before, Evie. You like to solve problems by punching them. You can't do that here."

Deep inside Scotland Yard, Eva glanced through the one-way glass at the two punks handcuffed to the interrogation table. She sighed. Eva really wanted to punch them. But she knew it would only lead to legal issues, which would serve the punks, not justice. "Okay, fine. No punching."

"Or kicking."

"Paul!"

Her friend and handler's face broke into a cheeky expression. "MI5 and Metro are bending a whole mess of rules to let you have first crack at these clowns, so don't waste your five minutes, alright?"

"I won't."

"I know."

After the attack, the reaction had been rapid and methodical. Rather than fall into shock or panic, the MI6 personnel strapped on their game faces and hurled themselves into defending the SIS building. The police on the ground had enveloped the two punks in a blanket of blue uniforms and hustled them into a waiting van, which sped off in the blink of an eye.

The damage was mostly superficial; it had been an orchestrated strike. It had inflicted far less damage than the embassy attack, but for Eva, it was far more personal. This was her place, her people.

The Metropolitan Police's invitation would not have come easily. This was a domestic incident, not at all within MI6's jurisdiction, but given the highly personal nature of the attack, MI5 had persuaded Metro to provide limited access. Eva could only imagine the favours Paul had called in to make it happen.

Perhaps even more surprising was that Eva had been made lead agent on the search for Horatio Lancing. This gave her all sorts of leeway, including being the first to interrogate the two idiots from the bridge.

As they waited for Eva to be ushered in, Paul said, "I don't know about you, but didn't the attack seem a little... I don't know..."

"Lame?" Eva asked.

"Yes! Exactly, lame." Paul tugged on his vest. "It's vastly different to the Russian embassy situation. Those devices would have been smuggled in under tight security, and may have been there for some time before detonation. The Russians still don't know how it was done. This?" He motioned to the two clowns behind glass. "Seems like it was carried out by the Amateur Theatrical Society."

He was right. The embassy bombing was horrific, and brutally effective. The murder of the spy in Budapest would have to have been carried out with equal precision. Even the most inexperienced CIA agent would be formidable when cornered, but these two teenagers seemed thoroughly incompetent by comparison. Why let yourself get spotted out the front of your target, and with the actual weapons on you? It was as idiotic as it was doomed to failure. It was like storming Buckingham Palace with a rolled-up newspaper and a unicycle. Eva needed to know why.

"Where's Alexie?" she asked.

"Back at the hotel. In light of the incident, we thought it best for the questioning to wait," Paul replied. "We'll tee it up after this, if you're still up for it?"

Before Eva could respond, a bespectacled, middle-aged gent opened the door of the interrogation room and crooked a finger, motioning Eva into the room. Once inside, he left her to it. Just the two terrorists and her. Game on.

As Eva strode into the room, the teenagers' eyes bored into her, looking her up and down like a slab of meat. The lust in their eyes made it plain they viewed her as a sexual object, not a threat. That was their first mistake.

"As you refuse to give the police your names, I'm going to call you Gavin." She pointed to the youngest of the two. She squinted at the older one, who sneered. "You seem like a Trent."

"Fuck you."

"Settle down, Trent. We only just met." She paced in front of them. "Okay boys, let's see what you're up against." Eva counted on her fingers. "Destruction of public property, preparation of terrorist acts, possession of devices and materials for use in terrorist acts…"

The two sat up, startled.

Eva went on. "Commission, preparation and instigation of terrorism. Then there are the mundane ones: attempted murder, and if any of the people rushed to hospital don't pull through…" She shook her head gravely.

None of the injuries suffered by MI6 staff were life threatening. There were lots of cuts and bruises. One person was likely to lose an earlobe, but no one would die. Eva would keep that to herself for now, though.

She went on. "Well, let's just say if anyone doesn't make it, we'll add murder to your long list of offences." She gazed at her fingers in mock confusion. "Seems like I'm going to need more hands. I haven't even really gotten started yet."

Their faces were no longer predatory. They were terrified. Fear seeped from every pore. Hardened criminals they weren't.

"What do you mean, 'terrorism and murder'?" Gavin asked in a breaking voice. "We didn't do nothing!"

"Oh yes you did, my dear Gavin." Eva knew she had them now, but she did her best not to show it. "You see, you're very much connected. Forensics have already advised that the RPGs that hit the SIS headquarters were from the same model you lads were carrying, so you're up on those charges, whether you pulled the trigger or not. It's being classified as a coordinated attack, which means you're going down for the lot. Every charge. Every. Single. One. In short, mates," She leaned over the table and stared them each in the eyes, "you're fucked."

Gavin bounced in his chair, frantically glancing about as if an escape route would materialise at any moment. "Nah, mate, listen, it wasn't us, it was the prize rack."

"Shut up!" shouted Trent.

Eva's forehead crinkled in confusion. "What's a prize rack?"

"Keep yer trap shut!" Trent yelled at Gavin.

Gavin ignored him. "A geezer, on the internet. He set it all up. That's 'is name, Prize Rack."

Eva scoffed. "No one's called Prize Rack."

"I'm warning you." Trent strained against his handcuffs.

"He is! That's 'is name, I swear. Prize Rack."

Eva was simultaneously elated and confused. The two teenagers were far easier to crack than she'd anticipated, but she had no idea what they were actually on about.

"So, this... Prize Rack fellow, did you ever meet?"

"Nah, just messages on WhatsApp," Gavin replied.

Eva imagined that the police listening in were scrambling to search the phones the two had been caught with.

"Why did this person want you to blow up MI6?"

Gavin shook his head, speaking fast. "We weren't going to blow up nothin'. Press a button, fifty thousand quid, that's what the bloke said. Prize Rack."

"Is that what human life is worth to you, mate? Fifty thousand?"

"Nah, that's not it at all, guv." Gavin tried to wipe sweat from his brow, but the handcuffs made it impossible. "He swore youse was so heavily fortified there ain't no way nothin' could get through, right? 'e said it was all—" he clicked his fingers, as if trying to find the right words.

Trent sighed, as if resigned to giving Eva everything. He said, "Sound and fury."

Gavin clicked his fingers again. "That's it! Sound and fury. That's what 'e said. Prize Rack."

Eva folded her arms. "And then is heard no more; it is a tale told by an idiot, full of sound and fury, signifying nothing."

The two stared at her as if she'd asked them to explain the theory of relativity in Mandarin.

"Sorry, wrong audience. It's Shakespeare. *Macbeth*." She paused. "It's a play by an old geezer." Trying to get back on track, she asked the question she was here for. "What does the name Horatio Lancing mean to you?"

The two frowned at one another and simultaneously shrugged. "Never heard of him."

"Right, so..." Eva paused. "Wait, what?"

"Who is he then?" Trent asked.

Stunned, Eva asked, "Wait on. How can you not know who Horatio Lancing is?"

The two exchanged glances. Their confusion seemed genuine.

"You've never heard the name, like, ever?" she asked. "That's like saying you've never heard of Steve Jobs."

"Who?"

Eva stared at them. Either these two were world-class poker players or they really were dumber than a box of hammers. She needed to move on; she only had limited time.

"Why were you on the bridge, and not with the others across the river?"

Gavin sniffed. "Well, we didn't know there was others, yeah? We was there lookin' for the best places to aim."

In Eva's expert opinion, the two in front of her were, in the nicest possible way, complete fucking morons. They were scoping the place armed. What sort of idiot would do that with all the security cameras about? Had they never used Google Street View? Probably not, if they didn't know who Steve Jobs was.

"Why didn't you attack when the other missiles hit?" she asked.

The two gazed at one another sheepishly.

Letting out a sigh, Gavin said, "We don't know why them others fired. We had two hours before we was meant to fire the thing. Thirteen thirty, he said, be ready. They was going to give us the signal to fire, but we had to be ready by thirteen thirty. I re-read the message a hundred times. Thirteen thirty, not a minute later."

Eva tilted her head in confusion. "The attack was at one thirty."

"Yeah?" Gavin shrugged his shoulders.

With a frown, Eva said, "One thirty is thirteen thirty."

Gavin gave a slight shake of his head. "No, it's not. It's three thirty."

Eva turned to the glass window and shook her head in disbelief. She could only imagine what was taking place behind the one-way glass.

"Look, lady," Trent said, fear strangling his words, "we ain't bad blokes. If we tell you everything, we'll get off, yeah?"

Pursing her lips, Eva shook her head sadly. "I'm afraid, sunshine, the only place you'll be getting off is in a prison shower. You boys are going away for a long time."

If they had gone any whiter they would have been clear. A tsunami of panic washed over them.

"Guys," Eva softened her voice, "I know you're not criminal masterminds. You're clearly confused by verbs."

She received blank looks in return.

"You know, doing words."

More blank looks.

She went on. "If you cooperate fully and they can find who sent you those messages, you might get some leniency, but boys, you royally fucked up. You might want to accept that and cooperate. There's no alternative."

As if on cue there was a knock on the door. The bespectacled gent stuck his head around the door, and this time he looked far cheerier.

"Times up."

Eva nodded, and said nothing as she left. Paul was waiting outside in the hall.

He sighed and nodded at the room Eva had just exited.

"We're not dealing with Plato here."

"We're not even dealing with Pluto." Eva ran her fingers through her hair. "Pisstain spunktrumpets, they're dumb."

"If we can get into their phones we might be able to find out who gave the order." Paul sighed. "Although, to be perfectly frank, I'd bet pounds to pudding it will be a wasted effort. Whoever organised this is far smarter than this lot." He nodded towards the door.

"My shoes are smarter than this lot."

Walking down the corridor, Eva's mind raced. Like the two freelancers in Saint Petersburg, these two weren't spies or enemy combatants. They were private contractors out for a buck. They appeared to have been hired for one thing, rather than being part of the overall scheme.

"Do you know what they were talking about with the prize rack thing?" Eva asked.

"Not really, but…"

"But what?"

"There is a Russian word, prizrak. Perhaps that's what they meant."

"Maybe. What does it mean?"

"Ghost."

The trip back to MI6 was a long one. The building had been cordoned off, with multiple circles of security and every street surrounding Vauxhall Cross shut down. Eva lost count of the security checkpoints they went through.

When they'd finally made their way inside, they went straight to Paul's office. Without asking, he poured two large scotches and handed one to Eva. "You've earned this."

That was a big compliment from her superior. She'd done well with the interrogation. Unfortunately, it had probably aided MI5 and Metro more than it had her case. She was no closer to finding Harry than when she left Wakefield Prison.

About to say as much to Paul, Eva was cut short as Trev came stumbling into the room holding a computer tablet, a panicky expression splashed across his features.

"We're under attack!"

Paul maintained his stoic expression. "You're about four hours too late, Trevor."

Trev shook his head vigorously. "No no no, not that. Cyber attack." He inhaled deeply to centre himself. "All the IT firewalls have been breached, every protocol has been overrun. Pretty much every secured server has been compromised. Not just us, all of Five Eyes and some more. CIA, Mossad, DGSE. Everything's been hacked."

Eva put down her drink. "You'll need to explain it in non-techo terms."

The pain on Trev's face was obvious. He scratched the back of his neck. "Okay. Imagine Five Eyes as five dams, all interconnected. Each intelligence agency has a sea of intelligence data. CIA, us, the Aussies. When we want to, we can flow information. It can be a trickle or a flood, we get to decide, right? Well, someone has popped all the spillways or whatever you call them. Everything's flowing out. All of it."

Paul sat up. "How do we stop it?"

"We've got people literally pulling cables. We don't know what's secure and what's not, so we're yanking everything. Any cable connected to the outside world is being pulled out. It will take time, though. Who knows what will be stolen before we seal it up."

Paul pushed away his drink, his expression grave.

"How did this happen, Trev?" Eva asked.

Trev let out a frustrated exhale. "There's a standing IT protocol. If we're ever under physical attack, protocol dictates that we shut down all external connection in case it's a coordinated cyber attack."

Eva nodded. "Makes sense."

"Except, it didn't happen this afternoon."

"It didn't?"

"The exact opposite happened."

Paul's head shot up. "You'll need to explain this to me. In detail."

Trev nodded. "As far as I can make out, someone put code into our systems overriding the protocol. Who knows, it could have been there for months. As soon as we thought we'd instigated the shutdown procedure, the barn doors flew open, so to speak." He sat and took a big sip of Eva's drink. Stress permeated from the kid. "But not in a particularly glaring way, not one that would raise alarms. We thought the shutdown had occurred, and went to help the injured. But in the background the hack didn't just open up pipes to our systems, it opened up pipes to Five Eyes and more, and started extracting their information as well, impersonating us."

"This was a coordinated attack. Planned," Paul said. It was a statement, not a question.

"Yeah, yeah, most definitely. Someone planted the code and exploited it. They were ready for it. As soon as the lockdown started, someone accessed a shit tonne of intelligence data and cracked it open like a coconut. The code itself would never have worked, we would have spotted it instantly—the two things had to occur together. Without the lockdown protocol being instigated, the piece of code would have just sat there. This was planned. Someone knew what they were doing."

To calm his nerves, Eva patted Trev's hand. She took back her drink and downed a large swig. This was a lot to take in.

"Is this what Alexie was going to tell us?" Eva asked. "Did we fuck up the timing?"

"Maybe." Paul rubbed his stubbled chin.

"Where is Alexie now?" Eva asked.

"I assume still back at the hotel. Why?"

Overcome with an inexplicable sense of dread, Eva said, "Can you get his security detail on the phone?"

Paul frowned, but did as Eva requested. He dialled the number. Waiting for an answer, his expression doubled down. "Huh. No answer."

Eva's sense of dread wasn't going away. Paul called the station chief and was advised that he would receive an update ASAP. The next few minutes were agonisingly slow. It was times like these Eva wished she bit her nails. Or that you could smoke in government offices. The three sat in silence, staring at the phone on Paul's desk.

For ten minutes, all that could be heard was the ticking of the clock. When the phone finally rang, they all jumped. Paul answered formally. Within seconds, his face fell, and a weighty expression splashed across his features. He hung up with a sombre sigh.

"It's as you feared, Evie. The security detail is dead. Two agents." He rubbed his hand over his face. "Alexie is gone. There's... there's a lot of blood."

"What happened?"

"The blood isn't from the agents. Looks like the old bastard didn't go down without a fight. There's... there's so much blood, Evie. The agents attending say it's doubtful an old man could have survived long after sustaining injuries like that. I'm sorry."

"Why would they take him?"

"I assume to find out what he'd told us." He sighed. "They checked the hotel footage—it's blank. All of it erased."

Trev gave a slight shake of his head. "I don't get it."

"We've been fucked, Trev. Royally and without lube. Whoever was behind this didn't want Alexie to tell us what he knew.

They've been planning this for a long time. It's not a smash and grab, this took finesse. It took—"

"An IT mastermind?" Paul asked pointedly.

*Blueberry fuckmuffins.* He was right. This had to be related to Harry. It had to be. But to what end? One thing was certain, every major Western spy agency had just had the covers ripped off it. Intelligence sources were no longer safe. The age of secrets was over.

# CHAPTER FIVE

"Did you punch them?" Bishop stuffed a forkful of salad in his mouth.

"No. Why does everyone keep asking me that?" Eva flung her hands into the air and squared her jaw. "I was respectful of the rule of law and to the chain of command. I treated those two punks with all due respect of His Majesty's government and appointed agencies."

It was dark outside. Eva and Bishop sat in the deserted MI6 cafeteria, eating salad and doing their best to make sense of the day.

"My apologies," Bishop said. "Perhaps I should rephrase. Did you want to punch them?"

"Oh Christ yes. I've never wanted to throat punch anyone more in my life. And believe me, they definitely need some sense beaten into them."

Bishop flashed his million-dollar smile and went back to his salad. Talking about Gavin and Trent's stupidity was a welcome distraction from what was really on Eva's mind: Harry McFuck-Face Lancing.

Casually, Bishop said, "It's not your fault, you know? Whoever took Alexie, you couldn't have foreseen it. We were under attack, we had to concentrate on that, or more people could have been hurt."

"There were more people hurt, Bishop."

"I mean more than those two agents."

"And Alexie."

"I suppose." Bishop didn't seem terribly upset at the possible passing of an old KGB agent. He hadn't been a fan of inviting the fox into the henhouse in the first place.

Still despondent about the loss of the Alexie and the two agents, Eva floated in a miasma of her own self-pity. No trace of Alexie had been found. More blood had been discovered in the car park of the hotel, but from there, nothing. Experts had confirmed what Paul had told Eva: it was unlikely any human being could survive for long after losing that much blood. Alexie was as good as dead.

Eva could have kicked herself if she was that flexible. She should have foreseen the attacks somehow. She was a spy, she should have deduced that this would happen. Now it seemed all too obvious. The phone call from Harry, then discovered that he was missing, then a huge cyber attack on the world's spy agencies. There may as well have been a huge red flashing neon arrow above Harry's head. Now all they had to do was find him.

Eva had put out feelers throughout the world. She'd contacted all the places she could recall visiting with Harry, every associate, driver, anyone who might have a tenuous link to her ex. She'd called his favourite restaurants, hotels, places of business and obscure associates, and asked them all to tell her if he turned up. Traipsing around the planet, Eva had once known Harry's moves intimately. She had to use that knowledge to her advantage, but so far nothing had turned up. She'd have to wait, which wasn't exactly her strong suit.

"We'll find Lancing, Eva. You'll have your revenge, I assure you."

Was Bishop reading her mind again? Eva really hoped not. Sometimes her mind ran off with inappropriate thoughts.

Picturing Bishop naked in front of a fire on a bearskin rug was the most recent one. She blinked several times to remove the image from her mind. It didn't work.

She stabbed her salad with more force than was necessary. "I'm sure we will. But right now," Eva sighed and glanced around the empty cafeteria, "everything can go fuck itself with a cactus."

Bishop laughed, a roguish, manly laugh. His eyes twinkled. "You're rather adorable when you're frustrated."

Hefting an eyebrow, Eva assessed her companion. "Is this where you offer to take me back to your place to alleviate my frustration, Bishop?"

He shook his head. "I would never be so boorish. I assure you, my dear, if you were to accompany me to my apartment, frustration would be the furthest thing from your mind."

Bishop was charming, Eva had to give him that. Then again, so was Harry. She'd fallen for her ex's charm and he'd hurt her like no one had. Loch had been all charm, too, and so had countless men before them. So many charming men. All of them had wounded her, one way or another. Was she destined to relive the same mistakes over and over?

She narrowed her eyes at Bishop.

He tilted his head, a tiny mischievous grin crossing his soft lips. "What?"

When he didn't receive an answer, Bishop went over to the condiment section and came back with a bottle of chilli sauce. He ingloriously squeezed it over his salad.

"What the twat waffle are you doing, man?" Eva was horrified.

"What? This? Hot sauce boosts your metabolism for hours after you eat it, which helps with weight management."

"There's not an ounce of fat on your body."

Bishop winked. "I know."

Adjusting her gaze, Eva stared at the ceiling. This wasn't helping her. She needed to get back to the topic at hand.

Paul was off dealing with the ramifications of the greatest intelligence breach in history. Heads would roll. Eva wondered if hers would be the first on the chopping block. She'd had a lead on

Harry and hung up on him, she'd failed to protect Alexie, and the breach had probably been perpetrated by her ex. She only hoped Paul and Bishop would be spared.

As he left to deal with the aftermath, Paul had been uncharacteristically blasé. On his way out of his office he'd said, "That's just the way the way espionage goes sometimes."

They weren't exactly the most inspiring words Eva had ever heard. Not quite up there with Churchill's wartime speeches, or King's "I have a dream". Who was she kidding? The lyrics to the Black Eyed Peas' *My Humps* offered more inspiration than that.

Not in the mood for her kale and pomegranate salad, Eva pushed it away. She craved a hamburger. With thick fries and onion rings. There was no chance she'd get that kind of meal here.

She sneered at the salad. She needed carbs.

While Bishop ate, elsewhere in the building the search was on for whoever had perpetrated the cyber attack. Only an MI6 IT person could have placed the code that the raid had triggered—apparently it could not have been introduced from the outside. Trev and his team of IT boffins were investigating. They believed the code would have been there for at least two months when the last patch was applied. Someone had been planning this for a long time.

As soon as the cyber attack was triggered, MI6 went into lockdown again. Every server, PC, phone and pocket calculator was searched for the missing data. According to Trev, the instigator of the data download had to be within MI6 itself. After that, they could have gone anywhere, but they had to be physically in the building to trigger it. It was scary to think that they had a saboteur and traitor within their midst. So far none of the stolen data had been found. It must have gone somewhere; it was only a matter of time before it appeared. In the interim, MI6 was tearing itself apart.

Meanwhile, the world edged closer to the brink of a new Cold War. News of the data theft had reached the media, although not the full extent and hadn't garnered much air time. The news coverage was focused on the RPG attack and the aftermath. If the full extent of the cyber attack was known it would only amplify tensions. As would the discovery that an ex-KGB informant had been kidnapped and likely killed.

Not that Russia hadn't been mentioned in the speculation about who had carried out the attack. Accusations of retaliation for the embassy attack were quickly flung about. News of the murdered CIA agent had become public, and this only fuelled the wildfire. Vitriol had ratcheted up and fear seeped into reporting as people grew genuinely concerned about how far this could go. Some news agencies went as far as predicting that the war could turn hot, or even that nuclear weapons could be deployed. It was MI6's job to stop that from happening.

Swirling thoughts of global politics made Eva push her salad even further away. "How the hell did someone crack a state-of-the art IT defence system?"

Her fellow operative took a final mouthful of his salad and dabbed his mouth with a napkin. "Someone. Hmmm. Could be anyone, I guess, anyone at all." Bishop put his fist to his chin. "Now, let me think, do you know anyone who has a penchant for hacking impenetrable IT systems and holding the world for ransom? Any names come to mind at all?"

Eva sneered. "Very funny, you prancing cologne ad. You're going to say Harry, aren't you?"

"Of course I am, Eva. That should be obvious, even to you."

"What do you mean, 'even to me'?"

Bishop sighed. Uncharacteristically, he seemed to be trying to avoid revving her up. "You're going to have to let go of your Horatio Lancing baggage if you're going to survive this, Eva. It will only slow you down."

As much as she hated to admit it, he was right. She wasn't about to tell Bishop that, though. "You never liked him, did you?"

"He did threaten every nation on Earth." Bishop sat up stiffly. "Don't refer to him like I met him once and thought he chewed oddly. Your ex did try to kill me, Eva."

"I'll be honest, most of my exes would probably try to kill you."

Aghast, Bishop asked, "What's wrong with me?"

"How long do you have?"

Bishop waggled a finger at her. "Don't deflect. Lancing is the most likely son of a bitch to be behind this. He has a history of stealing data and using it to his own ends, blackmailing governments, and he knows the ins and outs of IT systems. Hell, half the servers here have his name on them. If you made an identikit picture of who was most likely, his stupid face would come up every time."

"I know."

"And as well as all that... wait, you know? Well... good."

"Of course I know. I'm not as stupid as your dinner choices, Bishop. But I'm wondering why Harry hasn't called me back. He was so keen to talk to me during the embassy bombing, but once I hung up on him, nothing. If he was so eager for a chat, why the radio silence?"

Bishop's accusatory finger hung in mid-air. "That..." he lowered his digit, "is a very good point."

"I do make those occasionally."

"I must say, I always look forward to the thrust of your points."

Images of sweaty bodies and bearskin rugs came dancing into her mind again. *Stupid brain.*

Before Eva could come up with a retort, her phone rang. She answered, but not before issuing Bishop with a tired eye roll.

It was Callahan. "Can you please come down to security, Miss Destruction?"

"Why?"

"There's a package. You... can you come down please, Miss? It's... you need to see this."

Eva frowned and hung up, then stood, and jerked her head for Bishop to follow. In the few minutes it took to get to security, Eva's mind raced. What could be awaiting her? The best-case scenario was that someone had grabbed Harry and dropped him off in reception tied up with a bright pink bow. Optimistic, sure, but Eva was a glass-half-full kind of girl.

When they arrived, Callahan's face was grave. "This came in an hour ago by courier, addressed to you. We gave it the usual checks and our systems alerted us to… Well, it didn't get through."

"Why not?"

Callahan held up the small cardboard box. The brown paper wrapping had been carefully cut away and the top lid was open. Inside, lying on a bed of crushed red crepe paper was shiny bullet, a .45 calibre by the look of it.

Eva lifted her eyebrow at Callahan.

As if answering an unuttered question, he said, "Dusted for prints. It's clean. No return address. Courier picked it up from the front of a council estate. No help there."

Tentatively, Eva reached down and picked the bullet up. It was relatively light, like most bullets. It was amazing that such a small thing could terminate a life in an instant.

There was something odd about it. She held it to her nose. The bullet smelled of perfume.

Bishop smelt it too. "There was a bloke on the other side in the '60s who used to go around—"

"The Perfume Assassin?" Eva said. "Yeah, I've heard the story."

"We never did find out who it was, but I thought they would have been dead long before now."

It seemed a lot of dead spies weren't quite as lifeless as first thought. Eva rolled the bullet between her fingers. No matter which way you looked at it, someone had sent her a death threat.

Eva needed this.

Only one glass of wine in, she was already feeling better. As much as she could, given the circumstances. Nancy sat opposite and topped up her glass. Well, less topping, more drowning.

They were at a suburban Italian restaurant halfway between their apartments. They sat across from one another at a little table on the pavement, a large concrete flower pot between them and the road. Dusk was ambling across the sky, and a light breeze moved around the last vestiges of summer. The little place on the leafy South Kensington street had served them well over the years, with many a story told over the crisp white tablecloths.

The restaurant wasn't far from MI6, and occasionally Eva had a slight twang of panic that she'd see someone from work who might want to say hi. That would be a difficult conversation to have in front of her best friend.

Nancy put the bottle of sauvignon blanc back into the ice bucket and continued her story about a co-worker who had been dismissed for stealing office supplies, even though she was on a seven-figure salary. The familiarity of the scene calmed Eva.

If the bullet was meant to rattle her, it had only partially worked. A vague threat only meant she was vaguely troubled. She'd faced down terrible foes in her time, ones with far more direct menace. She didn't know who had sent her the bullet, so she didn't know if she should take it seriously. But she was smart enough not to dismiss it. It seemed likely to be a deadly warning. Or promise.

Why would Eva be targeted for assassination? She hadn't extracted any worthwhile information from Alexie besides the fact that Harry had escaped, but MI6 already knew that. So why murder her? To what end? She didn't know who was behind it all.

There was no way Harry would order her assassination. As fervently as she knew the world wasn't flat, Eva was absolutely certain Harry would kill himself before he would see any harm come to her. There wasn't a fragment of an atom in her body that believed Harry would allow her to be harmed.

With nothing further to go on, Eva's mission right now was to get drunk. It was the weekend, after all. Wasn't that what regular citizens did on the weekend? There was a good chance she'd be one of those soon enough. Heads would surely roll for the security breach. She had been summoned by name to Saint Petersburg and failed to get the information they needed. And now her charge was likely dead, the promised intelligence gone with him.

Nobody knew for sure where the breached data had gone, but

everyone understood it wasn't anywhere good. It was only a matter of time before Eva was asked to tender her resignation.

She felt a big night coming on. She desperately needed to forget the world of espionage for a while. It would still be there tomorrow. She'd neglected her friend for too long, and they had much to catch up on. Not that Eva could tell Nancy much. Perhaps one day when they were old and grey and considered "disruptive influences" at the nursing home, Eva might let her friend in on some of her exploits. Maybe. She'd have fifty years to figure out the best way to tell her.

It wasn't just work that Eva wished she could talk to Nancy about. There was also the little matter of Bishop. Did she care for him or was he just something shiny she'd been distracted by? Was he another in the endlessly long line of bad boys she was attracted to? Nancy was particularly good at asking the hard questions that helped Eva figure out her feelings. But she couldn't tell her about Bishop.

Nancy would see through any talk of a co-worker in an instant. As far as Nancy was concerned, Eva only worked in a café. She didn't have co-workers, apart from Anchor, who Nancy had met multiple times. Nancy knew he wasn't Eva's type. For a start, he was gay. Also, he was nice.

If Eva mentioned Bishop, Nancy would grill her about how they met, how they kept bumping into each other and, most tellingly, why Eva hadn't mentioned him before. No, Eva couldn't bring up Bishop without the whole house of cards falling down around Eva's ears. Nancy knew her too well. Best to let her friend do most of the talking and go along for the ride.

Eva laughed as Nancy told her tale. Her animated hands flew about, emphasising pertinent points. After their recent estrangement, Eva was glad to have her best friend back.

The sun began to set as they waved down the waiter, Simon. They'd been there so often he knew them by name. They ordered a second bottle and some bruschetta as a starter. For the first time in a long time, Eva relaxed. Tonight, the world could take care of itself. She was going to be a human being for once. Maybe she would bring up Bishop if she was drunk enough. Perhaps she could frame him as a regular customer or something. If she waited until Nancy was tipsy she'd be less inclined to question everything through the lens of logic.

One thing was for sure, Eva was determined to have a normal night. And that's exactly what she did.

Until the gunshot.

The first distinctive pop came just before the waiter collapsed on the pavement. At first Nancy laughed, thinking Simon had tripped over again; there was a precedent. Then she saw the blood. Nancy was the first to scream. She wasn't the last. Several diners cried out when they saw that Simon's white dress pants were steadily turning crimson.

Eva's head darted around, searching for threats. She was about to shout at everyone to get down when her wine glass exploded, showering her in fragments. She flipped the table and got behind it. It would be good for obscuring sight, but not for stopping bullets. Eva grabbed Nancy by the neck and pulled her behind the solid concrete pot plant, out of the line of fire. They were too far from the restaurant to make it inside without being exposed.

"You lot, inside!" Eva shouted at the patrons near the entrance who were staring blankly at the scene. They were civilians, their minds were unable to flick from domestic life to imminent threat. Eva had already made that shift. "Now!" Turning her attention to the restaurant customers inside, she added, "Get away from the windows. Everyone back!"

Thankfully, they did exactly as asked. Two men grasped Simon under the arms and dragged him inside. Only Nancy and Eva were left outside, exposed behind the large pot plant. Eva automatically reached for her gun, which was tucked into the back of her jeans, then hesitated. Nancy was terrified. She worked in finance; she wasn't trained for this. Gunfights were rare in the banking sector.

A bullet ripped through the wood of the table, stabbing light through the smoking hole. They couldn't stay behind the pot plant for long, but there was no way they would make it into the restaurant without being mowed down. Eva had no choice.

Extracting her Sig Sauer pistol, Eva chambered a round and held it between her hands, barrel skyward.

Nancy's eyes went wide. "What the feck are you doing? Where the bloody hell did you get that thing?"

Eva ignored the question and raised herself up on her hindquarters. She spared a second to peer between the table and the pot plant. The gunfire could only be coming from a limited number of sniper nests. She mentally calculated the prime locations where she would set up and worked back from there. The suburb was densely populated; she couldn't fire wildly. She had to have a definite target or innocent people would get hurt.

Just as she pulled her head back to safety, wood splintered, creating another hole in the table. The shooter was trying to goad them into making a rash move. Eva snuck a glance around the edge of the table. There. The van, facing the other way with its doors open, behind the VW Beetle. Too close for a sniper nest. Eva wondered why they were so close. They must have set up in haste, and the natural curvature of the road meant they couldn't get further away. That, and finding a park in central London was a nightmare. Their position gave Eva a slight advantage. She was within striking distance, if she could get a decent shot.

Time to act. Her body tensed. She crouched, ready to move.

Nancy's hand clamped down on Eva's forearm. "What are you doing?" Panic, meshed with disbelief, stained her words. "You're not a ninja."

"No, Nance, I'm not." Eva breathed out slowly. "I'm a fucking spy."

Disbelief was slapped across Nancy's face. She had no frame of reference for any of this. No one would. Eva hoped she hadn't ended their friendship.

Although she was ready for action, Eva halted. Maybe Nance was right. She wasn't a ninja. A frontal assault on a prepared sniper was reckless, especially when it meant leaving her best friend vulnerable. She needed a distraction. She knew exactly what to do.

Sliding her gun between the table and the pot plant, Eva loosed two bullets to let the sniper know she wasn't having any of their shenanigans. It would give them the slightest reprieve before the sniper made their next move. The response was a flurry of bullets that peppered the pot plant. Nancy shrieked.

Pulling out her phone, Eva called the one person she knew she could always rely on.

He answered on the first ring.

She skipped the small talk. "Where are you? I need you."

"Words I've longed to hear." His voice was self-confident, as always.

"Can you hear the gunfire, smartarse?"

"I'm in the car park." His voice was suddenly devoid of swagger, edged with concern. "Where are you?"

Eva gave him the location and explained the situation.

"Two minutes." He hung up.

Fear scorching her words, Nancy asked, "Who did you call?"

"My partner."

"Who the hell are you?" Nancy asked in disbelief.

"Spy partner." Even under fire, Eva managed a grin.

"I repeat, who the hell are you?"

Eva ignored the jibe. She knew that was the terror speaking. She stared into her best friend's eyes. "When I fire, you run for the door, you got me?"

In return, Nancy simply shook her head, her eyes watery. "I don't understand what's going on."

Extracting a hair tie from her bag, Eva fixed her hair in a ponytail. "I'm a spy, Nance, I work for MI6. I have been for a couple of years. I'm sorry I never told you, but I wanted to protect you." She peered around the corner of the plant. "Which I'm obviously fucking useless at." She sighed. "Look, if we get out of this we'll have a big old chat, but right now," she pulled back the hammer of her pistol, "I need you to run."

After another volley of shots against the rapidly crumbling

flower pot, Eva slipped her pistol between the pot and table and fired three rounds. They were blind shots, not precisely aimed. They would have hit the van somewhere, but were unlikely to be on target. If Eva took the time to aim properly, the sniper would have her before she could shoot. She'd be dead in an instant. All she needed to do was keep the sniper occupied until her distraction arrived.

There was a hesitant silence, as if the sniper was surprised that Eva was fighting back. If that was the case, he didn't know her at all. There was no angry reprisal via a return hail of bullets. Her adversary was waiting for the right shot. The sniper was patient, she'd give him that.

From the south came the roar of an engine. Eva grinned, and Nancy recoiled slightly, wondering if her friend had truly gone mad.

"Cavalry," Eva explained. "Keep an eye on the road, you'll want to see this."

Rounding the corner at a ludicrous speed was an Indian Scout motorbike. Astride the beast was Bishop, resplendent in his tight-fitting suit, no helmet. He was a madman. But he was her madman.

Bishop hurtled towards them at an insane pace. It was only when he was within metres of them that he slammed on the brakes. The bike's rear wheel slid to the right. Instead of fighting it, Bishop went with it. He steered the bike into the skid and rose to a standing position. The bike steadily lost momentum, and as it toppled, Bishop strode off the bike like he was stepping off a yacht.

As the motorbike went skidding along the asphalt, Bishop stood in the middle of the road and pulled a pistol from his shoulder holster. Loosing shots at the van, he took cover on the opposite side of the street, behind a parked Mercedes. The sniper peppered the car with bullets.

Eva had her distraction.

Bishop turned to Eva and Nancy. "Ladies." He tipped an imaginary hat. "Lovely night for it."

"Who the feck is that?" Nancy asked Eva.

"Bishop."

Under her breath, Nancy muttered, "He's gorgeous."

"I know." Eva fired a shot into the van. "Trouble is, he knows it too."

Bishop and Eva exchanged hand signals and completed their silent conversation with a nod. They had a plan. All they needed to do was execute it.

Eva turned to Nancy. "Now, if you'll excuse me, I have to shoot someone."

Right on cue, Bishop released a barrage of shots at the van and took cover. As expected, the sniper launched vengeance on the newcomer. That was all Eva needed.

Standing, she rounded the pot plant and walked calmly down the centre of the street, unloading her pistol at the van. Eva fired at a steady pace, never giving the sniper a moment's reprieve.

She clenched her teeth as she fired. This arsehole had come into her neighbourhood, shot up her restaurant and almost killed her best friend. She wasn't having any of it. Eva was pissed. And slightly tipsy.

The full clip empty, she ejected it onto the ground and slapped in her reserve. Bishop fired to keep the van occupied. Eva's brief pause must have given the shooter hope that she was spent. His mistake. She hadn't even warmed up yet.

The sniper raised his head and put his eye to the scope. His last mistake.

Eva aimed her bullet directly at the largest mass—his head. Instead of hitting the centre of his forehead like she'd wanted, the bullet struck down the barrel of the scope, which erupted in explosion of metal, plastic and glass. The sniper reeled backwards, pawing at the hole where his eye had once been. The scream was primitive and pitiful.

Perhaps she was more encumbered by drink than she'd thought. She rarely missed. Eva's pace didn't let up. She strode towards him, gun forward. Bishop joined her.

The driver's side door of the van swung open and a burly man in a white coat exited. He was clasping an Uzi submachine gun. He swung the weapon towards the two spies.

Eva simply said, "No."

Bishop and Eva placed a bullet in each of his shoulder blades, rendering him incapacitated, but still alive. He dropped to the ground, writhing in pain.

Walking around the vehicle, Eva checked for any more attackers. There weren't any more. The two assassins they'd taken down were screaming in agony and weren't going anywhere.

There was no self-congratulatory back slapping between the MI6 agents. This wasn't something to celebrate.

"Where'd you get the bike?" Eva asked.

"Craig from Finance."

"That was generous of him."

"It will be."

"Will be?"

"When I ask if it's okay to borrow his bike."

"Ah," Eva said, glancing over at the scratched-up motorbike that lay on its side. "Thanks for coming to my rescue."

A curious expression crossed Bishop's face. He gave a slight shake of his head. "Eva, you know I didn't save you, right?"

Eva tilted her head curiously.

He went on. "I didn't rescue you, you saved yourself. I merely gave you the chance to do what you do so well. You're far more capable than you realise."

"I think you did more than just distracting them, dude. You did good."

Bishop slid a warm hand along her jawline, his thumb caressing her cheek. "I hope you consider me more than a mere distraction."

For a moment Eva nuzzled into his caress, then suddenly realised what she was doing.

Gently, she pushed his hand away. "I have to get back to…" She pointed a thumb towards the restaurant.

"Of course."

Too many thoughts were pinging about in Eva's already wired

brain. One of them was the bearskin rug again. She shook it loose. There were far more important things going on.

On her way back to the restaurant, the owner, Giovani, poked his head out the front door. "Is it over?"

"For now." Eva peeked behind her. "Better call the police, and an ambulance. Tell them to alert MI5, they'll want in on this."

Confused, Giovani said, "We already called the police."

"Good work."

Walking back to the table she had been casually sharing with Nancy only minutes before, Eva said, "I thought I told you to run." She extended a hand to help her friend up.

Standing, Nancy said, "I was too fecking petrified my legs wouldn't work. I think I peed my pants a little too."

Eva smiled. "That happens."

She tucked the gun into the waistband of her jeans. Nancy watched the pistol as she did, then gawped at her friend with a blank expression.

Tilting her head, Eva said, "Are you going to say anything?"

There was silence for a moment. Nancy pulled out the upended bottle from the ice bucket and issued a deep sigh. "I think we're going to need more wine."

# CHAPTER SIX

"You shot them up pretty good there, Ms Destruction." The Chief of the Secret Intelligence Service, Elizabeth Crompton, eyed Eva over her extremely large art deco desk. She was mid-fifties, had birdlike features, and was officious. It was Eva's first time meeting her.

Eva balanced a cup and saucer awkwardly on her knee. Paul was by her side, sitting formally. "In my defence, I didn't punch them."

A polite expression crossed the Chief's thin lips. "No, you did not."

The new head of MI6 stirred her tea, the spoon clinking against the china. The room was deathly silent. It was a little too reserved, too impersonal. Not for the first time, Eva wondered if she was about to be fired.

"You are fine?"

"Oh yeah, sure. Not the first scrape I've been in." She paused, adding, "Ma'am."

Chief Crompton was the first female leader MI6 had ever had. Never deployed in the field, she'd nevertheless risen through the ranks steadily. After the fallout of Eva's last mission, a routing of senior MI6 leadership had occurred. Crompton was the last one standing. There were unpacked boxes on the floor, and the room smelt of fresh paint.

"Your first mission for us was apprehending Mr Lancing. Would you say there is a possibility that some party has deduced that the person most qualified to do so again is the first person to dispose of?"

Eva gulped uncomfortably. "Maybe. We're still looking into it."

"I see." A sliver of a smile. "How goes the search for Lancing?" she asked in a manner that was meant to appear casual.

"I'm waiting for a spec report later this morning, but leads are thin on the ground," Eva said. In order to fill the silence, she added, "I've used every phone number and contact I can think of from my previous... mission, but no replies. He's well and truly gone to ground."

Eva glanced at Paul, who was mysteriously quiet. Perhaps it was because this was Eva's first official meeting with the big boss, and he didn't want to step on his friend's toes. Or perhaps it was the fact that someone had been taking pot-shots at his wife the night before.

The Chief nodded and continued to clink her spoon about the cup. Did her tea really require that much stirring? "The attempt on your life? Connected to the infamous Perfume Assassin?"

"Perhaps. Or somebody trying to make us think it was. It doesn't matter all that much either way, since we never figured out who it was back in the day, ma'am." Eva sighed. Why was she being so formal? It wasn't her. "Apart from that, we don't know who it could be. I mean, sure, I've been rude to a few hairdressers, and left many a parking officer questioning their life choices, but assassination is a big call. Even if I did offer some suggestions about the potential rectal use of the parking officer's ticketing machine."

"Quite." The Chief's polite smile was gossamer thin. "Nobody has found the body of Alaksiej Barinov?"

Eva shook her head. "I'm afraid not. We're not one hundred

percent sure he's dead, but it seems likely. Though nothing has come up."

"I see." More stirring. "Perhaps, given all these Cold War connections, it is time to rethink our approach?"

"Ma'am?" It was Paul's first word in over five minutes.

"Let us assume for a moment that this Perfume Assassin is the same KGB agent from years ago. If one is to catch an old spy, perhaps one needs to think like an old spy." The chief continued to move her spoon about.

The stirring thing was really getting on Eva's tits. Seconds away from reaching across and slapping the spoon from the Chief's hand, Eva put her own tea cup on the floor. "I don't understand."

"I'm thinking that we are aware of people who perhaps know these men, Barinov and The Assassin, best. I will concede it has been a number of years, but I'm wondering if we're missing some basics here. Perhaps we could draw on the plethora of experience from our past ranks, those who dealt with these customers previously, and leverage their knowledge."

"You mean past operatives, from the Service?"

The Chief gave a curt nod. "I'll draw up a list of names."

Paul gave Eva a sideways glance. He didn't much care for the idea, clearly. "Very good ma'am."

"That will be all." The Chief placed her spoon on the saucer, where it rang like a ceramic bell, dismissing them both.

The two rose awkwardly, exchanging expressions only two familiar friends could about the strange little meeting. They bid their farewells and headed for the door.

"And Eva?"

"Yes Chief?"

"Get the sons of bitches who did this to us. I want to see them pay, you understand me?"

Maybe she didn't have as big a stick up her arse as Eva thought. Maybe just a small one. Like a twig. Or a toothpick.

"Yes ma'am."

As Eva shut the door the Chief was already on her computer, her focus elsewhere. It was a quiet walk down the hall.

Eva couldn't believe she'd had to tell Nancy she was a spy. After the police, MI5 and MI6 had all their piece, the two friends went back to Eva's and polished off another bottle of wine. Nancy had many questions, and Eva answered as many as she could without breaching the Official Secrets Act. Nancy appeared to have taken the news well, but Eva knew her best friend better than that. Nancy would need time to process the information and truly decide where she stood. There was no question Eva would give her all the time she needed.

The other item playing on her mind was the fact that someone wanted to kill her. Was the attack on spy agencies related to the Russian bombing? What about the assassination attempt on her? If so, why? To Eva, the security breaches still smelt of Harry, but the assassination attempt didn't.

Harry had once held the world to ransom. Now every major Western spy agency had been attacked while he was a free man. It was too coincidental. But hiring someone to kill her? He'd never do that. Ironically, Eva would stake her life on it. But if that was the case, then what was going on?

Entering the lift, Eva asked, "How's Nancy?"

"Wavering between Zen calm and manic hysteria."

"So, nothing's changed then?"

Paul's stony face told Eva it was no laughing matter.

"She's going to need some time, Evie. This has shaken her, shaken me, in fact. I'm fine with you being shot at…"

"Thanks very much."

"… But when my wife gets in the line of fire, that's overstepping the mark. Now it's personal. The gloves are off. We need to take it to them, and as the Chief said, make them pay." Each word came with a stab of a finger, his jaw tight. "I don't care what it takes, we're bringing hell down upon those abhorrent bastards. No matter what the cost is, what rules we break, we get them, you understand me? We crush their very souls."

Eva nodded. She had never seen her friend so full of righteous anger. They'd pushed Paul too far, and now his eyes fired with rage.

More to herself than to Paul, she said, "Demons run when a good man goes to war."

The elevator pinged at their floor.

Tilting his head, Paul said, "What's that from? Tennyson?"

"Doctor Who."

"Ah. Close." The smallest of amused looks reassured Eva that Paul was still there under the exterior of hardened vengeance.

They entered Paul's office and found Bishop waiting on the lounge. He appeared ready for them, or a GQ photo shoot. Nancy was right, he was gorgeous. Not for the first time that day, Eva wanted to fold into his arms. For comfort. At least, that's what she kept saying in her head. Other parts of her were less convinced.

"How's the missus, Paul?"

Paul took his position behind his desk. "Stunned like an abattoir cow."

"Paul!"

Genuinely surprised by the reaction, he quickly added, "I meant the stunned part, not the cow bit... obviously."

Bishop and Eva stifled a laugh and sat. While Paul logged into his computer, Bishop leaned over. "How are you?"

"I'm okay, thanks."

"No." Bishop's face took on a purposeful expression. "Don't give me the reflex answer. How are you, really?"

Eva blinked. She wasn't used to people delving deeper. Bishop was right, of course. She wasn't fine. Someone had tried to kill her and had damn well nearly succeeded if it wasn't for the person genuinely asking after her welfare. It wasn't something easily shaken off. Bishop knew that better than anyone.

"Messed up, but getting there."

The answer seemed to satisfy Bishop. He nodded and stroked her hand gently. Eva's skin tingled at the warmth of his touch.

Without preface, Paul asked, "What have you got from the two... gentlemen who were shooting at Evie and my beloved?"

Sitting up, Bishop said, "Initially there was a lot of screaming and crying for their mothers."

Paul harrumphed. "After that?"

"They haven't said a word. We've IDed them, though. One Anton Petrovitch and Nikolay Ilyich. We did some digging, and it looks like their bank balances received a hefty injection of funds from an untraceable Cayman Island account four days ago."

"Well, that's the money for the hit, then," Eva said.

"Seems like it." Bishop nodded. "But there's a difference to this one than the last few."

"Huh?"

"The two from the pursuit car in Saint Petersburg and the two knuckleheads from the bridge were private contractors. These two weren't. Well, they are, but they're not."

Eva wiggled uncomfortably in her chair. "Right. So, when you said there was a difference, you meant my sentence made sense and yours didn't?"

Bishop crinkled his nose. "You get awfully snippy when you shoot people, have you noticed?"

"Bishop!"

"Alright, you two," Paul said in a schoolmasterly tone. He motioned for Bishop to continue.

"The two blokes you shot were apparently private contractors. But…"

"But?"

"They are also ex-SVR."

"Great." Eva threw her hands in the air. "That's exactly what we need now, Russian Secret Service involvement. How ex?"

"Two months."

"Holy Bolsheviks. They may as well have come straight from the Kremlin in full dress uniform."

Turning to Paul, Eva saw the conflict bubbling below the surface. On one hand, he wanted to hunt down the bastards responsible for shooting up South Kensington and nearly killing his wife. On the other, if word got out that two former Russian spies had attempted an assassination a stone's throw from MI6 and the halls of British government, there would be a major diplomatic and political shitstorm.

They let it sink in for a moment. Eva could have sworn there was a chill in the air. It may have been the oncoming Cold War.

Glancing in Paul's direction, Bishop said, "Have you shown her the paper?"

A grimace crossed Paul's face. "I hadn't decided if I was going to tell her yet."

"Good thing I mentioned it then?" Bishop beamed.

"Quite."

Flinging her head between the two like she was watching a Wimbledon final, Eva asked, "What paper?"

With a grunt, Paul opened a drawer and placed the paper on the desk.

"It's a newspaper," Eva said curiously. "We still have those?"

"Page thirty-one." Paul paused. "The obituaries."

Half curious, half hesitant, Eva turned to the page. There they were, a full page of obituaries. Some brief, some overly long and flowery. She imagined there was a reason the obits section of the paper kept going when other sections like jobs or housing had long ago traversed over to the digital realm. She supposed old people were simultaneously the most likely to read it and to know anyone mentioned. Then she saw it.

It was brief. It stated that the deceased had served their country bravely and had sadly lost their life. A ceremony was to be held the next day at 1 pm at Brompton Oratory. No flowers.

Eva read the obit curiously. She glanced up at Bishop and Paul, who seemed as perplexed as she was. Mainly because the name of the deceased was familiar. Of course, it would be. It was her name. It was official, it seemed. Eva Destruction was dead.

Knightsbridge was ominously quiet. It was the middle of the day, yet there seemed to be far less foot traffic in the central London neighbourhood than usual. Close to the museum district, near

Harrods, it seemed odd to Eva that so few people were wandering about. It was virtually deserted. Except for the close to twenty MI6 operational staff stationed at various points surrounding Brompton Oratory church.

Everyone who read the obituary had had the same reaction that Eva had.

"It's a minge-punching bellend-slapping trap."

Well, perhaps some had sworn less.

The initial, and still most likely, response was that Eva was being set up. Clandestine meetings in churches hadn't garnered a lot of positive results recently. There had already been a direct attempt on her life, and the funeral notice called her out by name.

But still, Eva was intrigued. So were MI6. What if the message was something else? What if this *wasn't* from the Perfume Assassin? Her organisation was desperate for any leads. There was no way they could ignore the message.

Unlike her previous meeting in Saint Petersburg, where Bishop had been her only backup, this time she had far more support. As Eva entered the church she saw at least five familiar faces. Operational staff from various departments had taken up positions throughout the house of worship. None acknowledged her arrival. There were probably more staff she didn't recognise. For all she knew, Jimmy the office boy was hiding in the organ with a sniper rifle.

The church wasn't set up for a funeral. There were no photos of Eva Destruction, and nobody handed out booklets or gave any indication it was a funeral service at all. The priest at the front seemed to be readying for mass. With no further instruction, Eva took a seat on a middle pew and waited.

Brompton Oratory had a shady espionage history. During the Cold War, the KGB had used the church as a dead letter box on countless occasions. Packages from agents and their handlers were left behind pillars and under pews, providing the Soviets with boundless top-secret material. The infamous Kim Philby himself had provided the USSR with critical information within the confines of the Roman Catholic church.

Was that why this church had been chosen? Or was someone wasting her time? Eva had been in more churches in the past week than in the last ten years.

The church a quarter full, the priest began his mass. For an hour and twenty minutes Eva half-listened to the droning, monotonous voice of Father Bridgeman as he prattled on about a donkey who had made unleavened bread and offered it to a leper. Or something. Eva wasn't really paying attention.

Then the priest called for communion. Eva wasn't a hypocrite, so always steadfastly refused to take communion, even at good friends' weddings, so she stayed where she was, and watched several worshippers dawdle towards the altar.

After blessing two elderly men, a middle-aged woman stepped forward to take communion. After blessing her, the priest mumbled, "Body of Christ, are you Eva Destruction?"

Eva sat up. Had she heard correctly? Was she going mad?

"Did you hear that?" she asked quietly.

"Hear what?" Bishop asked through her earpiece.

"I just… shut up."

"You asked me a question," Bishop replied indignantly.

With increased intensity, Eva watched the priest. The next man received the Eucharist normally. Then a young, conservatively dressed woman knelt before him.

"Body of Christ, are you Eva Destruction?"

The woman was confused, but shook her head. He continued on as normal.

Next in line was an elderly parishioner, dressed up to the nines in her finest for church. The priest nodded at her and commenced his communion. "Body of Christ, are you Eva Destruction?"

Each time he said it, the priest's face was hopeful. Each time, his expectations were dashed. Eva could hardly leave the man disappointed. She virtually leapt out of her seat and joined the line for Holy Communion.

When she finally reached the front of the line, the priest said, "Body of Christ, are you Eva Destruction?"

"Yeah, ah, I'm Eva Destruction."

The priest baulked, as if surprised he had finally received an answer. "Really? That's marvellous." He leaned in conspiratorially and whispered, "Please come and see me after mass. I have a message for you."

Providing a nod in answer, Eva went back to her pew. "Did you get..."

"I got it," Bishop replied. "This is really odd, Eva."

"As odd as chilli sauce on a salad?"

Bishop sighed. "Like I said, snippy."

Ten minutes later, mass was done. Most parishioners had left, although a few MI6 agents lingered. Bishop walked through the entrance. He had a way about him that appeared casual, no matter the circumstance. The spy looked as at home in a church as he did at a beachside luau. It was quite a talent. He took up position near the door, helping elderly parishioners put away the prayer books.

Waiting until the priest was alone, Eva approached and, ignoring subtleties, asked, "What's this about?"

"Well, you see, a man came by and..." He looked hesitantly about the church, as if searching for undesirables. Little did he know the only people left were himself and half of the London Secret Service. He flicked his head, gesturing for her to follow him into the vestry, through a small door behind the altar. Subtle, he wasn't.

Bishop nodded to Eva, silently telling her he would be ready if anything happened. He had her back, like always. Eva followed the priest in, and he closed the door behind them.

"A man," the priest said quietly. "He came by yesterday and provided an extremely generous donation to the restoration fund. You see, it's a very old building, and with the pollution and all, our repair bills often stack up. We've asked the National Trust for additional funds for the—"

"The man?" Eva asked impatiently.

"Oh yes. He said the donation was conditional upon me

agreeing to hand a lady called Eva Destruction an envelope at this mass. It had to be you and it had to be now. I thought, well, if that's all that's required, one little envelope..." He pulled out an envelope from beneath a pile of bibles. Hesitantly, he handed it over. He seemed embarrassed now. "It was a very generous endowment."

"So you said."

Eva tore it open and read the brief message. She checked her watch.

"Bishop, we need to move, now."

"Oh, I'm not a bishop," the priest said.

Ignoring him, Eva yanked open the door. Bishop was standing there, ready.

She turned to the priest. "I'm afraid you'll need to answer some questions."

"Questions?" the priest asked, confused. "Who wants to ask me questions?"

Stepping out from the vestry, the priest saw ten MI6 agents staring at him sternly.

"Oh my."

Bounding out of the church, Eva shoved the message into Bishop's hand. "We have less than ten minutes to be at 2 Whitehall Court. Notify Ops. think we're going on a treasure hunt."

The two ran down the road, heading for Bishop's recently repaired Audi, which was parked near the corner.

"Whitehall Court? Really?" Bishop asked as they ran. "You know that used to be—"

"I know. And check out at who we need to ask for."

Bishop glanced at the message and scowled. "If I was Australian I'd ask if someone was taking the piss."

Eva smirked. "Good to see I'm rubbing off on you."

"Eva, my dear, you can rub off on me any time."

"No time for innuendo, Bishop!"

Slowing as they neared the car, Bishop shook his head sadly, "You do make it so hard."

Eva rolled her eyes as Bishop tossed her the keys. She unlocked the car and they dove in. The drive would normally take fifteen minutes. They had to make it in far less than ten. There was no discussion about who would drive.

Eva hit the start button, threw the car into gear and took off like a rocket.

"Bet you can't do it in five," Bishop said, half teasing.

Jerking the wheel, Eva threw the car around the corner, skidding as it went. Bishop was thrown against the door and scrambled for the grab handle on the roof to right himself. "Woah." He fumbled to click on his seatbelt. "I just had this repaired, Eva."

Staring at the windscreen and leaning forward, amusement tickled Eva's lips. She floored it.

Four minutes and thirty-eight second later, they skidded to a halt at 2 Whitehall Court, right in front of the Royal Horseguards hotel.

Bishop's face was white. "I still don't know how you fit between those buses." His fingernails dug into the leather seat. "You're not allowed to mount the footpath like that."

"We're here." Eva ignored his whining.

They exited the vehicle, scanning for threats. En route, Bishop had called in their destination, but there wasn't enough time to have agents in position. They were on their own.

They both knew the address. Everyone at MI6 did. The old building once housed the Foreign Section of the Secret Service Bureau. The foundation of MI6.

As they walked towards the entrance, a voice yelled, "You can't park there!"

They turned to see a pudgy, red-faced middle-aged man marching towards them.

"Look at all the men telling me what to do," Eva said quietly to Bishop as she walked briskly. "I must really be achieving today."

"You there! I say! You can't park—"

The man was silenced when Eva and Bishop lifted their jackets in unison to show pistols holstered beneath. They had no time for niceties. The pudgy little man couldn't scramble away fast enough.

Eva checked her watch. They had time, but not much. They

burst into the reception of the Royal Horseguards hotel, hands on weapons, expecting anything. They didn't get anything. Unless you counted a startled receptionist clutching his vest.

There didn't appear to be anyone else in reception, just some high-backed chairs. Eva asked for the person named in the message, but the well-groomed gent at reception shook his head in confusion. Not that Eva expected to meet the person named on the note. Eva found it unlikely that Mansfield Cummings would be hanging out at the Royal Horseguards. Mainly because he'd been dead close to a hundred years. Cummings was the first director of MI6.

She was well and truly being played with.

And not in a good way.

From behind one of the high-backed chairs came a hacking cough. Eva raised an eyebrow at her partner. Their hands went back to their pistols. Slowly, they made their way towards the chair.

Before Eva could see who was sitting there, a brittle male voice said, "You are one minute late."

His accent was thick. Russian. For the briefest of moments Eva hoped it was Alexie. But as she rounded the chair, her hopes were dashed. It was an elderly male, but not Alexie.

The infirm old man appeared frail, but his eyes betrayed him. They were sharp as a Damascus sword.

"What's this about?" Eva asked.

"What are these things always about?" He sat upright. "The fate of the world, Miss Destruction. The fate of the world."

# CHAPTER SEVEN

"The fate of the world, eh?"

*Ominous*. Okay.

Eva narrowed her eyes. "So, who are—?"

"My name is Boris Nikolayev," the old man interrupted. "I once worked for Komitet Gosudarstvennoy Bezopasnosti. Your people used to call me by codename, Snow Leopard."

Eva smiled. "Snow Leopard hey?" She sat next to him. "Lucky it's cold today."

The old man shook his head. "Nyet. I come from Siberia; everywhere is too hot."

Bishop stepped away and pulled out his phone, no doubt to hook the rest of MI6 into Eva's conversation. She was still wired up, with her earpiece in.

With a sigh, she folded her arms. "I'm going to have to be completely honest with you, Boris. I'm kind of getting over mysterious ex-KGB types."

The ex-agent seemed to take no offence at the statement. He nodded. "You were stupid to trust Alexie Barinov."

So he knew Alexie. Not only that, he knew they had spoken. *Who is this guy?*

"Why would you say that?" Eva asked.

"He is very untrustworthy man."

Normally opposed to harming the elderly, Eva was willing to make an exception in this guy's case. "Why, because he was ex-KGB?"

"Da."

"You're ex-KGB."

Boris shrugged.

Not entirely sure where this was headed, Eva said, "Nice little game with the funeral notice and the Cummings bit. Cute."

Boris frowned. "I needed to get your attention. I am retired old man and do not get out often. I can have fun if I want."

"Right." Eva wasn't buying any of this guy's shtick. There was something about his manner that rubbed her the wrong way.

"Why did you say Alexie was untrustworthy?"

"Because is true."

"Not that it matters anyway. He's dead."

Boris shook his head. "Bah! He not dead."

He was really getting on Eva's nerves now. "The pool of blood left on the hotel carpet says otherwise, champ."

"Is not his blood. I assume he had someone else place it there. He does not care for sight of blood." He waved his hand. "We made fun of this back in the day."

"Why would you think he's not dead? Two agents were killed as well. Our agents. He was going to reveal information to us and was killed to—"

Boris clicked his nicotine-stained fingers to silence Eva, like she was a dog. It took all her strength not to leap over and smack the side of his head. The old spy bent down and pulled a battered suit-case out from under the coffee table. He opened the suitcase to reveal a musty stack of files and took a manila folder from the top of the pile. Placing it on the table, he turned it towards Eva.

"This picture taken yesterday in Frankfurt. I hope I look so well when I am dead, da?"

He handed her a crystal-clear colour photograph of Alexie walking down a cobblestoned street, talking on a mobile phone. A billboard in the background advertised a Marvel superhero movie that was about to come out.

Eva frowned. Not taking her eyes off the photo, she said, "Maybe he was kidnapped?"

"Perhaps. Tell me, in your experience, do kidnapped men walk around airports and buy duty-free whiskey? I am curious."

"What are you saying?"

The old man sniffed, inhaling a huge glob of phlegm as he did so. "Who do you think killed your agents in the hotel?"

"We're not sure, but we assumed it was whoever kidnapped Alexie."

"Wrong. You assume wrong."

A sense of dread clawed at Eva's chest. She recalled the report: no sign of forced entry. "Alexie killed them?"

A slow nod.

"Why would he do that?"

He tilted his head, and Eva's cogs went into overdrive. She backtracked over all she knew, took everything apart and reassembled it.

As if jolted by electricity, Eva leapt up. The coffee table wobbled and almost fell. She paid it no mind.

"Oh fuck."

Concerned, Bishop approached. She waved him away.

"You're live with Ops," a posh voice said through Eva's earpiece.

"Oh fuckity fucking fuck nuggets with a side order of fuckballs. That weasel-dicked twat-faced spunktrumpet."

"I assume I'm listening to Eva Destruction," said a voice that sounded very much like the new chief of MI6.

"What is it, Evie?" Paul asked through the earpiece.

Eva paced. "In the event of attack, procedure dictates MI6 clear all entrances, right? Get everyone out of harm's way. Shit. He didn't go through X-ray."

"What are you babbling about, Evie?" Paul asked, a hint of concern in his voice. "We don't want people hurt. We want our staff out of danger."

With a nod to nobody in particular, Eva was only half listening. "Alexie strung us along, Paul. Told us all the juicy bits we wanted to hear. I bet he hired those goons who chased us in Saint Petersburg, to make the whole thing seem more urgent. When Alexie got to MI6 he had a case with him, an old briefcase. A tattered old thing—I didn't give it much thought. But when the idiots on the bridge were spotted, we rushed him through security, right past the X-ray machine. Then the RPGs hit and the network was unbolted."

The thoughts were coming rapidly now. She knew she was talking too fast. "Trev said the hack could only be exploited by someone within the MI6 building. Physically, they had to be there. Alexie was in the building, Paul! We only brought him into headquarters after he dropped the news about Harry, but we let him in. He must have had something in the case that got into our internal systems through the wi-fi. He coordinated the attacks to get him inside at the right time, so he could trigger the code to open everything up. We invited the wolf into our burrow and he ripped our throats out."

She flopped into her chair. It was her fault. Eva had been played, thoroughly and without mercy. Just when she'd been starting to think she had a handle on the spy business, she was thoroughly disgraced by a grand master of the game.

Alexie had told them everything they wanted to hear, everything that would get him inside SIS headquarters. He'd sprinkled just enough truth to keep them salivating, giving them exactly what they thought they wanted. And now MI6 had been torn open and every Western spy agency had been caught with their pants down and their genitals gently flapping in the breeze.

"Boris, how did you get this photo? How did you know about Alexie, about me?"

"I am an old spy. Old spies do not have many friends. What friends we do have are old spies too, da? I had old friends disappear. I do not like mysteries. Like said, I am retired old man. I have time, so I investigate. Some of my friends die in suspicious circumstances. I do not like suspicious circumstances. They make me suspicious. Other acquaintances, Barinov was one, he got job and moved away. Nobody gives old spy job unless up to no good. I start to dig."

"You must have been very bored."

Boris ignored the quip. "I track old friend to Frankfurt. I also find Barinov."

Eva was still having a hard time reconciling the grandfatherly Alexie with the perpetrator of the attack—or Prizrak, as the two idiots from the bridge knew him. What Boris had told her put everything into place. Why hadn't she seen it? All logic pointed to Alexie being the one who had taken them down. Eva had to keep reminding herself the old man hadn't been a friendly local green-grocer, but the dreaded Red Scorpion.

"You say Alexie isn't to be trusted. He is working for the other side?"

"Who is other side?"

Feeling stupid, Eva said, "The KGB?"

"You do know this is not still a thing, little girl?"

"I heard a rumour." Eva winced at being called "little girl", but let it slide to keep the conversation on track. "Who is he working for?" She gulped. "Harry Lancing?"

"Nyet, at least I do not think so. It is Lancing fault, but that Capitalist swine is not behind it."

"His fault?"

"The hacking. Taking of information. This is Horatio Lancing technology, but I do not believe he is the man with the agenda."

Eva was annoyed to find herself overcome with a sense of relief. She shouldn't have been. She hated Harry. Didn't she?

Boris went on. "No, the men behind this, they use Lancing's machinery, his technology to tunnel into these agencies. But different methods, I think. Lancing, he is like velvet touch…"

Eva would have blushed at the thought of Harry's touch if she was given to blushing. She wasn't.

"…but these men use sledgehammer. They have no finesse. No art. Who attacks a secret service agency with rocket launcher? I will tell you. Idiots, that is who."

In the corner of reception, Bishop stared at Eva intently, impatient to be part of the conversation. He'd have to wait.

"Do you know about Lancing's whereabouts?"

"I suspect he is not where he is supposed to be." Boris studied Eva's face for a reaction. When none came, he shrugged. "I believe Lancing to be involved with this, either voluntarily or not, but he is not running operation."

There was no way Eva could trust this man's say-so on face value. She knew nothing about him. But she desperately wanted to believe the last thing he had said. Please don't let her ex-boyfriend be the one making a grab for power over the entire world. He'd tried once, and it hadn't ended well for either of them.

"Why should I trust you?" Eva asked. "I trusted an ex-KGB agent recently and it bit my toned white arse."

"Is good to be cautious. Means good spy. I am not saying it is all truth, for I am lowly farmer's son. But I am saying is truth best to my knowledge."

Eva asks, "Why me? Why reach out to me?"

"Because you know Lancing, have a history of taking down bad men who threaten world. Plus, you are very pretty."

"That's equal parts complimentary and insulting."

"This is Russian way. You want nice, you move to Canada."

Thinking back to the package she received, Eva asked a question MI6 had never been able to get a direct answer to. "What do you know of the Perfume Assassin?"

"Is stupid hubris man."

"Do you know who it was?"

"Da."

Eva waited. The elderly ex-agent stared back at her.

"Are you going to tell me?"

"As soon as you ask me."

She grunted. "Who was the Perfume Assassin?"

"Alexie Barinov." Boris leaned over to his suitcase. "I have file here somewhere."

Eva's fist thumped the table, causing Boris to jump. "That son of a bitch sent me a bullet in the mail."

"Then you should be dead," Boris said matter-of-factly. "He was always good at what he did."

"Yeah, well, he must be slipping." She eyed Bishop pacing in the corner and sighed. "Plus, I had some help."

Bishop gave her the slightest of nods.

Replaying part of the conversation in her mind, Eva said, "Who was the spy you tracked to Frankfurt?"

"I am sorry? I am old man, hearing going."

"The other spy. You said you found Alexie by tracking another ex-colleague of yours. Who was it? Maybe we have them on file, too."

"Ah," Boris said, suddenly cagey. "I was hoping you would not ask me this question."

"Why not? You've been very forthcoming so far," Eva said with a tinge of sarcasm. She wasn't completely on board with Boris yet. Everything seemed to check out, but there was something about him Eva didn't trust. She had to concede that would apply to any ex-KGB agent these days.

"I think... I think I will be like your spy movies on this subject. This is needs to know basis, yes?"

Clenching and re-clenching her fists, Eva was ready to throttle the old guy. He had given them information, then wilfully withheld more. Her mind spinning, Eva tried to piece everything together. The Russian embassy bombing, the murder of the CIA agent in Budapest, Harry's escape, Alexie's betrayal, the attack on MI6 systems and whatever had led Boris to follow Alexie to Frankfurt. There was a lot to take in. How did it all tie together?

"Fine. Is there anything you can tell us? Like, for example, who is behind all of this?"

"Perhaps." Boris's face became darker. "Perhaps not." A shrug. "Nyet."

Eva was ready to punch something. She needed to act. She'd been passive for far too long.

"But," said Boris, "I have suspicion. I believe there is political element to all this. There would be no reason for such public targets if not." He leant in. "There is agenda here. He has major plan, we must find what it is."

"Who? Who has a plan?"

Boris checked his watch. "Would you like to meet him?"

~

It was the second time in a week Eva had travelled to Russia. She was annoyed for two reasons. Firstly, her last expedition hadn't ended well, and this trip appeared equally fraught. Secondly, she didn't seem to be entitled to frequent flyer miles. She should really look into that.

Gazing out the plane window, the sprawling suburbs of Moscow spread out across the horizon. The city seemed to stretch out forever—not all that surprising, given it was Europe's biggest city. From the sky it appeared like most metropolises, but up close Eva imagined it would be something else entirely.

Eva had never been to Moscow and would normally be excited about discovering something new. She wasn't. Her stomach was doing backflips. She wasn't a tourist. She was a spy on mission into what had once been the most feared heartland of MI6's most dreaded enemy. Her mission was to find out if that was the case once more.

Bishop was in the back of the plane—in economy, much to his disgust. It was thought that, as they had entered Saint Petersburg together, they should arrive in Moscow separately, and under different names, just in case. As Eva was lead agent, she got to choose who flew first class. She hoped Bishop was enjoying the lack of legroom.

Over the course of the three-and-a-half-hour flight, Boris had said little, besides ordering more and more vodka. That, and complaining incessantly about not being able to smoke, the explanation of his frequent rasping coughs. Any normal man would have passed out after the amount the old spy had drunk, or, more likely, be clinically dead. But the ex-KGB agent appeared as sober as when he had boarded. Boris took full advantage of the service in first class. Eva might not earn frequent flyer rewards, but at least they could travel in style.

After their initial meeting Eva had researched the Snow Leopard. There wasn't a lot on file. Nothing connecting him to the events in Warsaw and The Amanda Bourke Affair, although that wasn't altogether surprising. The KGB had run a faultless operation. Either Snow Leopard was only a low-level operative, or he had been supremely good at what he did.

Eva wasn't sure about Boris. It could have been her experience with Alexie, which had jaded her, or perhaps it was his abrasive manner. The fact that he wouldn't give up the reason he'd been in Frankfurt and able to track Alexie was troubling. It could have been his old spy instincts, or perhaps something more sinister. Or it could simply be Eva's super-spy spidey sense, if that was a thing. It probably wasn't, but Eva kind of hoped it was.

As the pilot announced that passengers should prepare for landing, Eva went through what they knew, or at least what they thought they knew, in light of Boris's revelations. The Perfume Assassin and the hit on Eva—Alexie, although the reasoning behind it seemed murky. The RPG attack on MI6—Alexie. Eva would bet her right nut—if she had one—that Prizrak was Alexie's alias. The cyber attack on MI6 and the other agencies—Alexie? But, although he may have grabbed the information, the old man would never have the wherewithal to hack a state-of-the-art IT system. So that one had a big old question mark.

Who was she kidding? It wasn't much of a question mark. If she was honest with herself, it would be more of an exclamation point. There was only one name that could be linked to Alexie's successful cyber attack.

Who was behind the explosion at the Russian embassy and the murder of the CIA agent, however, was still up for debate. They seemed at odds with the immediate end goals of the other attacks—unless ratcheting up international tensions was the end goal.

"How exactly did you link all the events and this person we're seeing?" Eva asked.

Boris waggled his glass at the cabin steward, asking for a refill.

While he waited, he lowered his voice, "This man we are seeing, he was with Alexie in Frankfurt."

"His lover?"

"No. Not like that. He is much younger than Alexie. Even though the man we will see, what is phrase? Swings this way. That is what you young people say, da?"

"Something like that. Did you get a photo of them together?"

"Nyet, they moved too quickly."

*How convenient*, Eva thought.

"I know this man, Durov," Boris said. "Everyone with passing interest in politics in Russia know this man. Soon whole world will know him. He is to become very famous."

"Why, Boris? What's he doing?"

"Come next election he will be Russian President."

"I think I'm going to have a permanent kink in my neck." Bishop rubbed the back of his head as he limped down the wide pathway. "I may need surgery. How do regular people do it?"

"Fly without bitching?" Eva raised an eyebrow.

"Travel economy. They're treated like cattle. It's inhuman."

Eva rolled her eyes. Boris seemed indifferent to the conversation. The trio ambled down the spacious footpath of the All-Russian Exhibition Centre in north-eastern Moscow. It was originally built as a Soviet-era exhibition centre and amusement park. The section they were in was dominated by a hundred-metre-high monument. It celebrated the launch of Sputnik and was humbly called "The Monument to the Conquerors of Space". Not exactly subtle.

Up ahead, a crowd milled about in front of an auditorium. Placards bore pictures of Daegan Durov. He looked to be in his early forties, with dark hair. He was good-looking, for a politician. A large portion of the crowd appeared to be women.

Since Boris mentioned his name, Eva had done some digging on Daegan Durov. Born and raised in Moscow, he became part of the radical left at university before abruptly deciding to join the Russian Federation army. Instead of alienating both sides, they each claimed him as their own; a comment on the man, rather than on either party, Eva decided.

Entering parliament at the age of thirty-six, a mere five years later he threw his hat in the ring for the presidency. Given Russia's less than stellar history with homosexuality, Durov's ascension was nothing short of miraculous. His sexuality barely rated a mention, even from the far right. His campaign was less than a week old, and while the candidate had a decent following, few believed he had the numbers to usurp the current leadership. Even though the fledgling new government had been racked with scandal and incompetence, it was tipped to retain power.

Following the civil war, there had been a routing of the old guard. Russians were yearning for something new, something strong. Some saw this brash young upstart as the key to the future they craved. Many commentators said he would be a real challenger in four to eight years, but not yet.

Taking in the towering monument and Soviet-era park, Eva asked Boris, "Why have the rally here?"

"He is politician. He is making grand political statement."

"Which is?"

"Russia was once world leader in science, military, philosophy, in a great many things. Vote for him and he will make it so again."

"He's going to say that exactly?" Eva asked sceptically.

Boris frowned. "Since when did politician say what they mean, little girl?"

He had a point. A chauvinistic one, sure, but a point nonetheless.

They entered the rally as inconspicuously as they could, and stood at the back of the packed auditorium. Red banners adorned every available space, and throngs of expectant, mostly young people eagerly found a seat. The mood was jubilant, but reserved. Almost like a rock gig where everyone in the crowd was about to see their favourite artist.

The lights dimmed and the music trumpeted through the

sound system. It was like an old Soviet march, but with a techno beat. Eva had to admit it was both catchy and stirring. Spotlights circled around the audience in time with the music. As the song reached its crescendo, the spotlights hit the centre of the stage and a smiling Daegan Durov walked out. He waved to the crowd and they responded with rapturous applause.

The man knew how to make an entrance, that was for sure.

Over the next thirty minutes, Durov kept the enthusiastic audience spellbound by his expert oratory. Eva didn't speak much Russian, but the MI6-issued translator in her ear did all the heavy lifting.

Never veering into negativity, Durov hammered home his main point in various ways. Essentially, it all boiled down to one thing— Russia was once great, but its leadership had grown fat and complacent, and it needed a new, young, trailblazer to make it a world leader in the 21st century. Durov had a wise charm about him, like a young Barack Obama with a bit of edgy rock star thrown in.

Russian pundits gave his campaign little chance. They said he'd be a worthy challenger... in about ten years. Too young, too inexperienced, too nice, was the general take. The current President, Nicholai Sokolov, was likely to hang on to power. Watching Durov, Eva wondered if the country was missing an opportunity. If Eva were Russian, she'd certainly give Durov the time of day.

Then she remembered why they were there. According to Boris, this smiling, affable politician was the cause of the chaos of the last few weeks. Or so Boris believed. To be honest, Eva couldn't see it. Where was the venom against the evil West? Where was the vitriol, rallying for patriotism and the need to create another Iron Curtain? Why would an up-and-coming politician mingle with the man responsible for an attack on MI6 and the Russian embassy in London?

Eva wondered if Boris was wasting their time. She certainly hadn't warmed to the gruff old geezer. While his pictures of a live Alexie were compelling, they certainly didn't implicate the man on the stage before them. That was purely on the old KGB operative's word. After the rally they would be grilling Boris, that much was certain.

All too soon it was over, and the lights came on. Young, pretty men and women dotted the audience with computer pads, eagerly signing people up to Durov's cause. Durov's attractive acolytes seemed to hone in on the better-dressed members of the audience; some were even greeted by name. It was a slickly run machine.

"We go now." Boris elbowed Eva.

He seemed keen to leave, as if reluctant to be seen at the rally. Boris hobbled faster than Eva had seen him move before. The normally shuffling old man practically tore towards the front entrance. Bishop and Eva struggled to keep up.

As the timeworn ex-KGB agent reached the main doors, a much younger man in an expensive suit stepped out of the shadows, obstructing Boris's exit. Even though he had deliberately blocked the old man's path, the young man gazed past Boris.

"Miss Eva Destruction?"

Eva's internal alarm automatically sounded. No one had been alerted to her arrival in Moscow. She had travelled under a false name. Her hand automatically went to the rear of her jacket.

The man before her appeared unperturbed by her reaction. He simply stood before them, calmly awaiting her reply. He had black slicked-back hair and appeared to be a cross between a sleazy waiter and an apprentice henchman.

"Yes?" Eva finally managed to say.

"My name is Anatoly. I have been asked to invite you to meet someone."

Eva gave Bishop a slight shake of her head, indicating he should stand down. She had this.

Addressing the new arrival, Eva asked, "And who might that be?"

"The next President of the Russian Federation."

# CHAPTER EIGHT

"Why the fuck does everyone want to see me lately?" Eva asked as she followed Anatoly down the subterranean hallway under the convention centre.

"I'm afraid I can't speak for other people," Anatoly replied formally.

"Can you speak for Durov?"

"I would never presume to be so bold."

"Can you speak for yourself, then?"

"On occasion, but only when I'm allowed."

Eva stared at him.

Anatoly smirked slightly. "This is joke."

"I have to be honest, I still struggle with the whole Russian humour thing."

The two of them strolled down the concrete passageway, their footsteps echoing off the bare, colourless walls. The original plan was to watch Durov's rally and then place him under observation to see if they could tie him to Alexie or the breached data.

It was a long shot, sure, but a man running for the head of the Russian government being seen cavorting with the man who had exposed their secrets was something MI6 couldn't ignore. At least, that was the plan. In her brief stint as a spy, Eva had come to realise that all the planning in the world amounted to a flaming pile of monkey turds when the bullets started flying.

Adaptability was the key. Like, when a challenger for one of the most powerful countries on earth asks you for a chat, you go with it.

They came to a red door with a faded star. Anatoly rapped three times. A faint "Zakhodi" could be heard from the other side. The assistant opened the door and motioned for Eva to enter, while he remained in the hallway. It seemed he was not permitted an audience with his master this time.

The door closed quietly behind her and Eva stepped forward. The room was oddly dim. This being an entertainment centre, she had expected the harsh illumination of fluorescent lights every-where. Had they dimmed the lights especially for this meeting? Given the theatrics of Durov's stage performance, Eva wouldn't have been surprised. It seemed every aspect of his life was choreo-graphed.

"Good evening, Miss Destruction." His private voice was more sedate than his stage one. It carried a more severe edge. "I hope you enjoyed the rally."

Durov stood in the half-light at the back of the room, standing to attention. His English was perfect. No hint of any particular accent, his vowels and consonants were so rounded they were virtually circular, his enunciation crystal clear.

"I seem to be quite popular in Russian circles lately." Eva stepped forward. Durov remained motionless, so she stopped her advance. There seemed to be a no-man's-land between them. "I'd ask how you knew I was here, but it seems you have ways of picking people out of the crowd."

"We use technology to our advantage, not unlike a former boyfriend of yours, wouldn't you say?"

Mentioning her ex was never the best way to get into Eva's good books.

"Danny Bannerman? I don't see how my high-school boyfriend

is relevant here. He was pretty technologically inept. Pretty sure he couldn't even spell ATM."

"I had heard you were amusing, Destruction."

"I have my moments."

"It is a shame I was misinformed." He folded his hands in front of his crotch.

The contrast between his on-stage and in-person personas was startling. The man before her had an air of contempt, and all the warmth of an arctic tundra.

"Why am I here, Durov?"

"That's what I would like to know, Destruction. Why *are* you here?"

"What can I say? I'm a sucker for a rally."

A bored tut escaped Durov's mouth, like a father annoyed at his child's puerile attempt at humour. He stared at Eva for a long time, daring her to break the awkward silence.

For no apparent reason, a cruel half-smile crossed his lips. It was virtually a sneer. Eva suddenly felt vulnerable. A distinct chill ran down her spine. There was something eminently threatening about this inanimate man. Without moving her eyes from Durov, she assessed the room for escape routes, mentally calculating ways to flee or fight her way out if she was forced to.

"I am curious as to why MI6 would take it upon themselves to patronise my little get-together, and with one of my country's most esteemed former intelligence operatives as well. I am most curious, I must say."

The man wasn't short of information.

"Would you believe I'm just a humble tourist?"

Durov frowned. "Nobody with the name Eva Destruction is a humble anything."

Eva said nothing. Silence swirled around them.

"I am surprised they gave someone like you the task of finding Lancing and the missing data."

Now he sounded like he had too much information. And he was condescending.

"Someone like me?"

Durov glowered. It was the expression of someone who was aware they'd said something offensive, but who felt it was beneath them to care. "Someone more qualified."

"Someone with a penis?" Eva's nails dug into her palms.

Giving a shrug, Durov inspected his flawless fingernails and gave a bored sigh. "Don't confuse tokenism with equality. MI6 are setting you up for failure, surely you understand this? 'Oh look, we gave this pathetic woman an opportunity to be in charge, and look what happened. Oh well, we tried, back to the patriarchy. Let's meet down the strip club.'" He gave a derisive laugh. "You're pitiful. You think a few scraps from the master's table equates to egalitarianism. You'd best learn while you're in my country: you don't ask for power, you take it."

Normally Eva would savagely knock down each and every one of the puerile arguments Durov put forward, but now wasn't the time. Her feminist forebears would be turning in their graves, but she had to stay on mission. Did that mean she was evolving into a better agent? It was hard to decide if biting her tongue in the face of sexism was learning adaptability or acceding to prejudice.

It was hard to believe Durov could be so blatantly sexist. He was a gay man in Russia, where until recently his lifestyle had been vilified and criminalised. Surely he would be more understanding? Obviously not. Eva guessed one type of oppression didn't automatically negate another. Regardless, she had to get the conversation back on track.

"You put on quite the show. You must really—"

With a wave of his hand, Durov cut her short. This topic of conversation bored him. Eva would have loved to keep going, just to annoy him, but it seemed he had other ideas.

Taking one step forward into the light, Durov tilted his head. "Contrary to what you may have heard, I do not wish to take over the world, Miss Destruction."

Surprisingly, Eva hadn't heard that, but it was telling that Durov thought she had.

"No?" Eva asked.

"No. I only want to secure the best possible future for my country."

"So you've stopped running for office?"

He gave a small, polite laugh. "I take back what I said, Destruction. You are funny. I enjoy a sense of humour in a woman—so rare, I find."

Eva fumed at the patronising compliment, packaged in a wrapping of sexism. The old cliché of women not being funny perpetuated by men uncomfortable with women being smarter than they were. She chose not to take what it was clearly intended to be—bait.

Durov took another step forward, his head lowered, and stared at her intensely. "We seem to be getting along famously—"

"Do we?"

"—so I wish to offer you some advice. Go home. Take whatever intelligence you have..."

Eva didn't know if he was talking about spying or making a personal slight.

"... and waddle off to whatever hole you came from. You're not welcome in my country. You will find nothing of interest here. Stop wasting your time and mine by investigating whatever crazed imaginings you've been fed by a sad, tired old man."

Behind her back, Eva cracked her knuckles. "Thank you for your feedback. It will be filed in the appropriate place."

"And that is?"

"Up your arse."

"Charming." Durov sniffed, as if suddenly tired of the conversation. "It's a pity you won't have a chance to enjoy your time in Moscow. I think you would have liked our nightclub scene very much."

"Not really one for nightclubs myself."

"No, I expect not. That would be more for Candy Stripe, I would think."

The chill down Eva's spine turned to ice, and her breath hitched. Candy Stripe was a cover profile set up for her on a previous mission to Macau. Knowing she was MI6 was one thing, but this was something else entirely. How the glowing fuck would Durov know about her former cover name?

"How do you know that name?" Eva asked coldly.

"You would be amazed at what I know."

"Only someone who had access to the breached MI6 data would have that information."

"Really?" Durov shook his head, feigning surprise. "According to the media, the breach only involved low-level information of little importance. I do hope you're not telling me otherwise, Miss Destruction?" Durov took two steps forward, now so close that Eva could feel his breath. His voice was low, but carried an unnatural hint of menace.

"Because if someone held that information it would be a very dangerous situation, wouldn't you say? The power they could wield would be unfathomable, the influence unmatched in human history." He shook his head slowly, keeping his eyes locked on hers. "Imagine how much control they would have over world events... over—" he stared into Eva's eyes, "people. I would say, theoretically, of course, that someone who held that much power would be most formidable. With that information, they could make a man do anything." He took one final step, bringing them nose to nose. "They would be someone you should never, ever cross. I imagine the consequences would be most deadly."

He stepped back and smiled. Suddenly he was the genial stage politician from earlier. The metamorphosis was astounding. He extended his hand.

"Miss Destruction, it has been a pleasure. Take care on your return trip."

Too stunned for words, Eva took his hand and shook. Durov beamed and walked away briskly, exiting via the door she had come through.

Standing completely alone in the austere room, Eva felt like she was covered in a thin film of slime.

It was several moments before Eva could move again. The confrontation was greater than the sum of its parts. Had they had found the man who was behind it all? Perhaps. The walking dissociative identity disorder that was Durov seemed too well informed and menacing to be coincidental. The man knew too much, was too combative for Eva to have misinterpreted what he'd said. But he'd given her nothing concrete to tie him to events. Nothing that would hold up in court, that is.

Marching out of the room, Eva found Bishop and Boris outside in the cold park. They were milling about at the base of the Monument to the Conquerors of Space. She gave them a brief rundown of the altercation and suggested they get the hell out of there.

As they walked to their hotel, Eva replayed the conversation in her head. She hadn't imagined it. Durov had petrified her. It was more than his words or his manner. His presence had a malevolence she found difficult to explain. The man had shaken her like few in her life ever had. She didn't know what to do with the tension.

When they reached the hotel, Eva escorted Boris to his suite and told Bishop to go to his room like he was a petulant schoolboy. Bishop didn't take kindly to that, but she was lead agent, so she told him to suck it up. Durov's sexist remarks had got under her skin, and she needed to assert a certain level of control. She was aware of how stupid it was, but figured Bishop knew her well enough to not take offence. She hoped.

Once Boris was safely in his room, Eva went to Bishop's. When he opened the door, she barged past him and opened the minibar. She took out a tiny bottle of Jack Daniels and downed it in one gulp, then did the same to a bottle of vodka. As she opened a bottle of gin, she turned to a startled Bishop. "You better order more booze, you're running low."

It was obvious Eva was more shaken than she realised. This wasn't her. She had faced down other dangerous men before; why had Durov shaken her so? She wondered if the answer was at the bottom of the bottle of gin. After tossing it back, she determined that it wasn't, but decided to keep looking just in case.

Bishop cast Eva a curious glance. "You drank all my alcohol." He gave her a playful pout. "That was impolite."

Ignoring him, Eva held up two half-bottles of chardonnay and merlot, weighing up which to open first. Was it a good idea to mix her drinks like this? She didn't care.

Eva decided she wasn't in the mood for Bishop's playful mocking. "Fuck your manners."

"Only my manners? Eva, you disappoint me."

Bishop could shift from playful to seductive so suddenly it was alarming. She put down the bottle. "I assure you, Bishop, I never disappoint."

Tilting his head in acquiescence, Bishop grinned. "I don't doubt it."

Damn he was a good-looking bastard.

"What's this about, Eva?" He pointed an elbow to the growing pile of empty bottles. His voice was soft, non-confrontational. Almost, dare she say it, caring. "You come barging into my room and down all the cheap booze—are you okay?"

Eva turned towards him and gently placed her arse on the desk. It was a sturdy desk. Arching her back, she leaned her head to one side. "You don't like me coming in your room?"

"You can come in my room any time." There was that lady-killer smile again. "Last time you visited my hotel room we both ended up naked."

"That was a mistake." Eva kept her voice even, although she did allow her memory to recall it. It was quite a memory.

"I don't remember finding anything amiss." Bishop slid his hands into his pockets. "Quite the opposite, in fact."

"No, I mean the fact that we had no clothes on, it wasn't planned, it just… Bishop, could you please stop undressing me with your eyes."

"Is there another way you would like me to undress you?"

Eva sighed. "You're insufferable."

Taking a step forward, Bishop ran his fingertips gently along Eva's arm. She didn't shy away from the touch. It felt good. More than good.

In a whisper, Bishop said, "Admit it, you're falling for me, Eva."

She slid her hand down his back. "Why would I fall for you? You're emotionally unavailable."

"That's ridiculous. I am emotionally available." Bishop gave his head a slight shake. "Just not to women."

Eva pulled herself up, realising she was about to hurtle down an emotional hill where she didn't know how to stop. They were on a mission. This was Bishop. What the hell was she thinking?

Turning to grab two glasses, she poured the merlot. Eva used the movement as an excuse to put some distance between the two of them.

*Holy duck-queefing fuck puddles. What were you about to do, woman?*

Eva took a moment to compose herself. To his credit, Bishop let her. She needed to pull herself together. She'd almost done exactly what her libido wanted her to. That was generally an ill-advised course of action.

Taking a sip to buy some time, Eva said, "I often wonder how you became who you are, Bishop."

"Well, there was a radioactive spider and some gamma rays, and I seem to recall a super serum of some description."

"You're not a superhero, dude."

"Aren't I?"

"No, I mean how did you become this rogue? What made you create this cocoon of cad around you? What happened in your life to cause you to be this way? Who hurt you?"

All humour fell away from Bishop's face. He put the glass down and walked to the centre of the room, making some pretence about searching for something. Eva saw the hurt in his eyes. She normally praised herself on her marksmanship, and it seemed her remarks had hit far too close to the target.

"I'm sorry Bishop, I didn't mean to…"

"No, don't be silly, I'm fine," he said in a way that clearly meant the exact opposite. "We should really focus on the mission."

"Right," Eva said. "What do we do now?"

"Call the boss."

～

"Can I state again for the record that this is the dumbest idea since I thought I could pull off a fringe."

"This isn't a stupid idea, Evie." Paul's tone was as convincing as a Nigerian prince's email.

"It really is." Eva pulled at her skirt.

She sat in a small reception area talking to Paul on the phone. Completely out of character, she was dressed in a pencil skirt and formal blazer. It had been bought in a hurry and wasn't sitting right, which seemed fitting, because neither was the reason for the meeting.

"You're lead agent. It falls to you," Paul said.

"Surely this is a diplomatic issue. The ambassador—"

"Wasn't there," Paul interrupted. "You were. If we're going to defuse this situation we need—"

"Defuse?" Eva laughed.

"Yes, defuse. We're hurtling towards another Cold War, Evie. We need to relieve some of this pressure. If we can alert the Russians that we suspect one of their own is behind it all, we'll go some way towards avoiding further conflict. They can start their own parallel investigation. The way both sides are acting, this thing could escalate to an armed conflict within weeks. Russia has already dispatched its aircraft carrier from Gdańsk, and the Americans have moved their own into the Mediterranean. Tensions are high, make no mistake. One spark and the whole powder keg will blow. You need to make sure it doesn't get to that."

*No pressure.* Fail and they'd have World War III on their hands. Piece of piss. For her next trick, Eva would cure cancer, eliminate world hunger and stop manspreading on public transport.

Blowing out a lungful of air, Eva took in her surroundings. The place was quiet as a tomb, and about as welcoming. Lavish was an accurate word. As was opulent. Deep red carpet, extravagant gold filigree—it was a lot to take in.

Eva had never dreamt she'd see inside the Kremlin. Now she wished it had remained a dream. Like most people, she had thought of the Kremlin as a few onion-shaped towers. It wasn't until she'd researched it that she'd realised it was so much more. Besides the twenty towers, there were numerous grand buildings within the huge fortified walls, including palaces—five of them, to be exact. There were also several cathedrals, as well as the head-quarters of the most important government agencies.

Despite the grand scale of the Kremlin, the reception area she sat in was tiny. But what it lacked in space it more than made up for in ostentatious ornamentation.

She wished she had her gun.

Bishop had not been allowed in. Inviting one MI6 agent into the hallowed halls was fraught; allowing two was tantamount to the fall of the Berlin Wall. Her partner was no doubt outside, brooding.

Eva's little run-in with Durov the night before had led to a sleepless night. It wasn't the only thing that had. Frustration does that to a girl. Was Bishop right? Was she falling for him? Did she want to keep falling? What would happen when she landed? She had to put that aside for now. Regardless of what he may think, Bishop wasn't more important than the fate of the world. She had to focus.

Squirming in her uncomfortable suit, Eva waited for the Under-secretary of the Assistant to the Sub-Chief of the Junior Attaché of the somethingorother. MI6 and the GRU had no official ties. There were no formal lines of communication. This meeting had been organised through backchannels and diplomatic hoops. Officially, Eva wasn't there. She was an agricultural envoy for an EU investi-gation committee. MI6 had no knowledge of how seriously the other side were taking this meeting, but the fact that she was meeting a nobody underling of a nobody underling suggested not very.

Eva still didn't know what she was going to say. That she'd met Durov and he was creepy as fuck? While true, that probably wouldn't help their cause. Eva smoothed her skirt. She couldn't have been more uncomfortable if she tried.

From the other side of the door, footsteps came echoing across the marble floor. The door creaked open and a pimply uniformed man, virtually a teen, in a ridiculously large military hat bowed at her.

"You, come, please."

He pivoted on the spot and marched out before Eva could answer. She scurried after him as quickly as she could. The pencil skirt didn't help. Shuffling to catch up with the young officer, Eva managed a moment of awe.

It was hard to believe she was being escorted through the Kremlin. Earlier in the morning she'd walked through Red Square, which was enough to create a sense of astonishment in itself. Then she'd passed through the fortified walls of the Kremlin, which sent a quiver through her entire body. The complex was far larger than she'd anticipated. She'd spied the Grand Kremlin Palace immediately. Like everything else in Russia, it was ridiculously big. She'd been steered away from the seat of government and ushered into a small building at the complex's outskirts.

Now it seemed that the officer was leading her back towards the Grand Kremlin Palace again. Either that, or the exit.

Waddling along as fast as her skirt allowed, Eva drew even with the young man. "I was told I was meeting with the Junior Attaché for the sub-something…"

"I'm afraid the meeting will not take place today."

That was all he said. He continued his march, and Eva continued her struggle to keep up. Instead of turning right, the way she'd come in, the officer turned left, directly through an entrance into the palace.

Eva halted. "Hang on, this is…"

Two guards at the doorway saluted the young officer as he charged forward. Eva ran to keep pace. For the next several minutes she was led through elaborately decorated hallways, filled with priceless artworks, statues, suits of armour and marble busts. She would have loved to slow down and admire the artistry and lavishness of it all, but their pace offered no such luxury.

Just as Eva was getting winded, the officer slowed down. They came to a set of large double doors, above them an imposing marble staircase snaking in two, providing a grand entrance to whoever descended.

The young officer finally came to a stop and nodded towards the doors.

"Do I...?" Eva asked, making a door-opening gesture with her hands.

The officer nodded and stood as rigid as one of the suits of armour. It seemed this was as far as he went.

Eva yanked the door open. Inside was a beautiful, giant ballroom. It was so stunningly decorated even Louis XIV might have told them to calm the fuck down. At the centre of the grand hall were two thrones, positioned opposite each other. The right one was vacant. Behind the other stood a long man, with an equally long face. He wore formal gloves and an elaborate coachman's jacket. On the throne sat...

*Holy shitgibblets.*

Eva blinked several times to decide if she was imagining things. Her shock must have been apparent, because the gentleman on the throne motioned for her to come over and sit.

It seemed the President of the Russian Federation wanted to see her. Eva was reasonably certain she was about to throw up.

How had a low-level informal discussion suddenly escalated into a meeting with one of the most powerful men in the world? Eva conceded she was pretty interesting, but to be bumped up to head of state was a dramatic turn of events. Even Paul's influence couldn't make this meeting happen. Something was going on in the background that she wasn't privy to.

Clomping over in her ill-fitting formal shoes, the walk to the centre of the ballroom seemed to take forever. The majesty of the room was in comic contrasted to the clatter of her cheap footwear. She didn't have the right attire for such an important meeting. She certainly didn't have the mental preparation.

Of course, she knew of the President. He had been appointed after the chaos of the civil war. Eva equated his selection as the Russian head of state as the equivalent of Steven Bradbury, an Australian speed skater who won a gold medal at the Winter

Olympics when every one of his opponents fell over in the final. President Sokolov had ended up as President in pretty much the same way. He'd been the last man standing when the rubble settled.

Eva greeted the President formally with a bow.

The puffy cheeked middle-aged man beamed at her. "English," he said with a thick Russian accent, shaking his head. He pointed to the man behind him. who must have been his interpreter.

Eva nodded her understanding. He gestured for her to sit on the throne opposite. Eva did as she was told.

The President proceeded to speak in Russian, gesturing genially, talking about something at length. Eva wished she had her translating device, but it was deemed impudent to take such technology into the "enemy's" lair. While the President spoke, Eva tried to remain calm and focused.

The interpreter listened intently and nodded politely once the President had finished.

The long man smiled courteously at Eva and said, "You're a dirty whore who deserves to die."

"What!" Eva shot out of her seat.

The President seemed as shocked as Eva. He barked in Russian at the interpreter.

"What did he say?" Eva demanded of the interpreter.

He spoke several words in Russian to the President, who seemed to calm slightly but was as agitated as Eva.

The interpreter said, "Oh, he formally thanked you for coming." He displayed a row of yellowed teeth. "I was the one who called you a whore."

"Why would you say that?" Eva's eyes darted around the ballroom as she tried to work out what was happening.

"Well, isn't it true?" the interpreter asked civilly. "You look like a dirty whore."

"What the fuck is going on?"

"This."

From beneath the coachman's jacket the interpreter pulled out a Walther PPK pistol and aimed it at Eva. She reeled backwards. She was in the centre of a ballroom—there was no way she could outrun a pistol before she reached a door. She found herself moving away from him nonetheless. President Sokolov screamed at the interpreter—Eva assumed he was demanding to know what the hell was going on. That made two of them.

Without another word, the interpreter aimed the gun at the President and pulled the trigger. The back of the President's head blew out, splashing blood and brains all over the throne.

Eva's mouth hung open in shock. *What the fuck is going on?*

As politely as he had first greeted her, the interpreter said, "One moment, please."

He sprayed his gloved hands with a little bottle he had extracted from his pocket. Smiling his yellow smile, he then tucked the bottle back in his coat. He waved the gun around casually, taking his time. But instead of targeting Eva, the thin man aimed the weapon at his own face.

Eva cried out, "No!"

With a grim frown, the interpreter pulled the trigger. His face exploded in a sickening splatter of red, and the tall man slumped to the floor. The gun clanked across the parquetry.

Open mouthed, Eva hyperventilated, trying to make sense of what had happened. The ballroom was inhumanly silent. Blood seeped from the two bodies, and a sickening sea of crimson spread across the floor. A knock at the far door made her jump. A Russian voice called from the other side. The tone sounded like someone was asking if everything was alright in there.

Eva's mind raced. The President of Russia was dead. His interpreter was dead. It would be blamed on her. No one would believe that a man would kill the President and then shoot himself in the face. That was clearly insane. She was being framed—both her and MI6.

Someone had gone to a lot of trouble to get a British Secret Service agent in the same room as the President, along with someone willing to sacrifice themselves without hesitation. A cataclysmic world event had occurred before Eva's eyes.

Paul would be so proud. Eva had totally defused the situation.

Her eyes darted around the room. No escape. No weapons. Security would burst in at any second. She was in the middle of the fortified Kremlin. The security of every major Russian military, intelligence and civilian agency was between her and the outside world.

The banging on the door grew louder.

Eva had to decide on her next move. She only had seconds left. Reaching down, she ripped the side of her skirt, then, bending into a crouch, Eva broke into a run.

# CHAPTER NINE

Kremlin literally meant "fortress inside a city".

All Eva had to do was find her way out of the fortress without being captured or killed. Simple.

If she stumbled, if she fell, the world would fall into chaos, and the cataclysmic effects would last for decades. There was no doubt that if she was captured, MI6 would be blamed. World War I had been triggered when a prince was shot by a radical. This was far more serious. A Secret Service agent assassinating a head of state? The ramifications would be catastrophic.

It was up to Eva to prevent that from happening. The stability of the world depended on her surviving the next few minutes. The responsibility was massive, but so would be the consequences if she failed.

At least if Eva was caught, she would have completed Paul's task. She would have put an end to the new Cold War, just like he'd asked—it would turn hot within days. A foreign agent murdering a head of state was a declaration of war. No diplomatic manoeuvring would avert it. The Russian people would go mad. There would be severe retaliation, and with no clear leadership at the top, there was no telling how the nation would react. The nuclear option may even come into play. Every new world leader likes to start their tenure with a show of strength, to demonstrate their power. It was likely that whoever was appointed the new head of the Russian Federation would do likewise.

Eva's only saving grace was that the meeting hadn't been official. It had been slapped together by backchannels, and the only official record was the agricultural envoy that never existed.

Eva could only assume Durov was behind the insane assassination. Or Alexie. Most likely both. What influence must they have to make a man kill his own President and take his own life? She recalled what Durov had said to her about the security breach data. "They could make a man do anything with that information."

But right now, Eva had to focus.

She sprinted across the ballroom, away from the rapping on the door. As she flung the door open and stumbled into the hallway, she wished they'd had longer to prepare, and to plan possible escape routes. She gathered her thoughts. If she ran in the hallways, any security camera footage could be used to claim she fled the scene. If she strolled, that would at least give MI6 plausible deniability. It took all her self-control not to sprint, but she held it together.

Walking briskly, she pulled out her phone. It took two agonising rings before Bishop answered.

"Hi Eva. How's it going?"

"I'm not going to lie," she said, panting heavily, "could be better."

She gave him a rundown of events. Stunned silence was his initial response.

"We need to get you out of there," Bishop finally said.

"You fucking think?"

So far Eva had passed only a handful of people in the corridors. None of them had paid her any attention. A woman in a suit would be common in what was essentially Russia's version of the White House. Her pace was as hurried as she dared.

"Bishop," she whispered. "Don't come after me."

"If it comes down to—"

"Promise me," Eva said firmly. "Promise me you won't do anything mental."

There was no immediate answer. Eva knew perfectly well that her partner would burn the Kremlin to the ground if it meant getting her to safety. A Bishop rampage was a beautiful thing to witness, but it would be the worst possible strategy in this situation. It would only end in them both dying. She'd gladly lay down her life if it meant Bishop remained safe.

What did that mean? Did she just admit to caring for Bishop? Marching quickly down the wide hallway, she pushed the thoughts down firmly.

A tapping sound came through her phone—she assumed Bishop was attacking his computer.

"Eva, I need you to turn on the geolocation on your phone and activate the MARC beacon."

While Eva's phone appeared to be an off-the-shelf mobile device, it had a few tricks up its sleeve.

"MI6 has a map of the Kremlin?" she asked quietly.

"A map-ish," Bishop replied. Eva could tell he was only half-listening, busy working on his computer. "We've drawn it up over the years from different intelligence sources, but we've never tested it out. No time like the present."

If anyone was going to get her out of this alive it would be her partner.

"Bishop," Eva said, rounding a corner to another vacant hallway, "I'm scared."

It was probably the first time Eva had ever uttered those words, certainly to Bishop. Bishop didn't respond—probably because he knew they were words Eva wouldn't use lightly. Through all their harrowing exploits, Eva had never said anything like that. Never before had her actions carried so much weight.

"Okay, I've got you," Bishop said. "Take the next left."

"Did you hear what I said, Bishop, I said I'm—"

"You need to treat this like war, Eva. Your first priority is to stay alive for the next minute."

"Then what?"

"Then we work on the next minute. Then the next."

"Until?"

"Until we're sitting on a beach in the Maldives."

How did he do that? Even in this situation, he could make her smile. "I like this plan."

"Suddenly I do too. I'll even buy you a bikini."

"You get me out of this, I won't need the bikini."

Bishop coughed, then his voice turned serious. "When you're in the next corridor, take the second right. There's a broom closet, second door on the left—or at least, there was in the '90s."

Eva came to a halt. A small sign in Cyrillic letters adorned the door. Eva held up her phone, which translated it for her. "Communications." It was locked. Eva could pick it, but why bother? She needed escape, not sabotage.

"It's a comms cabinet now. Next suggestion?"

Before Bishop could answer, a piercing wail assaulted her ears.

"That's a siren," Eva shouted into the phone. "I'm screwed."

"It could be a good siren."

"Have you ever heard of a good siren, Bishop?"

"There could be. Like when they give the all clear. That's a good siren."

"Pretty sure this isn't one of those, dude."

"You're right of course. Look, Eva, I'm going to put you on hold."

And that's exactly what he did. Here she was, standing in the middle of a Kremlin hallway, siren shrieking, and Bishop put her on fucking hold? What was he doing? Ordering a pizza?

A few excruciating seconds later, Bishop came back on the line. "Alright. We apparently have a gent on the inside. I'm going to direct you to him."

"A gent?"

"A Russian gent, yes. Ops have been alerted to your plight, we're mobilising assets as we speak. The chap in question has been with us for a number of years, but he's not answering his phone right now. Regardless, there's a code word to give him: 'Hummingbird'. He should look after you."

"I'm not liking the word 'should'."

"It's the best we've got right now."

With the incessant alarm still ringing, Bishop directed Eva up two flights of stairs and further into the belly of the beast. Like Trev, the gent in question worked in IT. Without giving too much detail, Bishop told Eva he'd been feeding them mid-level information for the better part of a decade. He, according to Bishop, was a 'good egg'. She'd settle for any type of egg right now. Although she could murder a Cadbury Creme Egg if anyone was offering.

Bishop told her the contact's name was Ivan Markoski. Eva didn't care what his name was. It could be Chad Douche-canoe for all she cared, so long as he could help.

The reaction in the palace was odd. People milled about, not entirely sure what they should do. It wasn't a fire siren, which had clear instructions and evacuation protocols. This was different. Eva expected to hear an announcement over the loudspeakers providing her description and precise whereabouts, but so far it hadn't happened.

Following Bishop's last instruction, Eva turned to face a small door among a sea of small doors. She knocked politely.

"You should knock," Bishop suggested helpfully.

"Thanks, I'll try that."

Eva knocked again, but there was no response. She opened the door and it creaked quietly. Poking her head inside, she saw a tiny room overfilled with racks of computer equipment. In the centre of the room was an old solid wooden desk overflowing with monitors in various states of repair. A man in his thirties sat in front of the desk.

Eva sighed. "Found him."

"Well, say hello," Bishop said encouragingly.

"I would, but it's not going to make much difference." Eva was numb. "His throat's been slashed, Bishop. He's dead. We've been made."

"Run."

Eva didn't need to be told twice. Or once, for that matter. Before Bishop had even uttered the word she was already in the hall and moving as fast as decorum would allow. She had faith in Bishop but knew no map or words of encouragement could change the inevitable. Eva was going to be caught, put on show for all the world, and executed. She'd faced down threats before, but saw no way out of this.

The dead informant must have been exposed by the data breach. But the GRU weren't known for slashing throats. They were more about shining lights in faces and the occasional polonium poisoning of those they disagreed with. This was different. This was brutal. This was a message.

There were more beeps as people joined the conference call, trying to help. Eva knew it was futile. Her pace slowed. There was no use rushing when she had nowhere to rush to. Her thoughts now centred on whether it was best to surrender and try and explain, rather than pursuing this pointless attempt to escape.

"Eva?" It was a new voice. A female one. "I know things seem grim, love, but we're working on getting you out." The Chief of MI6's voice carried genuine concern.

"I'll do my best not to be captured for the good of the Service and—"

"Sod the fucking Service, Eva. Save your arse. I've read your files, I know you are an extremely capable young woman. You've faced harrowing situations before and always prevailed. Always. Remember that. Keep putting one foot in front of the other. We'll get you out of there. You have my word."

Even in her frightened state, Eva was overcome with pride, and a slight sense of shame that she'd misjudged the Chief on their first meeting. She was feistier than Eva had realised, and had far less of a stick up her arse. If she ever got out of this Eva might even ask the Chief out for a beer. But first she had to get out.

"What's the plan?" Eva asked with new determination.

"Cause a bit of mayhem," the Chief said.

Eva grinned. "My favourite thing."

~

For the next five minutes, Eva miraculously evaded capture. Several packs of panicked soldiers had run past her down various passageways. The fact that they paid her no mind told her she wasn't public enemy number one. Yet.

It seemed bizarre. Surely the young officer who had escorted her to the ballroom could describe her appearance? Wouldn't Eva be the prime suspect? Wouldn't there be an instruction to appre-hend any dark-haired woman with tattoos who couldn't speak a word of Russian? Someone had gone to a lot of trouble to frame her, so why weren't they framing her? It certainly wasn't Eva's skills that had gotten her this far. Essentially, she'd been wandering around aimlessly.

There was more at play here.

The staff at headquarters were doing their best to keep her safe. They tried to contact any assets friendly to their cause within the walls of the Kremlin. None answered, which was concerning in itself. The current strategy was to find her a place to hide until things quietened down. That really wasn't her style. Eva wasn't one to hide.

On her way to a third-floor back room that may or may not have once been an infirmary, a suit appeared in the corridor before her. Keeping her head down, Eva marched forward, moving to the left to avoid the man. He stepped to the same side, shadowing her move and blocking her path. Eva changed direction again and he moved to intercept her. Doing her best to appear annoyed, like any office worker, she huffed, and planted her hands on her hips.

Eva finally looked at the man. He was handsome, in a scruffy kind of way, with a rough and ready three-day growth. He looked on the verge of wrestling a bear, or driving across Mexico at a moment's notice. With dark hair, a chiselled jaw and a dimple on his chin, he radiated a young Mickey Rourke's smoulder. Eva tried not to drool.

"Can I help you? You seem lost." His English was flawless.

Eva knew better than to answer. It was a classic ruse: speak in your opponent's native language, enticing them to answer and give away who they are. Trouble was, Eva couldn't reply in Russian. She spoke three languages, but Russian wasn't one of them.

Gesturing to indicate she didn't have time for the man, Eva put the phone to her ear as if taking a call. Bishop hadn't hung up and remained her lifeline to the outside world, and hopefully salvation. Other voices had come and gone, but Bishop had stayed, there for whenever she needed reassurance. Bishop was her rock.

Avoiding the man, Eva determinedly marched down the hallway to no destination at all. Unfortunately, her friendly companion wasn't about to give up so easily. He kept pace with her, smiling amiably.

"If I was English I would say you are in a spot of bother. But I am not English, so I will use an American phrase about being up shit creek without the availability of a paddle."

Perhaps his English wasn't as flawless as she thought. His pronunciation was impeccable, but he wasn't well-versed in idioms.

On the phone, Bishop said, "That voice, it sounds…"

Eva ignored her partner and made a series of grunts, as if she were listening to a fascinating conversation at the other end of the line.

The dark-haired man seemed unconcerned that Eva was pretending to be on a call. He chuckled genially and said, "If that is MI6 on your phone, it may be best if you place me on speaker so I can address all levels of authority at once. I do hate to repeat myself."

Without thinking, Eva stopped walking and stared open-mouthed at the man.

"I mean, we're frightfully short on time, I thought it best to get to the heart of the matter. If I was to be overly dramatic I would suggest that the fate of the world depends on what happens between us in the next few minutes."

It wasn't the first time she'd heard those words. Usually they were slurred by a drunk guy at a nightclub who exhaled toxic stale breath that reeked of alcohol. It was, however, the first time it was likely to be true.

"My name is Oleg." His tone was pleasant, as if they were being introduced at a garden party. "I can get you out of here."

"What did he say his name was?" Bishop shrieked.

Ignoring her compatriot on the phone, Eva said in English, "You can?"

"Listen very carefully Eva." Bishop's voice was low and forceful. "Shoot *him* in the face."

Clenching her teeth, Eva said into the phone, "He's saying he can help, Bishop."

Oleg's face was overcome with surprise. "Bishop? MI6 Bishop?" Oleg let loose a full-body laugh. "This is too much. Tell him I say hello. He must be having the kittens, no, leopards. You have made my week now. This is excellent."

It seemed Oleg and Bishop had a history, and not a fond one— at least not for Bishop. *Diddums.* There was more at stake than Bishop's precious ego. Her neck, for one. The fate of the world, for another. Eva quite liked her neck. Oleg seemed to be taking an interest in it too, but Eva had more important things on her mind than Oleg's longing glance.

"Where are you from?"

"A little town near Vladivostok."

"Funny. Which agency?"

"GRU. I was one of the few members of staff to approve your off-the-record attendance today. Your name is Destruction, yes?"

Eva nodded. "Then why help me? You don't know I wasn't responsible for what happened."

His smile brought out his dimples. "I do not believe you shot our President. I know MI6 are stupid, but I do not believe they are *that* stupid."

"Do you want to shoot him now?" Bishop asked. "I bet you want to shoot him now, don't you?"

Eva did her best to block out the baiting. She tucked the phone in her pocket to silence her partner for a bit. She needed to focus.

"I can get you out," Oleg said, "but we must not draw any attention to ourselves, do you understand?"

Eva said, "I wish you'd said that about three minutes ago."

"Why is that?" Oleg asked.

As if on cue, a different alarm, more urgent than the previous one, blared. A fire alarm.

"What did you do?" He frowned.

Eva struck a thumb at her chest. "Like you said, the name is Destruction."

Several minutes before, Eva had found an unoccupied office, a pack of cigarettes and, more importantly, a lighter. Gathering all the paper she could find, she created a little bonfire in a garbage bin. The original thinking was that any distraction was a good distraction.

Eva fought to keep the amusement from showing on her face. "I know we only just met, but you'll learn I tend to have trouble keeping a low profile."

Oleg walked briskly towards the stairwell. "This is not such a good thing for a spy, I think."

"It's probably something I could work on." She pushed open the fire door. "How do you plan on getting me out?"

The two of them descended the stairs at pace, leaping three at a time, Eva in front.

A shout emanated from below. Standing on a landing, a young soldier in a large red peaked hat shouted at them. He held up his own pass, pointing. Although Eva didn't know what he was saying, the message was clear enough. *Can't you hear the alarm? Show me your pass!*

Still bounding towards him, Eva maintained her momentum. With a final leap, she drew back her fist and bore down on the soldier, striking him squarely in the jaw. His head spun, almost snapping off. Using her downward momentum, she grabbed the front of his jacket and pulled him over her body, flinging him further down the stairwell. His head struck the wall and he rolled several times then flopped to a halt, face down.

Oleg stepped over him, seemingly unperturbed by Eva's actions. "Come, more people will soon be here."

Ignoring him, Eva placed two fingers on the young soldier's neck. There was a pulse; he was alive. Only then did she nod to Oleg. The GRU agent gave her a curious expression. "You are a most complex woman, I think, Destruction. I am beginning to like you."

Eva was grateful her phone was tucked in her pocket; she could only imagine what Bishop was saying. After two more flights of stairs, they reached a door. Oleg paused.

"There's a small courtyard, and beyond that, on the right, a door. After that is the car pool. We will not enter this yet. We will go left. There is officers' quarters, with change room. I will pick you a nice outfit. I am thinking a military motif."

A few minutes later, Eva emerged in the formal uniform of a Russian major, only one size too large. Eva thought she pulled off the smart outfit with aplomb. Not unsurprisingly, the officers' quarters were completely abandoned. It was no doubt against many Russian laws to impersonate a soldier, but as Eva had tactfully commented to Oleg, "Rules can go fuck themselves right now."

Stripping off her ill-fitting suit, she had donned the uniform in record time. Oleg made no attempt to turn away when Eva changed. She was so panicked she didn't even protest. There were more important things going on than one Russian's leering. Soon both of them were marching towards the car pool office, the GRU agent in the lead.

A young officer snapped to attention. Every soldier Eva saw seemed positively pre-pubescent.

Oleg snapped his fingers at a wall of keys and barked an order in Russian.

The soldier gazed at him with fear in his eyes and glanced from side to side, as if searching for someone more senior. He reluctantly shook his head, and replied with trepidation in his voice.

Rather than appear put out, Oleg chuckled amiably. He slapped his hand down on the soldier's shoulder congenially and spoke in a low voice. His manner may have been friendly, but Eva could tell his words were not.

The soldier scrambled for a set of keys and shoved them into Oleg's hands. He mumbled something that Eva took to mean, *you didn't get them from me.*

As the two of them walked briskly towards a set of civilian cars, Eva asked, "What did you say to him?"

Oleg shrugged. "Nothing much. I merely asked if he liked cold weather, because not giving me a car right now would get him stationed in Oymyakon."

"Which is?"

"Very far. Very cold. Very not nice."

Eva frowned approvingly. Oleg obviously had rank, and wasn't afraid to wave it about.

They piled into the car and before she'd even managed to fasten her seatbelt, Oleg was off. The car's tyres screeched on the concrete as they made their way up several levels before emerging into the dull sunshine. In the distance, a fire engine siren echoed through the streets.

The car pulled up at a final checkpoint, an old large metal gate. Moscow's streets were tantalisingly close through the bars. A much older soldier waved down the car.

"Pretend to be a man if you can," Oleg said under his breath.

Eyeballing the approaching officer, Eva mumbled, "I don't have time to grow a penis, but I can draw on a moustache with mascara if you give me a minute."

They didn't have a minute. The older officer approached the driver's door and shouted urgent-sounding words. Making a gesture with his hands, it was clear he wanted Oleg to back up and return to where they'd come from—not an option Eva cherished. When the officer saw Oleg's face, his back straightened, but there was no salute, even though it appeared he desperately wanted to.

A brief exchange followed. Oleg jabbed his finger at the gate and shouted insistently and with an air of authority, apparently ordering the gate be opened for important reasons. The guard, visibly upset at having to refuse a direct order, appeared to be appealing to Oleg's understanding that they were under an alert. Eva imagined if the guard knew the exact reason for the alert he wouldn't be wavering quite as much. The sirens became deafening as two fire engines screeched to a halt on the other side of the gate.

The driver of the fire engine honked his horn and shouted at the guard. Oleg shouted at the guard too. If Eva wasn't trying to be incognito she would have joined in. Visibly rattled, the guard threw up his hands and muttered something guttural-sounding, then headed back towards the guardhouse. He slapped a button and the gate slowly slid open. Oleg planted his foot and darted in front of the fire engine. The fire truck driver, who had just taken off, had to slam on the brakes to avoid colliding with them. He leaned out the window and yelled something as Oleg sped away. It sounded like the Russian equivalent of *up yours*.

Rain fell as the car's wheels rattled along Moscow's cobbled streets. Oleg sped the Lada Granta through the well-to-do streets surrounding the Kremlin. He said something as he darted through traffic, but his words seemed muffled to Eva. She couldn't focus. he said, it was unimportant.

It was too soon to assume she was safe. Very far from it, but by order of magnitude she was far safer outside the Kremlin than in it. Someone had put a lot of work into getting Eva in the room with the President so they could frame MI6 for the murder of a head of state. Once again, they'd been caught on the back foot, unaware and exposed.

*Enough.*

No more being caught out. No more dancing to the tune of others. The time for reacting was over.

As Eva stared at the rain-streaked window she was overcome with conviction, with a renewed sense of purpose. She had one end goal.

*Time to bring these fuckers down.*

Suddenly aware that she didn't know where they were headed, Eva asked with trepidation, "Where are we going?"

"A safe house," was all Oleg said. His smile was painted on, there was concern in his eyes.

She couldn't trust Oleg. Trusting Russians had gotten them to the brink of war. No matter what Oleg's intentions were, there was no way Eva could let him dictate what happened next. This was an MI6 operation. A shambles of an operation, sure, but an MI6 one nonetheless.

Spying the next set of lights, Eva readied herself to break loose and make a run for it. The bulge in Oleg's jacket told her he was armed, but Eva was prepared to deal with that if she needed to. One armed Russian was better than two thousand.

The phone in her pocket rang and she jumped. She was on edge, she needed to get a grip.

When she answered, all Bishop said was, "Hang on to something."

Fumbling for the grab handle, Eva saw the speeding Citroën before Oleg did. It t-boned Oleg's car and jolted them savagely to the right. Oleg's head struck the window, shattering it. The airbags deployed and everything turned white as choking powder filled the air. The car continued to careen towards the curb, which it struck with another jolt, flinging Oleg in the opposite direction. It was like being stuck in a pinball machine.

Momentarily stunned, Eva didn't know which way was up or down. Her car door was ripped open. Bishop stood before her, gun in hand, concern streaked across his face. He aimed his pistol at Oleg. He needn't have bothered. The GRU agent lay slumped in his seat, unconscious.

"Are you alright?" Bishop asked desperately.

"Yes," she managed to mumble. Her mouth was dry, her words slow and distant.

"We need to move."

Undoing her seatbelt, Bishop hoisted her out of the car. Passersby, having seen the crash, hovered nearby. Some shrieked upon seeing Bishop's gun. As he brought Eva to her feet, Bishop cast a hateful glance at Oleg's prone body. Eva read the expression as clear as a mile-high billboard: he'd love nothing more than to put a bullet between Oleg's eyes.

"We need to go," Eva wheezed.

Hovering for a moment, Bishop eventually nodded. He turned his back on the man he clearly had history with and threaded her arm over his shoulder, half-carrying, half-assisting her to scramble down the street. The sidewalk was thick with people, and they were soon absorbed into the crowd.

The area was thick with souvenir stores, Western high-end retail chains, Burger Kings and McDonald's. Powering down side streets, Bishop led them through department stores and car parks, until they finally slowed their pace after several blocks.

All the way, Bishop wore a curious expression. It was a melange of alarm, concern and determination. Mostly the last one. It was as if he would level the very city itself if it meant keeping Eva safe.

Travelling up two floors of the GUM department store, Bishop led Eva into an empty change room and locked the door behind them. Discarded garments were strewn across the floor. He gently lowered Eva onto a vacant chair and cupped her face in his hands. His determination had melted away. All that was left was concern.

He leaned in close. Eva could feel his breath on her face, the warmth of his skin. Without a word being spoken, Bishop leaned down and placed his lips on hers. They were softer than she'd imagined, but far more skilled. He kissed her with passion, his hand reaching for her lower back and pulling her close. His tongue intertwined with hers, swirling gently as his lips caressed her mouth.

As if suddenly aware of his action, he recoiled, his hand darting to his mouth.

"Oh my god, Eva, I'm so sorry. I was so caught up in... I never meant to..." He turned his head away, ashamed.

Eva reached for his arm. "Hey, hey." She pulled him closer and turned his chin towards her with a crooked finger. She gazed into his eyes. "Shut up and kiss me again."

That's exactly what he did.

# CHAPTER TEN

The extraction from Moscow was quick and efficient. The time between Bishop calling in their position and wheels up was less than two hours. Eva couldn't be anywhere near the Russian capital, and MI6 made sure that happened at lightning speed. She still wore her Russian major's uniform.

Inside the private jet, Eva watched the history-making event unfold on news websites. The initial reports were confused and contradictory. One said the President had fallen seriously ill. Another said he had been poisoned. One or two news services mentioned death, which others eagerly repeated, but with the stern caveat that the claim was unsubstantiated.

It wasn't until three hours after the event that a sombre, visibly reluctant official fronted a news conference. He walked up to a podium in front of a dozen Russian flags, camera flashes making the pale man appear even paler. It was only minutes before the translation appeared on news services. All the while, Eva felt bile rising in the back of her throat. *Don't say my name, don't say my name.*

After a brief preamble, the official read from a pre-prepared statement. He confirmed that yes, the President of Russia was dead. He silenced the shouts from the media with a wave of his hand, then continued. The cause of death was assassination by a firearm.

There was an audible gasp from the press. They hadn't been expecting that. The official used the hush to complete his statement. Currently the Kremlin was in lockdown. All agencies were cooperating, and authorities were confident they would find the perpetrator soon. This shocked the media out of their silence. Eva didn't understand what the press were shouting, but the connotation was clear. How could the President of their country be killed, in their own seat of power no less, and the murderer not have been apprehended already?

Relief flowed through her. There was a tiny chance she may not be identified. A very small one.

Growing visibly agitated, the official's jaw clenched. He cast a glance to the side of the stage, as if seeking assistance. None came.

Between gritted teeth, he said that representatives from other agencies would present to the press over the next few hours as more details came to light. He thanked the press, folded his paper and, to the howls of the press, walked away.

That was where all the news sites cut the footage. Live blogs appeared as banners, providing running updates as they occurred. The main gist was that the President of the Russian Federation had been murdered by "persons unknown". The rest was wild speculation.

Eva shut the laptop. There was no way of knowing if her picture was going to appear on the news services at some stage. Whether it did or not, it was far better to be in any country other than Russia. Someone had gone to extreme lengths to try and frame her and MI6. If they had evidence of her involvement, surely they would have used it by now. Far better to catch the "assassin" before she could leave the country. The lack of her picture appearing anywhere gave Eva a glimmer of hope that she would not be associated with the murder. Time would tell. For now, relief grew with every kilometre further she got from Moscow.

"We just cleared Russian airspace." Bishop emerged from the cockpit.

He'd left Eva to her news devouring. It was clear he wanted to talk about their kiss. There was hesitancy in his manner. Bishop was never hesitant about anything. The man was a walking monument to confidence. He'd asked if he could sit next to her for take-off; asked if she needed a water at least ten times. Hovering about, he seemed to realise what he was doing and moved away, but then apologised in case she took offence. He was like a nervous prom date trying to not appear too eager. It was adorable.

The fact that Eva didn't have regrets about the kiss was telling. There was a chance her senses were numb after her harrowing escape, but she suspected that wasn't it. She wanted Bishop. Running her thumb over her lips, she reconstructed the kiss in her mind. Sure, she'd thought about it before. It had even aided her on a quiet night at home sometimes. But in person? *Dayum.* The man had great technique, but there was more to it than that. Far more. There was genuine passion, capital D Desire. She wanted to know more. To have more. As she watched him call MI6 with a status update, she rolled her gaze over his well-fitted suit.

*You're in a whole mess of trouble, bitch.*

Eva thanked her brain for the informative update. It was nothing she didn't already know. Her heart had known well before the rest of her did—well, except certain other parts of her anatomy. Bishop turned in her direction as he spoke and gave her a wink and one of his incandescent smiles. She may as well have turned into a puddle.

Where to from here was up to them, but Eva was riding the enjoyable vibe that she knew she had to try to suppress. She had a lot to focus on in the next few hours, and as much as she'd like to, Bishop couldn't be one of those things.

He hung up and walked over. This time there was no hesitation as he sat next to her.

Bishop checked his watch. "You'll be debriefed in an hour."

"Dude, let a girl freshen up first."

"I meant at MI6, I didn't mean…"

"Wow." Eva pulled back in shock. "Since when have you missed a chance to drop a bit of innuendo?"

"I'm sorry, I just thought… I didn't want to…"

Eva slid her hand across his stubbled chin. He needed a shave. She'd like to see him shave. She'd like to see him do a great many things.

"It was a kiss, Bishop. I'd like more, but later. Right now we need to focus on other things, but that doesn't mean we can't be who we are."

"Of course." He nodded. "The boring fully-clothed debriefing…"

"Better."

"… is scheduled for sixteen hundred hours. Paul wanted to run it alone, but there will be a lot of bigwigs in there, so you'll need to be on your toes. Try to keep swears to under a hundred per minute if at all possible."

"I'll give it a crack, but I'm not promising anything, you glory-hole licking colon flap."

"Good girl. As long as you try, that's all I ask." Bishop smirked. He had such a nice smirk.

A thought had been festering in Eva's mind, and this seemed a good time to bring it up.

"Who is Oleg?" she asked. "It seems you have a history there."

Bishop's demeanour soured. "A story for another time."

"Was it mission-related or about a girl?"

His reply was stony. "Yes."

Was Eva jealous? Since when did she get jealous? This was new.

"I think we need to focus on the briefing." Bishop shifted in his seat. "You'll be grilled incessantly."

"No doubt. What did Paul say?"

"That was the biggest balls-up since Nero took up the fiddle and lit a fire so he didn't catch a chill." Paul handed her a whiskey.

Eva was thankful for her friend's honesty. She knew that already, but it was nice that Paul didn't sugar-coat it for her. The debrief had been as brutal as it had been long. She'd been subjected to five hours of non-stop questioning. She'd held her head high throughout, and apart from calling one member of MI6 an imperious cockspank, she was basically Mother Teresa.

Taking a sip of the scotch, her eyes virtually rolled back in her head. "My god, this tastes eleventy billion times better than it should. Thank you."

"Special batch. Hibiki, thirty years old. Been saving it for an occasion just like this."

Eva tilted her head. "For when one of your people gets accused of assassination?"

"That, or a cat birthday."

Paul was doing his best to cheer her up. Bless him. But he needn't have bothered—she was made of far sterner stuff. She was an MI6 agent. As she was adamant that she was going to find who put her in a room with the President. If she had to crawl through tunnels of glass, scale mountains of data, interrogate the Pope with a lead pipe, she'd find out who was responsible and bring them down. Eva had never been more determined in her life. People were going to pay. She didn't care what rules she broke along the way. If whoever did this knew anything about Eva Destruction they should be feeling warm piss flooding their pants right about now. She was going to see this through to the end.

Paul reclined in his chair. "Evie, you're not going to like this, but I may as well come straight out with it." He sighed. "You're off the case."

"What, why?"

"Well, there's the little fact that people believe you killed the President of Russia."

"That one time!"

"Sorry, Evie." Paul shifted in his chair uneasily. It put Eva on edge. Paul usually sat rigidly still. "There's talk…"

"There usually is."

"Some in the Foreign Office… low-level ones, mind, but officials nonetheless, are saying if it comes to light that we were there, the agent should be handed over to Russia. To ease tensions. At least, that's what the chatter is. Quite frankly, it's ridiculous. If the Ruskies had anything, Jesus, even suspected a foreign national was responsible, they would have been screaming blue murder well before now. But I thought you should know there was chatter."

"Nothing eases tension like a well-televised kangaroo court."

"If it comes to it, I want you to know that will never happen. With my last dying breath I would stop them from sacrificing you like that. Never going to happen, Evie."

"Thanks, Paul. I appreciate it. You didn't have to say it, but I appreciate that you did."

That was that. She was off the case. No finding who had really killed the Russian President and almost framed her for it. No finding Harry. No figuring out what Durov was up to. Or Alexie. Eva Destruction would be given a leave of absence and asked to lay low and take it easy.

Both people in the room knew that would never happen. Neither of them mentioned it.

"Why is it kangaroo court anyway?" Eva asked. "Is that racist? Should I be offended?"

"Probably. Do you have courts in Australia, or do you get all the relevant parties together for a booze-up and the last person standing wins?"

"Yeah, that's exactly how our court system works, Paul. Spot on."

Paul said that so few people knew about her Kremlin visit, they may have been so scared of anyone finding out they had kept it secret. Perhaps there were other factors at play. Eva wondered if it was Oleg who kept her name out of it. She couldn't be sure, but he seemed determined to stave off the worst diplomatic incident of the 21st century.

She found it curious that was officially off the case, but her friend was still talking about it. Bless him.

Eva took a sip, thinking through events. "Who was the tall

glass of water who pulled the trigger on President Sokolov and himself?"

"Ah," Paul said, waggling a finger, "that we do know. We had a file on him, Vasiliev. Shoddiest of shoddy customers. He played all sides. We paid him, so did the Yanks, and we're reasonably certain he had his hand in the pocket of the Chinese and Israelis, too. We thought we were the only ones who knew he had his hand in the cookie jar. It seems someone found out through the data breach, and somehow convinced him he needed to blow his brains out."

"That's some convincing."

"Quite. The bastard behind this has to be a data expert and a master in manipulation, plus one hell of a sadistic son-of-a-whore. A heady mix. We haven't the foggiest what made him pull the trigger. Being found with your hand in a lot of pockets doesn't seem a good enough reason to murder a head of state and commit suicide. He must have been protecting a loved one or something. The man obviously had his reasons."

"Durov is the one behind this, surely?" Eva swirled her glass.

"Seems almost certain. He appears to know how to read people perfectly. I have no doubt Durov told you he had the breached information so you would tell the Russians. He bet on it. That was his opening. He must have manipulated events so you had an audience with the President. This was all orchestrated Evie. We blindly walked into the spider's web."

"But did he though? He told me to get back into the hole, to go home."

Paul laughed quietly and tilted his head. "It's almost like he knew that ordering you to do something means you'd do the exact opposite."

Eva frowned. "That's not true."

"Evie, whatever you do, don't give me the finger."

Eva's eye twitched. She really, *really* wanted to give Paul the finger.

Behind his desk, Paul revelled in a cloud of smug. The lull in conversation made her mind wander. There was something she needed to say.

"I kissed Bishop. Well, he kissed me, then I kissed him back. Either way there was kissing. A lot of kissing. And inappropriate touching."

Paul raised an eyebrow. "Are you telling me this as your handler or your friend?"

"Friend. The other would be creepy."

He nodded, more towards his drink than Eva. "To be honest, I kind of already thought you were kissing and touching inappropriately."

It was Eva's turn to raise an eyebrow. "And you didn't say anything?"

"That's more Nancy's department. I sort of step in when she bitches about stuff behind your back."

Aghast, Eva said, "She bitches... yeah, okay, I can see that."

The two friends exchanged grins.

As casually as she could, Eva asked, "Who are you going to assign to find Harry?"

It was a loaded question and they both knew it.

With a swirl of his whiskey, Paul didn't meet her eye. "Preston."

"Preston?!" she shrieked. "That guy couldn't find the Great Pyramid of Cheops if you nailed his dick to it."

"Lucky we're not looking for pyramids, eh?" Paul poked his chin at Eva's empty glass, which she couldn't recall emptying. "Go home, get some rest. There will be follow-up tomorrow, but the worst is done with. Get some sleep, Evie. You did well today."

It was a lie, but a well-intentioned one. She hadn't done well at all. She'd walked into a trap, she'd almost started a world war and they were no closer to uncovering the truth.

Their conversation at an end, Eva was about to take her leave so Paul could get on with his work. Before she could say as much, her phone rang. Pulling it out of her pocket, she saw it was an unknown number with a lot of digits. With a series of hand gestures, Eva indicated that she would leave to take the call. Paul nodded in return, swivelling his chair towards his computer.

Before she pressed the answer button, Eva turned to her handler, and said, "Paul?"

He glanced her way and Eva flipped him the bird. He rolled his eyes and turned back to his computer.

As she strolled into the hallway, Eva said, "Hello?"

"Ms Destruction?"

"Yes?"

"This is Bernard from the Mandarin Oriental."

Eva had never gotten on well with the snooty little sycophant, but he was exceptionally good at his job at the high-end hotel.

"Oh yes, Bernard, how are you?"

"Well, thank you, Ms Destruction, I appreciate you asking. You, ah, requested I give you a call if certain circumstances were to arise…"

And so she had. Eva stopped walking and placed her hand on the wall for balance. In the space of a minute she had all she needed. Her previous complaints about being subject to events rather than grasping them by the short and curlies had just taken a dynamic shift. She thanked Bernard and hustled back to Paul's office.

"Didn't we just have a conversation?" Paul asked.

Eva sat without being asked. "Oh hey, remember when you took me off the case for finding Harry?"

"It was so long ago, I hardly recall."

"Yeah, you might have to let Preston down easy. I'm sure he'll be devastated—make sure you explain it to him slow. Maybe use crayons."

"Why would… Evie, what's going on?"

"That was one of my contacts. I pinged everyone I could think of who might give me a lead. This one pinged back."

"A lead? On Lancing?"

Eva nodded. "Want to nab the most wanted person on the planet?"

"Second-most. You're probably the first most wanted at the moment."

"Funny."

Paul leaned forward. "Where is he?"

"You need to put me back on the case, Paul. Reinstate me as lead agent."

"I... Are you blackmailing me, Aussie?"

"Me?" Eva asked, as innocent as a used-car salesman. "I would never contemplate such a thing. Let's call it aggressive persuasion."

"Let's cut the bullshit and call it blackmail, shall we?"

There was still humour in Paul's words, but far less than there had been a few minutes before. He steepled his fingers and furrowed his brow. Was he seriously thinking about not reinstating her and hoping she'd cough up the information voluntarily? He had to know you never played chicken with Eva Destruction.

He sighed heavily. "Fine, you're still lead. What do you need?"

"Get me on the next plane to Hong Kong."

# CHAPTER ELEVEN

"Will his new girlfriend Trixie be there?" Bishop asked.

"What, dude?" Eva asked amused.

"It seems like we're going to your ex's for dinner," Bishop said as the black limousine rushed through the neon-lit Hong Kong night. It was late, and few cars hindered their progress.

It was the first time the two of them had been alone since leaving Paul's office. The flight over had been packed with fellow agents. MI6 was leaving nothing to chance. They'd launch the King's corgis from a cannon if it meant apprehending Horatio Lancing. Eva and Bishop sat next to each other in the back of the car on the way to the hotel.

"I guess we are, yeah. And he doesn't know I'm bringing the current bloke with me," Eva added.

Bishop cocked an eyebrow. "Current?"

"Maybe current." She ran a finger down his trouser leg. "If you play your cards right."

"Cards? Like strip poker?"

"I'm awful at card games, Bishop."

His smile was luminescent. "I know."

Eva sighed. "Stop being such a good-looking bastard, could you?"

Bishop shrugged. "You may as well ask the sun to stop shining, the tides to cease or passengers to remain seated when the plane comes to a halt but the fasten seatbelt light is still on. Some things you have no power over."

She knew Bishop was doing his best to keep her mind off what was about to happen. Harry Lancing had exerted his power on her life yet again. Since the moment she'd first laid eyes on him in her coffee shop all those years ago, Eva had never been able to shake his influence. Even when he was meant to be locked away in the most secure prison on the planet he found a way to pull Eva into his chaotic orbit. Was now the time to rescind the power he had over her life? Was this finally the moment Eva could step out of his shadow?

On the flight over, the plan had been created, scrutinised, pulled apart and reconstructed. MI6 was taking no chances. The hotel would be sealed tight—a rat's flea would have little chance of escaping. It fell to Eva to be the bait. She would proceed to reception and call for him to come down. They would nab him there. If he refused to come down they would go get him themselves. The Operations team were confident they could achieve a simple extraction. But in Eva's experience, nothing was ever simple with Harry Lancing.

Like the moment before she'd stepped into the room at Wakefield Prison, Eva again wondered how she was going to react when she finally came face to face with the man who had once been her everything. Punching things was often a first reaction, but Eva doubted that would be the case now, although she was reluctant to rule it out entirely. Speaking of ruling things out...

"By the way, Bishop, you're not allowed to shoot him, okay?"

Mock appalled, he said, "Why would I do that?"

"Because he tried to kill you. Several times over. You're not exactly besties."

Holding a splayed palm to his chest, Bishop said, "I never hold a grudge."

"Yeah, you do." Eva sniggered. "All the time!"

"Name one time."

"Oleg," Eva said firmly. "You never told me why you wanted me to shoot him in the face."

Before Bishop could come up with a bullshit excuse to avoid answering, the driver informed them they were one minute from the target. The atmosphere in the car changed dramatically. Weapons were checked, even though they'd been checked ten times already. Eva was sure the agents in the five cars behind them were going through similar rituals.

Time to go on the offensive. Since the first explosion at the Russian embassy, they had been victims of events. That changed now. Eva slid her pistol into her shoulder holster and gave Bishop a nod. Game on.

As the car came to a stop, no orders were issued. There was no need. Everyone knew their role. As soon as Eva's foot hit the rain-drenched footpath ten other car doors swung open. The smattering of pedestrians reeled as black-clad men and women stormed towards the hotel, Eva in the lead.

Approaching the front of the ornate Mandarin Oriental, Eva did her best to suppress her memories of the hotel—mainly because they mostly involved writhing naked bodies. They weren't exactly helping her focus. There were more important things to think about right now. My, how her priorities had changed.

As the team of agents burst through the front door of the hotel, the two staff behind the counter shrieked. The lobby was empty. The armed squad took up positions at every exit.

Eva approached the startled hotel workers. "Hi. How's it going guys?"

The male, no older than twenty-five, flapped his lips several times before blurting, "Do you have a reservation?"

"No, sorry, dude. But we'll be out of your hair soon enough. Just need you to call room 1801 and ask him to come down. Let him know Eva is waiting. Put me on the phone if you need. Can you do that for me?"

The receptionist gave the heavily armed troops a sideways glance and clearly decided compliance was the best course of action. As his shaky hand reached for the receiver, the elevator pinged.

Half those present pivoted towards the sound, the other half covered the entrance. Eva admired their professionalism. The elevator doors slid open and a fit man in his forties emerged. He was dressed in sweats, a gym bag under his arm. Face buried in his phone, he stepped into the lobby.

In the split second before he lifted his head to take in the scene, Eva did her best to suppress a gasp. This was no fake, like the one in Wakefield. This was the real deal.

"Hey Harry."

The man lifted his head and went through a series of expressions in seconds. Initially shock, he soon beamed after realising it was Eva. Then he noticed the armed troops. He took a step back in shock. Finally, he focused his attention back towards Eva, and a boyish grin enveloped his face. "Hey Eva. I've missed you."

The troops kept to their orders and remained carved in marble until Eva gave the signal. Their restraint was impressive, given that they were facing the world's most wanted person. Or second-most.

She tilted her head. "Have you? That's nice." More casually than she felt, she added, "I went to visit you at prison."

"How thoughtful," Harry replied pleasantly, as if they were having a poolside chat.

"Someone else was in your place."

"Really?" Harry shook his head. "How odd. There must have been some mix-up."

"Must be. Bureaucracy, hey?" Eva rocked on her heels. "On an unrelated note, why aren't you there now? In prison?"

"I just popped out for some milk. They were running low."

Beneath the bravado, Eva knew Harry intimately enough to know he was scared. He was attempting to hold his head high, but underneath the charisma was a bubbling pot of despair. Surely he must have known he couldn't charm his way out?

She frowned. "You popped all the way to Hong Kong for milk?"

Harry winced. "Good-quality milk in Honkers."

Shaking her head, Eva tutted. "Even for you that's lame." She took a moment to take in the palatial surrounds of the Oriental. "I see you're hiding out in the most inconspicuous and threadbare accommodation."

A boyish shrug. "That's how you tracked me? Damn. I covered my tracks so carefully." He glanced at Eva. "But I should have taken into account the quality of my trackers."

There was no malice in his words. It was more respect.

"I guess I should have been more... Look, if I'm completely honest with you, I'm a bit out of sorts. There's twenty burly blokes pointing guns at me."

"And ladies."

"Oh good. The last thing I want is a sexist firing squad."

"They're not a firing squad, Harry. They're here to take you back to prison."

Frowning as he sagely nodded, Harry said, "What if I don't want to go?"

"They'll take you anyway," Eva said with a shrug. "You'll probably get punched more though. Just a tip."

Harry seemed to mull this over. He didn't have much of a choice. There was no escape, no talking his way out. His goose was so cooked it was charcoal.

It was a revelation to Eva that she didn't feel sorry for him. When she first brought him in years ago, even after she'd known the full extent of his Machiavellian schemes, she'd lost sleep over her actions. She'd never admit it, but she'd also shed tears. But now? Now she felt relief at the possibility of finally being rid of his influence once and for all. Was she really over Harry? She was dubious that it could be that easy. It couldn't be that easy. *Right?*

"It is nice to see you again, Eva. I miss you every day, that's no lie."

Taking a moment, Eva squinted at her former lover. She

assessed him from hair gel to sneakers. The realisation was as surprising as it was welcome.

"Huh. I really think I'm over you, Harry."

For the first time surprise splintered his carefully amiable façade. Her words had genuinely wounded him. *My god, the man is delusional if he thinks I'm still pining for him.*

Recovering, he gave her the boyish little laugh that had worked on her a thousand times before. "Over me? I always liked it when you were over me, Eva. Always most stimulating, for both of us."

Eva's face broke into a sad smile. "You're very charming, Harry. Always have been. But, as most men eventually find out, charm will only get you so far before someone calls you on your bullshit. Sorry to say your time is up."

Harry curiously followed Eva's hand as she raised it in front of her face. Within a second of clicking her fingers, eight troops descended upon him and shackled him in flexicuffs. The rest formed a secondary perimeter, cordoning Horatio Lancing off from the rest of the world.

Harry gave a slight shriek as he was shoved forward callously and the group moved as one towards the awaiting vehicles.

He managed to shoot Eva a smile. "Despite all this, I genuinely can't wait for our interrogation together. Sad, isn't it? I'll take any time I can with you."

Eva frowned. "Oh, I won't be conducting the interview."

Confusion creased Harry's pretty face. "You... you won't? Who will?"

From behind Eva, Bishop stepped out of the shadows. "Hi Horatio, remember me?" Harry's face fell as Bishop went on. "If I recall correctly, the last time we chatted you sentenced me to death. What larks we had, eh? I'd just like to say..."

"Him!" Harry was incensed, his gaze darting between Eva and Bishop. He futilely struggled to shake off the meaty hands of the two troops who had an iron-like grasp of his upper arms. He may as well have tried to shake off a mountain.

Bishop leaned in close. "... I look forward to conducting our little interrogation."

"Do you have any earmuffs?" Harry asked Eva politely in the back of the limousine.

The question was asked through a black bag, which had been placed over his head. Flanked by burly troops, Harry had his legs crossed in a relaxed pose. If it wasn't for the sack over his head, he could be mistaken for the person in control, not the one under arrest.

Eva, who had been doing her best to ignore her ex, asked in an annoyed voice, "What?"

"Earmuffs. Do you have any? It's just this silence is close to deafening, so I thought I could do with some. That's all."

Her ex probably thought he was being charismatic. Once upon a time Eva would have fallen for it. Harry was lucky Bishop was in the other vehicle. His mouth would have been taped shut by now. It had been deemed a good idea to have Bishop in the other car so the interrogation could be conducted fresh. Unfortunately, that meant Eva drew the short straw and had to ride with someone she'd rather never see again.

The first thing they did before piling Harry into the limo was check for any electronic devices. History had shown the man was capable of anything when given access to the outside world. Hell, he'd implanted an imposter and travelled halfway around the world with access to just one phone.

The man could never be underestimated. He'd made governments cower and the United Nations curse his very name. Eva had seen him manipulate billion-dollar business deals with a single well-chosen phrase, and cause a riot in the centre of London just to appear more sympathetic. The last thing they wanted was this man to have Wi-Fi and time on his hands. Nothing was more dangerous than Horatio Lancing with an internet connection.

"I'm not the bad guy here, Eva," Harry said in a voice so familiar. "Okay, yes, apart from all the law breaking and whatnot, but it was all for a reason. I'm the one doing the right thing, I've sacrificed myself for the greater good. Making governments look after their people, saving the environment, getting nations to work together for the betterment of all, these are noble things." There was an extended silence. "I can't help but think you're giving me the finger right about now."

The thought had occurred to her. "Harry, how many times do you need to be told the world doesn't want to be manipulated into thinking your way, or any other for that matter? People want free will—they want to decide for themselves."

"Governments aren't about free will! They're about winning the next election at any cost and getting away with all the self-interest they can."

The silence was longer this time. "I'm not getting into this debate again."

"Eva... I'm better than I was when last we... I've grown, realised things. I took on board the things you said to me last time. I know I can't do this on my own. It shouldn't be my lone voice. You taught me that. You taught me so much."

"Harry." Eva sighed and forced her voice to be less harsh. "Look. You need to stop trying to change the world. In a few minutes we'll be entering a facility where you'll be... let's just say you need to answer the questions posed, Harry. This isn't a game anymore, okay? People are dying. This is serious. You need to start acting like it."

The black hood nodded. "Okay. What do you want me to do?"

"Answer the questions."

"What if I don't want to?"

Gritting her teeth, Eva said, "Harry, there's only one way this is going to go down. Whether you like it or not, we're finally going to get some answers."

# CHAPTER TWELVE

The industrial park was like a ghost town on a Sunday night. MI6 had deemed Lancing's interrogation too time critical to wait for his arrival in London. The team were to grill Lancing in Hong Kong first, then sedate him and send him to MI6.

Each of the troops had taken up a defensive position. Every possible entrance point to the industrial park had several lines of security. Rocket launchers had been deployed in case. An Apache helicopter ensured there were no airborne surprises. How that had been approved by the Special Administrative Region's officials, Eva didn't know. Regardless, the lack of UK territory under her feet made her uncomfortable.

Before being shoved into the interrogation room Harry had been thoroughly searched and stripped of all possessions. His phone was already on its way back to London. He'd been scanned three times to check if he'd been implanted with a tracking device. Each scan had come up clean.

The interrogation room was like most interrogation rooms the world over. Stark white, one entrance, two chairs, one table, a two-way mirror, recording devices. Not for the first time, Eva regretted assigning Bishop the role of lead interrogator. Not that she wanted the role herself, but she feared Bishop would take his role... personally.

Standing casually beside Eva, Bishop loudly sipped on his tea. Harry sat alone in the room where he'd been roughly deposited three-quarters of an hour earlier.

"Not going to..." Eva nodded towards the mirrored glass.

"Like all good things in life, it's all about timing." Bishop's wicked grin told her he wasn't referring to interrogation techniques. Her partner loudly sipped from the Styrofoam cup.

Eva hefted an eyebrow. "How's the tea?"

"Ghastly." Bishop took another leisurely sip.

"You're just fucking with him now, aren't you?"

Bishop didn't even glance her way. "I haven't even started."

After another few minutes Bishop finally walked around the corner and opened the door to the room. He approached the table and reverently placed his tea on the edge, then walked away from Harry. Placing his hand on the top of the spare chair, Bishop dragged it loudly across the room. The bare walls amplified the scraping sound. When the chair was finally in place, Bishop sat opposite Harry and took a sip of his tea. They stared at one another for a full minute.

Finally, Bishop put the cup down. "Why do you keep altering the charging points on your mobile devices?"

"I... what?"

"The Lancing phones and pads, why do you keep changing the port? One year you're saying this is the new standard and the next you bring out the latest and greatest with a completely different port. It's very annoying."

Harry shook his head, confused. "That's not my... why would you ask me..."

"I just think it leads to a lot of e-waste, that's all. I would have thought there should be some industrial standard, like power points, you know?"

"There are a lot of issues at play there. Anti-colluding legislation, for starters, then there's each company's data throughput requirements. Lots of reasons, but that's not exactly my area of expertise. It's more up to department heads to—"

"Not your area of expertise?" Bishop interrupted. "I suppose not. But extracting data for your own purposes and using it to blackmail those in legitimate power? Now that's you all over, wouldn't you say?"

Eva had to hand it to him, Bishop knew how to keep his subject off-kilter. Interrogation 101: never ask the question your opponent expects.

"You're going to say I'm responsible for the MI6 data breach, aren't you? That I was behind it?"

Bishop shrugged. "Was I? I was just chatting about phone chargers."

"You didn't send armed troops halfway across the world to kidnap me so we could chat about phone chargers."

"I'm very interested in phone chargers."

There was no concealing Harry's infuriation. "Are you?"

"Oh yes. Fascinated."

Before Harry could respond, Bishop stood and walked out of the room. Without a word, he walked past Eva to the toilets. The door wasn't soundproof, and Eva could clearly hear him urinating. It took a minute before Bishop emerged. At least he washed his hands.

Sidling up to Eva, Bishop examined their captive. "Getting back to the conversation we were having at the Kremlin. Have you ever been to the Maldives?"

"Have I...? No."

Flapping his hand towards the interrogation room, he said, "When this is all over would you be interested in spending a couple of weeks in one of those cabins over the water? I'm reasonably certain you can even get them with slides into the ocean. Sound good?"

Eva crinkled her forehead and gave her partner a little laugh. "It does, actually. It really does."

Giving Eva a wink, Bishop strode off, re-entered the room and sat before a perplexed Harry. With a sniff, Bishop said nothing and stared at the prisoner. Harry stared back determinedly, but the shifting in his seat gave away his discomfort. Bishop continued to stare. For several minutes neither man spoke a word. Even Eva felt uncomfortable.

Out of nowhere, Bishop smiled. Continuing on as if he'd never left, he said, "I can't seem to get rid of some of these bloatware apps on my phone." He pulled out a Lancing mobile device. "Do you know if there's a trick to it? There's this fitness app I just can't seem to delete."

Harry threw his hands in the air. "What is this?" Eva saw he was rattled, something she had rarely witnessed. "You obviously want to know why I'm in Hong Kong, escaped prison and all. Just bloody ask me, alright?"

"You can tell me? That's marvellous." Bishop pulled his chair closer to the table. "But first, if you could..." Bishop held up the phone. "... I just need to get rid of a few apps. I'm running out of space."

With a push, Harry leaned back on his chair. "Whatever this is..." he waved his hands about, "... it won't work. I've negotiated multi-billion-dollar deals before breakfast—literally before breakfast—so I'd suggest you bring in Eva so she can ask some real questions."

"You'd like that, wouldn't you? Bring in the woman you've had on a string for years so you can try and manipulate her again. I'm sure you would. Hate to tell you this, but she's moved on."

*Oh badger shitnuggets.*

She should never have trusted Bishop to keep this professional. He was far too emotionally invested in the situation. In her.

Harry's eyes narrowed. The smallest of creases appeared in the corner of his mouth. Eva knew the look. He always had the same expression when he had someone beat.

Folding his arms, Harry tilted his head. "You're sleeping with her, aren't you?"

He couldn't bring himself to use her name, Eva noticed.

Bishop didn't miss a beat. "I can say unequivocally that Miss Destruction and myself have never engaged in any sexual activity. We have a lie detector outside if you'd like to put me to the test."

Eva knew it wouldn't be the truth for long. But it was nice to have it officially recorded for the MI6 archives. Maybe her partner knew exactly what he was doing. Harry was more uneasy than ever.

Rising, Bishop placed two fists on the table. "Now, you were saying something about prison?"

Harry growled. "Fine."

In the following few minutes the full story of Harry's escape came to light. Issuing a probing question here, leaving an awkwardly long silence there, Bishop extracted the full saga.

Harry had received a mobile phone smuggled into the prison. From there he had access to the world. A doppelganger was found and offered an unbelievable sum to impersonate Horatio Lancing, with a few cosmetic enhancements. His family's excessive debts were wiped out overnight, and contingencies were put in place if the deception was ever discovered. Harry refused to elaborate on what these were. The names of the guards and officials who had helped him were reeled off like a shopping list. It was ironic that the people who had helped Harry escape prison were about to head there themselves.

Once the story had been told in detail, Bishop asked, "For what purpose?"

"I'm sorry?"

"That's a lot of effort to go to. I'm wondering why."

Harry scoffed. "Have you ever been to prison?"

"Yes," Bishop replied without pause.

Simultaneously, Eva and Harry said, "What?"

Taking a moment to recover, Harry said, "I didn't want to be in prison anymore."

To Eva, the reply sounded hollow, somehow empty. Or it could have been the shock from hearing that Bishop had been locked up at some stage.

Bishop nodded. "Or perhaps you had a bigger idea. One that would require your presence on the other side of the bars. Something that would require the use of the world's secrets to manipulate world events. Somewhat of your forte, wouldn't you agree?"

"I already told you I didn't have anything to do with the MI6 data breach."

"No you didn't." Bishop scratched his chin. "You mentioned the breach without my prompting, but I assure you, you didn't deny your involvement. We can have a gander at the transcript if you would like."

"Well... okay, but it wasn't me behind it."

"Hmmm," Bishop mused. "I will most definitely take the word of a self-confessed prison escapee."

Harry lifted his head. "But I can tell you who did."

For the first time, Bishop's relentless confidence faltered, if only for a second. Eva sat up too. Everyone who was listening to the conversation was suddenly alert, despite the lack of sleep over the last forty-eight hours.

Harry must have seen it too. She saw his poise ratchet up slightly. For the first time Eva wondered who was actually in control of the conversation.

"I'm sure you and your people have drawn conclusions about how the data breach occurred. It's not arrogance to suggest my name would have been bandied about. They would be right about one thing, it was my technology used, but I assure you, it wasn't me pulling the trigger. I would never want the information to begin with."

Bishop took a sip of his tea. Surely it was cold by now. He took his time placing the cup back on the table. "And yet it was your technology behind it all, that's what you admitted, yes?"

"True, but I had no part in the events. I even tried to stop it. That's why I called Eva. She told you about it, I'm sure. The day of the Russian embassy bombing."

"Indeed. And yet everything has transpired regardless. You mustn't have tried very hard."

"I will admit things got away from me."

"Fascinating. Perhaps you could start giving specifics rather than making vague references to ambiguous notions. How about you tell us who is behind all this, if not you."

Harry's fists clenched and unclenched. Surely he would have known this question would come. He sighed. Staring at the table, he said, "His name is Durov. He's currently in the race for—"

"We know him," Bishop interrupted. "Eva met him. She's not a fan."

"Eva met..." Harry raised his head, confusion creasing his forehead. "Well anyway, we shared a similar opinion on the state of the planet. He wanted to achieve what I had once, giving power back to the people, not having them manipulated by mega-corporations and special-interest groups who bribe policymakers into compliance. He had the wherewithal to see it through. I thought I'd found a partner with the same world view. I was wrong. I thought I could control him. I was wrong. I thought I could find a way out of this mess." He stared at Bishop, genuine hurt in his eyes. "I was very wrong."

"I see," Bishop replied eventually. "I'm curious as to how Durov contacted you? I can't imagine him popping by Wakefield during visiting hours."

Harry raised an eyebrow. "Who do you think organised the phone to be smuggled in? It's not like I had spare bribe cash lying about my cell."

"So Durov sends you a phone, you have a few chats, find a kindred spirit, sing Kumbaya and he helps you break out of prison?"

"Nowhere near that simple, but essentially, yeah."

"Who funded all this? Who funded Durov?"

Harry's expression turned sheepish. "I had a few accounts stashed around the world that weren't frozen. A rainy day fund."

"You really must have gotten along famously for you to hand over all your cash like that."

"Like I said, I thought I could control him. I had no idea other elements were at work."

Taking a step closer to the glass, Eva wanted to scream, *ask him about the other elements!*

Instead, Bishop inspected his fingernails. "You called Eva. Right before the embassy bombing. Why?"

Harry's eyes became slits. "That's the second time you've mentioned Eva in a minute..." He turned to the mirror, to Eva. Without taking his eyes off the mirror, he addressed Bishop. "Are you sure you and Eva aren't..." He seemed incapable of finishing the sentence.

*Oh, giblet-slapping fuck-bunnies.*

"Why did you call her, Horatio?" Bishop pressed. "To talk about old times?"

Harry's head snapped back to Bishop. "I was protecting her. Like I always have."

Bishop folded his arms and said nothing.

Harry went on. "I was at Durov's facility. There were cameras set up. To see the embassy. I saw Eva, I knew it was her, in the corner of a screen. I ran out and called her, to warn her." He sighed. "It was right after that I got cold feet."

"Oh," Bishop said casually, "but before then, bombing people was just tickety boo."

A scowl creased Harry's face. "I thought it was going to be a small bomb, in an isolated part of the embassy, not..."

"Multiple bombs that killed eighteen people?" Bishop finished for him. "You say you gave Durov the tech to rip apart our data. Why?"

"I repeat again, I didn't know he was going to do that. I never wanted... Look, he was meant to use it to find information on his political opponents, to bring him to power. From there we could shape world events, make the world a better—"

"A better place for you and me?" Bishop broke into an off-key song. "There are ways to get there, if you care enough for the living."

Harry's face appeared pained. "Why are you singing?"

Undaunted, Bishop continued his toneless rendition. "Make a little space, make a better place." He puffed up his chest and ratcheted up his tune, "Heal the world, make it a better place, for you and for me!"

"Please stop."

"And the entire human race. There are people dying…"

"I'll pay anything, just stop singing."

"If you care enough for the living, make it a better place." Bishop spread his arms wide. "For you and for me!"

Blinking at Bishop, Harry stared. "What… what was that about?"

"Mainly that you're an idiot."

"I'm… why?"

"If you really believed the twaddle you're peddling," he waggled a finger at Harry, "which I seriously doubt, what makes you think you could change the world by bringing an opportunist like Durov to power?"

"He…" Harry sighed. "I thought he shared my view on the world. The mistake I made the first time was that I was front and centre. That didn't turn out so well. I'm more of a background kind of guy. I needed someone who could be the mouthpiece."

"You thought you'd found a puppet?"

"Not exactly…"

"I'm thinking that was it exactly."

Harry shrugged. Bishop was right. The two men sat across from one another. Eva was thankful for the breather. There was so much to digest.

Bishop swished the cold tea in the cup. "Why were you in Hong Kong?"

The shift in conversation gave Harry pause. "When I escaped and found out what Durov was up to I tried to stop it by calling Eva, but then it was too late. I went to ground, hiding from anyone who could send me back to prison and from Durov." Harry turned to the mirror, as if he saw Eva behind it. "Plus, I have fond memories of Hong Kong."

For the briefest of moments, Eva allowed herself to recall those memories too. She stamped them down just as quickly.

Extending his arms over his head, Bishop stretched. "Does the name Alaksiej Barinov mean anything to you? Also known as Alexie Barinov. AKA Red Scorpion. AKA the Perfume Assassin."

Bishop was good. He was very good. The crisscrossing of topics kept Harry from becoming comfortable. Once again, Harry's shock gave him away.

"The name has come up."

Bishop nodded. "In what context?"

"In the context of Durov."

"You've met him, Barinov?"

"I have. Can't say I was an admirer."

"So they're working together, Durov and Barinov?"

"You could say that."

Frowning approvingly, Bishop took his time before speaking. "United, they've inflicted quite some damage to our interests. You know these men. Is there something that potentially could hinder their union? I'm wondering, theoretically, if you were to contact one of these two men, perhaps you could convince them to turn on the other? Find a way to appeal to their baser instinct. Have one rat the other out."

Harry shook his head. "I highly doubt it."

"Why would that be?"

With a tilt of his head, Harry squinted at Bishop. Finally, his face cracked and he laughed. "You really don't know? I thought you people were in the espionage business."

"Know what?" Bishop was visibly uncomfortable.

Harry composed himself and leaned forward. "Durov is Alexie Baranov's son."

# CHAPTER THIRTEEN

"Paul, the game has changed. Get us the fuck out of here."

Mere minutes after Eva spoke those words into her phone, the entire entourage had mobilised and was on their way to the airport. The plane took off twenty minutes after she hung up.

Safely inside the private jet, Eva couldn't relax. She assumed it would be a long time before that would happen. A very long time.

Durov was Alexie's son? Of course he was. That was the critical piece that made everything make sense. Or at least some sense. A bit of sense. Alexie's motivation held a vague semblance of reasoning. He was creating a legacy for his offspring. It mad sense that an old Cold War spy would murder and manipulate events on a world scale, like the old days. He was bequeathing an inheritance like no one had before him. Alexie was creating a world leader using a lifetime of accumulated unscrupulous skills. And it was working.

Durov was making his play. The news was filled with his fiery oratory as he became the central figurehead for Russia's rage. This was the proof Russia needed to rid itself of the vile influence of the West and reclaim its rightful place as the world's leader. His approval rating was through the roof. He'd first won the left with his wise and inclusive views. Now his sabre-rattling vitriol was winning over the right. It was so well orchestrated Eva almost admired its execution. But she didn't. There was too much blood, with plenty more to come.

It wasn't like Russia didn't have a history of an ex-KGB agent manipulating events to grasp the seat of power. The only crimp in the plan seemed to be Eva's escape from the Kremlin. Without her there were only vague references to the assassination of the President by unknown "Western" perpetrators. The populace had obviously gobbled the story up, regardless of proof. Wrath had no time for facts.

Once in power, Durov would have the vast majority of people behind him. The plundered intelligence data would give he and Alexie an unparalleled ability to craft global events and control world leaders to dance to their tune. The plan was breathtaking in its audacity.

There were only a handful of people who knew the truth, and MI6 had the herculean task of trying to stop them. Eva glanced about the plane. She didn't know if it would be enough.

Harry lay sedated in the leather seat, his foppish hair covering his forehead. She tried to recall the times she'd watched him sleep, enthralled by his mere presence. She was no longer so beguiled, and yet... there was still something there. His gravity still possessed a power, but it was slipping. She truly was breaking free of his orbit.

Bishop was hunched over a laptop, filing his interrogation report. His face showed the exhaustion Eva felt. She knew he couldn't rest, not with what was at stake. When he took a moment to stretch, Eva leaned over.

"You did well back there."

He gave her a half nod. "Never mind that, how did you do?"

"Good. All good."

Laying an arm slowly over hers, Bishop held her hand firm and stared into her eyes. "Don't give me the reflex answer. I know it would have been tough seeing him again." He nodded at Harry's unconscious form. "More than tough. I want to know if you're okay, to see if I can help. Don't pretend that this was just another day in the office. I know it was far from that."

Not answering, Eva slipped her arms around Bishop and snuggled into his chest. The gesture felt odd with Harry mere metres away. Sure, he was knocked out, but she still had the vague feeling of perfidy. She did her best to shake it off, but it remained.

"Thank you for caring enough to ask," she finally said.

Bishop nuzzled his chin into her hair and inhaled deeply. Poor Bishop. She hadn't washed her hair in days, it wouldn't have been pleasant. In his arms, Eva suddenly felt heavy, as if the weight of the last week had been laid upon her. With a few blinks, she drifted off to sleep, distant memories of a man buying her a castle floating about her drowsy mind.

"Where exactly are we headed?" Eva asked.

She scurried to keep up with Paul as he marched down the halls of MI6. She hardly had time to sip her triple-shot espresso from her coffee shop.

"We need to track down Alexie, yes?" Paul didn't break stride.

"Obviously." Eva had some questions for the old spy, along with a distinct need to extract vengeance. The man had hired someone to take pot shots at Eva and her best friend. Plus, there was the whole starting a new world war thing. It was mostly the pot shots, though.

"Thanks to your old boyfriend's tech we're essentially trying to track someone who has their finger in every electric pie in the world."

"Wouldn't an electric pie be dangerous?" Eva asked goadingly.

Paul ignored the jibe. "Right now every major spy agency is effectively blind. We have no idea which source, operative or piece of intelligence has been compromised. Not a single tool we have, not a single method, can be trusted."

"So what are you saying, we give up?"

Paul gave her a sideways scowl. "Yes, that's it exactly. Let's all go home and hope the new Cold War just goes away. That kind of wishful thinking always works against tyrants." He gave a small chuckle to let her know he wasn't upset. "No, we simply don't use tools we have."

Polishing off the last of her coffee, Eva had a feeling she'd need a lot more before the day was out. "It kinda sounds a lot like giving up, dude."

"No, I didn't say that. I mean we use all the spy tools we can, ah, just not the modern ones."

Before Eva could tell Paul his answer made no sense, he thrust open the double doors to a large conference room. Inside, hunched around the boardroom table, were a group of men—only men—who wouldn't have been out of place in a retirement village.

The youngest of them would have been in his sixties. All were ravaged by age and grey hair to varying degrees. Their suits were well out of date, and for some the moniker of "shabby" would have been generous. Their billowing suits dated back to the '90s. The men briefly glanced towards Eva and Paul before returning to the piles of paper strewn across the conference table.

"Oh, I get it now," Eva said in a low voice to avoid being over-heard. "We're going to geriatric the bad guys into submission."

"Remember what the Chief said? If one is to catch an old spy, one needs to think like an old spy. She drew up a list of names." He waved his hand to indicate that the men before them were the manifestation of the list.

"What about Harry? I'm lead agent on bringing him in…"

"And you did that superbly. We're not tucking him back in the prison system just yet. He's being questioned, and we'll shake him for more information for as long as we can. Miraculously, someone made the sensible call of not bringing Lancing into Vauxhall Cross."

The two shared a knowing expression. Bringing in outsiders hadn't exactly gone well in recent times.

Paul went on. "When they're done with him he'll be facing a few additional trifling charges—escape, aiding and abetting trea-son, that kind of minor kerfuffle."

Harry would never be a free man. Given what he'd done first time around, it was always unlikely. After what he'd done recently, what he'd helped Durov do, intentionally or not, no parole board in the United Kingdom would ever allow him to walk free. He would die an old man, forgotten and alone. In the face of everything, the thought sickened Eva to the core.

Paul laid his hand on her shoulder. "You did great, Evie. You brought him in like we needed. You and your team extracted critical information that brought us closer to stopping this thing before it escalates any further." He lowered his voice. "I know it would have been tough. I can only imagine…"

Paul was one of the few people who knew how much she had truly loved Harry and had seen it firsthand.

"… but the hard part is out of the way. The next step," he gestured towards the old men, "is to track down Alexie and thwart his scheme once and for all."

"Did you just use 'thwart' in a sentence?"

"A terribly underused word. Like shenanigans, rapscallion and flapdoodle."

Eva forced out a smirk. "So, who are this lot?"

Paul stepped into the room. "Let me introduce you." He raised his voice. "Gentlemen." Once he had their attention, he went on. "This is Eva. Eva, this is Evans," he pointed, "aid to the Yanks at Teufelsburg, part of the ECHELON listening post in Berlin during the '60s, then went on to be station chief in Berlin, Washington and Vienna. Brent, lead agent in West Berlin when Red Scorpion was active, cultivated double agents over the wall. O'Neill, counterintelligence principal at MI5, 1975 to 1992." Paul recited their qualifications without referring to notes. There were no corrections.

Each man nodded in turn. It was an impressive list of resumes, no doubt representing decades of firsthand field experience. But Eva wasn't convinced it related in any way to their current crisis.

"Thank you, boy," Evans said, the most haggard of the group.

*Boy?* Paul didn't react to the word, but Eva wanted to. Didn't they know what position he held? What he'd achieved? To call a man of Paul's stature "boy" within his own organisation was tantamount to calling the Chief "Sweetie".

As if reading Eva's exasperation, Paul leaned over and whispered, "They all worked with my old man. A few met me back in the day, when I wore short pants." He paused, stared at them evenly. "Apparently some still see me as an eight-year-old kid."

Eva decided that now may not be the best time to argue the point. There were many reasons the dismissive attitude towards Paul rubbed her the wrong way, not least of which being her loyalty to her friend.

Paul made his apologies and explained he'd be back in a few minutes. While he was away, he suggested that everyone peruse the documents before them. Eva sat at the boardroom table and picked up the first piece of paper in front of her. It was a report from 1978, generated by a field office in Tel Aviv.

"Earl Grey, thanks darlin'."

Eva turned to the man who had uttered the words, Evans, the oldest of them by far. He resumed his scrutinising of the documents behind thick-rimmed glasses.

"What about it?" Eva asked.

"I'd love one." He didn't take his eyes off the paper in front of him.

"Me too." Eva shrugged.

"Off you pop then," Evans said, finally peering at her over his glasses.

"If you're implying, and let's hope for your wellbeing you're not, that I'm some sort of tea lady, I can fucking well assure you I'm not. As an added bonus, you should know I have no qualms about picking up an octogenarian and throwing him through a window. Just FYI."

Mouth agape in shock, Evans snapped his head back in shock. The others were watching the exchange with a mixture of amusement and bemusement.

"Well who the bloody hell are you?" Evans asked indignantly.

"I'm a field operative. A damn good one too."

"But you're… you're…"

"A woman?" Eva asked, eyebrow set to indignation.

"A New Zealander."

Eva stood. "Right, mate, you want to go feet or head first?"

"No offence, love," Evans said, in a half-hearted attempt at being conciliatory. "I had no idea you're an agent. You're too pretty for that. Back in my day they would have painted you on the side of a plane."

"There's absolutely no way I have an answer for that." Giving a slight shake of her head, Eva added, "Except maybe the window thing."

With amusement twinkling in his eyes, Brent spoke for the first time while holding up two palms. "Hey, we're all on the same side here. Pleasure to meet you, Eva." His eyes darted to the tattoos on her sleeves. "Have you, ah, been an, ah, operative long?"

"A few years. I've thwarted," she almost smiled at the word, "a few plots to destabilise world governments, terrorist schemes, assassination plans and governmental coup d'états. All successful missions, although…"

"Although?"

"I did lose a government-issued umbrella once."

"Umbrella?" Brent said. Amusement crossed his lips.

"Yeah. It was pink. Shame really."

Brent gave her a nod. "So, definitely not a tea lady?"

Eyes narrowing, Eva glared at Evans. "Not a tea lady. No."

Having quelled the open civil war, everyone went back to casually perusing the documents before them. With no direction as to what the group's function was, Eva picked up another random document and did the same. This one covered potential Soviet troop movements in Czechoslovakia from 1973. For several minutes the group sat in silence, apart from the rustle of paper and the occasional hacking cough.

As Eva was about to pipe up and ask what they were meant to be doing, the door creaked open. The others glanced up, disinterested, before resuming their reading. Eva was far more riveted than the others. Perhaps alarmed was more accurate. Having seen who Paul had escorted in, she assumed all hell was about to break loose.

Eyes darting about the room, Eva tried to work out who she could tackle to the ground when Paul announced what he was about to announce. There was no way these old Cold War warriors were going to take it with a genial laugh and some light banter. She wondered if they had enough strength in their old bones to hurl a chair across the room.

"Everyone," Paul sounded far more officious this time, "I have another introduction to make."

There were several groans from the group. Evans even tutted.

Paul went on. "This is Boris Nikolayev."

Boris nodded sheepishly, his old suitcase in hand. That got their attention. Every single one of them sat up, suddenly alert.

"As you could surmise from the name, he was once a member of the KGB."

"Snow Leopard," Brent whispered under his breath. "Jesus."

Boris crossed the floor and extended his hand to Eva. "I am sorry about the incident at the Kremlin. Most regrettable. I trust you survived unscathed."

She shook his hand and gave him a nod of thanks.

"Where have you been?" Eva asked in a hushed tone.

She'd been so caught up in her own events, she'd barely spared a thought for the old codger. All she knew was that MI6 had managed to bundle him out of Russia and he'd made his own way back to London.

"I have been... busy." He broke into a hoarse coughing fit. Sitting, he stowed his suitcase under the chair before flopping down into it.

"How those smokes treating you, Boris?" Eva asked. "Regretting not giving up the gaspers?"

"Nyet." He beat his chest proudly. "There are worse decisions, da? Like people who marry their prison penpals? That is worse life choice, surely?"

She had to chuckle at that one. Eva hoped their banter would show the other old spies there was little to fear. She was slowly coming around to the old curmudgeon. Without Boris's assistance they never would have gotten as far as they had. He may have been a gruff old chauvinist, but Eva was beginning to think there were some redeeming features under his hardened wrinkled shell.

"That was you?" O'Neill asked Eva in awe. "The Kremlin thing?"

"I didn't pull the trigger if that's what you're asking, but I was there." Eva raised both eyebrows. He seemed to know MI6 people were present. "You seem well informed for an ex-operative..."

O'Neill shrugged. "Once a spy, always a spy."

Eva recalled hearing the phrase once before. "We're all here to help track down the bastards who orchestrated the Kremlin catastrophe, among other things, and bring them down. Let's just say I have a vested interest in seeing them pay, and believe me, they will."

O'Neill and Brent exchanged glances, seeming to reassess Eva. They sat a little straighter and regarded her with less harsh eyes. She could detect an almost imperceptible increase in respect. Then again, it could have been the coffee finally kicking in.

Evans flapped his hand towards Boris. "What the bloody hell do you think you're doing, boy, bringing a Commie into these hallowed halls? We don't need the likes of..."

"What we need," Paul said, raising his voice to silence Evans, "is to use every available intelligence source we have. Boris here was indispensable in identifying one of our two main targets. He is to be trusted fully. And before you ask, the Chief herself suggested this. So if you have a problem with a directive from the head of MI6, I kindly thank you for your time and will gladly show you the door. If, however, you wish to contribute to the apprehension of the most dangerous wanted persons on the planet, then I would suggest you concentrate on the task at hand and stow the attitude. Am I making myself clear?"

Brent issued a small chuckle. "Someone's all grown up."

Paul glared at Evans. "Shame that can't be said for everyone." He clapped his hands together. "Alright, as we're all here, let's get this show on the road." He nodded towards Eva. "Ms Destruction is in charge and will be responsible for coordinating your efforts. In essence, she is your departmental lead."

"Me?" Eva asked in shock.

Unable to hide his amusement, Paul said, "Can you think of anyone more qualified? You've met the targets in the current day. You can guide these experts in leveraging their vast experience. Plus, I know your irrational fear of computers, so I thought this would be right up your alley."

He made a good case. Like always. She nodded, but made sure she gave Paul a displeased side eye anyway. It only fuelled his amusement.

"Right then, I'll leave you to it."

As he left, all eyes turned to Eva. Some more friendly than others.

"Well, we're not here to waste time on a load of flapdoodle, gents. Let's get started."

# CHAPTER FOURTEEN

For a long time, Eva didn't know where to start. The task seemed insurmountable. Collectively, the little group had over a century's worth of espionage experience. How was Eva meant to tap into that? Slowly she formulated a regimen. They identified all intelligence reports mentioning Red Scorpion or Alexie Barinov, noting times and particularly places where he had either been spotted or reported to have been. Then they listed all known associates and what was known about them, as well as, if they were alive, last known whereabouts and so forth. They also gave each Alexie reference a ranking based on how reliable the source was and if there were collaborating witnesses or associated evidence.

It was methodical, laborious work. A few of the reports had been filed by those in the room. Boris did his best to skirt the periphery. These weren't his reports, not his organisation. Not even his side of the war.

Superficially, Boris seemed unperturbed by his role as an outsider. It must have been the way of a spy. Being a fly on the wall would be as familiar as an old couch. The others treated him with caution, shielding reports so old they may as well have been declassified years ago. Eva did her best to involve the KGB veteran as much as possible, but his aloofness didn't aid matters.

With no idea if they were making any progress, Eva pressed on. By lunchtime they had filled half a wall with known associates, past locations and identified missions. All of it decades old and, Eva determined, completely useless.

They knew where Durov was. Every Russian news service, and the majority of international ones, were carrying his venom-fuelled rhetoric. The West bore the brunt of most of it, and the small remainder was directed at the ineptitude of various Russian governmental organisations for failing to apprehend those responsible for Sokolov's death. If only those listening knew the truth.

Without Alexie in custody or any evidence tying Durov to events, they had to leave him be. For now. Eva vowed his time would come.

Without knocking, Bishop strode in. Like always, he carried himself as though the room was his dominion alone. Every one of the old MI6 spies seemed more alert, and paid him homage, like he was lord of the manner.

They treated Paul like he was eight years old. For some, Eva was just a skirt. But of course they liked Bishop. He *looked* like a spy. Or at least what these guys envisaged they'd been like back in the day. Though Eva was sure none of them ever rocked a three-piece suit like Bishop.

He was a good-looking bastard, but the awe the others supplied him gave her pause. Bishop was like an old-school spy. Shouldn't that sound alarm bells? She would have thought she'd find herself attracted to an enlightened, feminist-leaning sort, not a throwback to the suave, self-assured, old-fashioned type. But all alarms were silent when it came to Bishop. She'd have to dedicate some time to that one. At some point. Just not now.

Pouring himself a glass of water, Bishop sat at the table. After brief introductions, he asked, "So what do we have?"

Eva gave a quick summation. When she said it out loud, the results from hours of painstaking work were even thinner than she'd first thought. Who was she kidding? If they were any thinner they'd have been see-through.

More to herself than anyone else in the room, Eva said, "We're not asking the right questions."

From the corner of her eye she saw Boris smile. Eva scratched the back of her head. Pulling a hair tie from her wrist, she fastened her hair into a ponytail.

"Right." She paced the room. "So we have all this information and intelligence, but it doesn't tell us squat about current motivations or actions." She lifted her coffee cup, only to find it empty. She didn't want to interrupt her line of thinking by fetching another. "We know Alexie and Durov were seen together in Frankfurt. We believe they're father and son. Alexie most likely killed or ordered the kill on the CIA agent in Budapest. The Russian embassy bombing in London has his fingerprints all over it. Everything flows from there." She shook her hands to encourage blood flow. She felt like she was on the verge of something. "We also know that Harry," she paused and eyed the group, "Horatio Lancing, provided the mechanism to attack MI6's computer infrastructure. Father and son are playing the long game."

"But what does..." Evans interrupted.

"Shut it," Bishop said, cutting him off. "Let her think."

Pacing laps in front of the boardroom table, Eva's mind raced.

Earlier, Eva had asked them all in turn, but besides Eva and Boris, no one in the room had ever been face to face with Alexie. But the ex-MI6 agents all knew the Red Scorpion by reputation. There was no doubt all had feared him, quite rightfully.

"What do we know of Alexie back in the day?" The question was rhetorical; no one dared interrupt her. "He was spotted in the field well into his forties. Isn't that old for a field agent?"

O'Neill shrugged. "It would be for MI6. You begin to lose the taste for danger after a while, and start looking after your own neck instead."

She nodded and pointed to the mounds of paper before her. "But he never pursued a higher office, was never promoted?"

"Not that we know of."

Eva nodded. "All these things he did… the assassinations," her mind briefly flicked back to her encounter with the Perfume Assassin, but she stamped it down, "the political manipulation, sabotage, stealing state secrets, engineering revolutions and then, nothing. It's like he disappeared."

"That's probably why we thought he was dead for so long," Bishop added, "and why that was never corrected. He went completely dark."

She nodded in Bishop's general direction. Eva was still on a roll. "But what's the trigger? Why would Alexie push all this onto his son? Everything about the man says he hides in the shadows, he is the epitome of a ghost, a splinter of an idea. He's not ambitious, yet he's pushing him onto the world stage, making his son the beneficiary of years of accumulated nefarious know-how. But in all his time, Alexie never pursued a promotion. Never seemed to move up in any of his roles. Yet his son wants to rule the world. Where did *Durov* get his ambition from?"

A throaty cough erupted in the corner of the room. Beaming, Boris waggled a finger at Eva. "I do something that happens rarely in my life. Not mean much to you, young lady, but is true. I wish to apologise."

"You do?" asked Eva. *This could be anything.*

"When we met, I said you were pretty, and I was little bit insulting, da?"

Eva shrugged. He was. She was slowly warming to the old bastard, but was still feeling far from friendly.

"I sit here and listen to old men bitch about old times."

The old men shifted in their seats, visibly agitated.

Boris ignored them. "They shuffle paper like old women and think they are doing something useful. Bah!" He threw a hand up dismissively. Again, he waved a finger in Eva's direction. "But you, young lady, you see information, but understand much more. You say you haven't asked right question, and then you ask the exact question you should. You are a very good spy, I think."

A pleased expression crossed her face. It was quite the compliment from someone with his experience. "Okay, so I asked the right question, but what does that have to do with—"

As Eva spoke, Boris dove into his battered old suitcase and rummaged around until he found what he was searching for. He tossed a photo face-down across the boardroom table and stopped Eva mid-sentence.

Before Eva could flip the photo, Boris rubbed his hands, glancing around nervously. "Are you familiar with Amanda Bourke Affair?"

Obviously, she was. Everyone in the room—shit, the building—knew. Aside from being one of the biggest scandals of the Cold War because an agent had disappeared, it was also when Paul's father had lost his life. Eva was glad Paul wasn't present.

"That bitch?" Evans spat.

"Oi," O'Neill piped up. "That's one of ours you're talking about, mate. Some respect."

Evans sneered in reply. "You ever meet her?" He waited for O'Neill to shake his head. "More front than Harrods. All sweet and innocent until she didn't get her way. I reckon she'd have got the top job if she hadn't been... you know." He eyed Eva as if saying the word "killed" would harm her delicate sensibilities. "Even back then, she had the bloody nerve to think she'd be chief one day. Talk about aspiration, right? There was no chance, obviously, as she was..." his voice tailed off and he cast Eva a sideways glance.

"A woman?" Eva glared daggers at Evans, daring him to reply.

"I wasn't going to say that, no," Evans said in a tone that told her it was exactly what he had been going to say. "From Liverpool is what I was going to say."

There was a time, not long ago, when Eva would have launched a tirade in Evans' direction, full of creative expletives about the tight interrelatedness of his parents and his penchant for animal husbandry. But now was not the time. Maybe she was growing? Maybe she was becoming part of the big espionage machine and losing herself. She hoped it wasn't the latter. She did enjoy her tirades.

Eva turned her attention back to Boris. "What about the Amanda Bourke Affair?"

"The woman. The one, the main one. Amanda Bourke. She was not killed in Warsaw. She," he inhaled deeply, eying off each of the old spies in the room, "she defected."

There were audible gasps from the group of hardened MI6 spies. Evans stood. Brent clenched his fists. It had always been suspected that Amanda Bourke could have defected, but there had been no evidence, and the lack of proof meant it had remained a theory.

"How do you know—" Eva began.

"Because Alexie and I were ones to take her back to Soviet Union."

Even though he was nervous, Eva detected a sense of pride in his words.

It took all of Eva's resolve to keep her eyes off the ageing secret agents in the room. Some of them would have surely worked on the Amanda Bourke disappearance. A number may have mourned her alleged passing. Every one of them would be livid to have their worst fears realised. One of their best and brightest had betrayed them in the most heinous of ways.

Doing her best to stamp down her shock, Eva went on. "What does this have to do with...?"

"I went back. To Frankfurt. I try to find Alexie, to take more photos for you. But I did not find Alexie. Or Durov. But someone was in the same apartment they were in."

Boris nodded at the photo beneath Eva's fingers. She flipped it over. It was a full colour photo of an older woman. The hair was grey, the lines on her face far more pronounced, but there was no doubt who it was.

"She was in Frankfurt," Boris said firmly. "Yesterday."

Simultaneously, Eva and Bishop said, "Amanda Bourke is alive?"

Boris's gaze lowered. "It has probably surprised many of your comrades," he jerked his head towards the other side of the table, but didn't dare look at them, "but, yes, Amanda Bourke is alive. She is in Frankfurt in the exact same apartment where Durov and Alexie Barinov were, and I do not know why."

*Jizz-juggling monkey flaps.*

This case was meant to be becoming clearer, not muddier. Now a supposedly dead spy had crept out from the woodwork, having defected decades ago, a traitor to her home country. What did it all mean?

A theory formed in Eva's mind. It was wild, and she knew it was a bigger stretch than pulling a rubber band all the way to Brighton. And yet it kind of made sense. The way a drunk person talking to a hedge at 3 am makes perfect sense. She had to run with it regardless, to see where it went.

Thankfully, the old spies remained silent, even though they must have been chomping at the bit to question Boris. Or lynch him.

"What happened to her once she was taken back to the USSR?" Eva asked.

Boris shrugged. "I do not know. My role was to get her over wall. I was surprised they did not make a, what is phrase? Song and dance? I am surprised the Politburo did not make a song and dance about another filthy capitalist embracing reason and seeking freedom within the glorious Soviet Union, blah, blah, blah." He shrugged. "Then again, I was never privy to workings of government and probably retained sanity because of this, da?"

"Do you know anything of what became of her once she crossed over?"

Boris shook his head. "Nyet."

"Did she marry?" Eva asked pointedly.

"I do not know." Another shrug. "I also do not know if she liked cheesecake." His frown reversed. "But your question, about ambition before was good question. For first time I began to think... well, a very strange thought."

Eva knew exactly how strange because she appeared to be having the same one. Was this the missing piece?

She turned to Bishop, who was bewildered by the conversation. "What do we know of Durov's parentage?"

"Next to nothing. The official story is he's an orphan… Oh shit, Eva. You're not suggesting Durov's parents are Alexie and Amanda Bourke, are you? That's—"

"Insane? It's not like everything else in this case is perfectly logical." Her pacing doubled down. "We couldn't source Durov's lust for power. His father was a man of shadows and manipulation, never one to seek the spotlight. Bourke, on the other hand…"

"She was always jolly ambitious," O'Neill piped in. "We joked she was going to be the first woman Prime Minister, or at least settle for Chief of the Service. Pretty sure it was only half joking. Even back then we thought she might do it, she had the bloody drive. The woman was smart, she'd have to be to get as far as she did back then as a female. Ambition? She had it by the truckload."

Evans scoffed. "It's a fucking long bow, darlin'."

Eva hefted an eyebrow. "Yeah, I know."

Bishop mirrored her eyebrow placement and added a smirk.

Addressing Evans, Eva added, "So I'll wait for your alternative theory."

Eva sat, thumped her feet on the table, folded her arms and stared at Evans. After a minute of glowering and uncomfortable silence, Bishop patted Eva on the shoulder and said, "Alright, point made, very good."

With her back to the others, she gave him a sly wink. Quietly, in a voice only he could hear, she asked, "Do you think I'm right?"

After a beautiful grin, Bishop whispered, "It's a wild theory. I'm not completely sold, but I'll tell you what, if you're right, I'll owe you a fiver."

"I'll hold you to that."

"Is that all you're going to hold me to?"

"Stop it."

He chuckled. "Never."

Eva chastised herself. This was no time for flirting. It was time to focus. So Boris and Alexie were in Warsaw when Amanda Bourke did her infamous disappearing act. There were questions

Eva wanted to ask Boris, but they could wait until they were free of the elderly MI6 spies. First and foremost, what had actually gone down in Warsaw? There were rumours, of course, there always were. Bad intelligence had been blamed, as had British leadership. The CIA was generally singled out for having botched the whole operation. Then there was the operative who had died during the affair. It was a historical footnote, a piece of information for espionage junkie websites. But for Eva it was far more personal than that. Again, she was thankful Paul had missed it all.

There was a knock at the door.

Paul poked his head in. "How are we all doing?" he asked with a genial smile.

*No no no no.*

*Scrotum-slapping muffbunnies.*

It was Evans who blurted the revelations. That Amanda Bourke had not only survived, but was alive. Not only that, but it was Boris, the man sitting in front of Paul, who had brought her over.

The collapse of Paul's expression was complete. His amiable disposition crumbled into stony intensity. His jaw was carved from marble. His fists contracted into balls of fury.

Between clenched teeth, Paul said, "My father was in Warsaw then."

Eva noted he didn't say his father *died* in Warsaw then.

Boris frowned. With a jut of his chin, he asked, "Who is father?"

"Steven Cavendish."

The years of field training, the decades of skills accumulated from practiced deceit were not enough to hide Boris's expression. Either the old spy was slipping or there was no way he could mask his horror. The old KGB agent's face dropped, and his eyes darted from side to side, searching for an escape. He slowly moved backwards, as if trying to slide into the shadows, but there was nothing to slide into. There was nothing but solid wall behind him.

"Boris," Eva said warily, "tell me you didn't..."

"I say nothing. Get me away from... get me out of here, now!"

"Deny it, man!" Paul yelled. "Tell me!"

Boris shook his head and continued to search for escape routes that didn't exist. Paul's face was molten lava, his body a coiled spring. He let forth a primeval snarl.

Eva was the first to react; Bishop was close behind. Soon five grown adults were struggling to hold back a single man with a lifetime of amassed rage. Paul's screams were primal. Genuine fear on his face, Boris had his back to the wall.

# CHAPTER FIFTEEN

As soon as they'd physically escorted Paul out of the room, Boris sealed up tighter than a cosmonaut's helmet. In the face of all requests, both screamed and calm, Boris refused to repudiate the assumption he was the one who had killed Paul's father killed in Warsaw. There were no assertions of innocence or otherwise. His lips may as well have been sewn shut.

The room was cleared. The old operatives were sent home, Bishop ushered Paul into his office and Eva was tasked with securing Boris. He sat before her in the closest available office. His stony resolve was absolute.

The man had helped MI6 in recent days. He'd opened their eyes to Alexie, who they'd otherwise have assumed dead. He'd pointed them towards Durov, who had quickly shown his hand. Boris had not only advised them that Amanda Bourke was alive, but that, according to his photos, she had been associating with the two main perpetrators of their pain. Eva had taken her own leaps about Bourke's role from there.

No matter how you sliced it, Boris had been instrumental in them getting this far.

Then again...

He had all but admitted he was the one responsible for Paul's father's death. Whether he had pulled the trigger or not, his shocked reaction and distinct lack of denial were tantamount to a confession. What happened from here? MI6 had in their grasp the perpetrator of one of the biggest scandals of the Cold War. But he could also be instrumental in saving them from a new one.

Eva needed a holiday.

Running her hands through hair long overdue for a wash, Eva glared at the ceiling and exhaled a frustrated breath. She wanted to be with her friend in his time of pain, but didn't know if Paul would feel the same way.

This was Eva's fault. All of it. It had been Boris who had initially contacted her. She'd tried to bring Boris into the old spy group and make them play nice. She wasn't responsible for Paul's father's death, but she sure as shit felt responsible for the revelation happening like it had.

She wanted to be with Bishop, too, but for her own selfish reasons. He would make her feel better, make her better. She knew it was illogical. But since when has love been logical?

*Woah. What was that?* Eva assumed stress was the reason the "L" word had seeped into her brain. Yes, definitely stress.

Stamping down the thought, she refocused on the topic at hand. Boris's revelation about Paul's father.

"Do you still have firing squad in this country?"

The haggard old face seemed to have aged in the last twenty minutes. Eva squinted at Boris, trying to get a read, but the old Russian may as well have been an Easter Island statue.

"No. The death penalty was done away with years ago."

A frown and a slight nod. "Officially. Given current circumstances, who know? It only takes a slight push for a nation to slip back into barbarity."

"Does that scare you? A firing squad?"

Boris let forth a raspy laugh. "I am old man. I have danced with death so many times we know each other's moves. I do not fear dying, little girl. I would not be helping you now if I did. I would be home with feet on coffee table yelling answer to game show question. No, my fate is my fate. But you," he narrowed his eyes, "you are another matter." Boris waved his weathered hand at Eva. "There is much to this story which revolves around you, da? Either because of you, or influenced by you. This odd, I think. You are very unique spy, Miss Eva Destruction."

Again, Boris's thoughts echoed hers. Given recent events, Eva wasn't going to argue. It was hard to reconcile her thoughts about this man she'd forged a grudging respect for. He was on their side, she was certain. Was all the help he'd given them recently irrelevant if he'd been the one to pull the trigger on Paul's dad? How could she deal with that? Every spy in the boardroom had killed people, she was sure. Many, if not all, of those kills were probably justified as being for the greater good. Did the ideological shifts since then negate the previous rationalisations? Could they ever? How long could one carry the ramifications of a split-second decision? Could any spy?

Eva stared hard at the old man. "Why did you help us? Why step back in after all these years?"

"Redemption." He tilted his weathered head. "Is this what you want me to say? Or some such notion? No. I am not noble man."

"Do you regret some of the things you did?"

"Does butcher have regret of cow he killed thirty years ago? I have no idea. Go ask butcher."

"You're saying you don't have remorse for killing Paul's dad, because..."

"I never said I kill Cavendish. But I regret them all, the deaths. That is my point. But I do not lose sleep over it."

More riddles. More enigmas wrapped in bullshit. Eva wasn't even sure what was true anymore. Was he responsible for Paul's dad's death or not?

She sighed. "Boris, why didn't you tell us about your role in the Amanda Bourke Affair? Or tell me, at least?"

A shrug with a frown. "I did not know of Cavendish lineage. How could I? What? Should I have told you about all the people I have encountered in my past and who they may and may not be related to? We would still be at our first meeting point, I think, da?"

Eva had had enough of skirting the issue. Circular spy talk was getting them no closer to the truth. "Did you kill Steven Cavendish?"

The very definition of stonewall stared back her.

"Dude, I'm trying to help you here. If you did, well, we'll try and find a way through it. If you didn't, then why the fuck are you carrying on like a politician caught with his pants down?"

"Why would politician have pants down? You mean like on privy?"

Eva crossed her arms and reflected Boris's stonewall back at him.

A sigh from the old spy. "Fine. It was not me, but I authorised weapons free. It was on my orders there was no restraint shown. Was not my bullet, but was my order."

So he didn't kill Paul's father. Eva was relieved, but only slightly. This was still on her. She was sure Paul wouldn't see it that way, but she had put him through this. It was her fault. Boris was right, much of this revolved around her. That also meant those she cared most about.

Boris shook his head as if reading her thoughts. "Nyet, Eva. Do not torture yourself about past things you cannot control." The tiniest of grins formed at the corner of Boris's wrinkled mouth. "Speaking of not being able to control your past... how is your old boyfriend? He have any more information?"

*Once a spy.* Eva knew better than to ask how Boris knew about Harry.

She was reasonably certain Harry didn't fall within the category of those she cared most about. Once, but no longer. The realisation was freeing.

Her thoughts strayed again to Bishop. They were well overdue for a heart to heart. And skin to skin, for that matter. They were overdue for a great many things. Some of them even involved having their clothes on. Not many.

Her mouth was pretty dry. She needed to quench a great many

things. Shaking her head to dislodge the thoughts of writhing sweaty bodies on bearskin rugs, Eva said, "Look, I don't know what's going to happen with you, Boris. I dare say you'll be put on ice for a bit while the legal bods figure out their options. Given the current state of international relations, I'm guessing a spy trade is pretty much out of the question."

Boris frowned so often it was almost a permanent feature. "Is firing squad still at dawn, or can I have breakfast first? I like this English breakfast, though needs more vodka."

At least *he* was jovial. Eva rolled her eyes. "No firing squad, but I'll ask if they can throw in a decent breakfast."

"Is good."

"Boris, we're going to find Alexie and Amanda. We're closing this down before it goes any further. Is there anything you can tell me that would give us an edge? Anything to help?"

Scratching his stubbled chin, Boris swished the thought around in his mind. "Amanda, at least back in day, was a true believer. She was Communist early, but never joined party because she knew she could never be spy if she did. Very ambitious, as your man said. Even when working with KGB, she put many of my comrades back in box, myself included. Always very smart, played long game." He rubbed the back of his head. "I told you about Alexie's distaste for blood. Maybe this will help." His eyes narrowed, as if accessing old memories. "Alexie, he had specialty. You old enough to recall terrible Russian coup in '91? Stupid military men in tanks thought they could restore USSR, you remember, da? Was no coup, more like Keystone Cops. Yeltsin was hailed as hero and Gorbachev never recovered—he was politically dead for not seeing it coming or stopping it once it did. The Soviet Union fell apart and Yeltsin was hero. Did ever strike you as odd? That such a coup even started and was so poorly executed? They did not take control of TV stations, and allowed Yeltsin on tank to give rousing speech. Odd, yes? Was all orchestrated by Alexie for Yeltsin. He staged it for Yeltsin's benefit.

"Remember assassination attempt on Rajiv Gandhi, the Indian Prime Minister? He was always in KGB pocket. What was his first state visit? Russia, of course. When his popularity was flagging in 1987, there was assassination attempt, just like his mother, but this one *he* survived. Then suddenly he was popular again." A mock surprised face. "These things we called Barinov Special. An attempted coup or assassination can be as effective as a real one, da?"

Unsure how any of this information could assist, Eva thanked him, and bid the old spy goodbye. He'd be placed under guard tonight, his fate uncertain. As she headed for the door, Boris snapped his fingers to get her attention. It still grated.

"If you would permit, some advice from an old, long-thought-dead spy. You are good agent, I think, Eva Destruction. Smart, resourceful. You have heart, probably most I have seen in MI6. I say to you, instinct and skill is good, but you also still have your humanity. You are not heartless, this is why *you* are good spy. You hold on to that, da? Your humanity defines you, never forget this. If you start to become unemotional, you leave. If it is no longer fun. Promise me, little girl? If you become cold-hearted like this withered old man, you go back to coffee shop and never look back. Can you promise this?"

Blinking several times to take it in, Eva slowly gave Boris a nod. "Okay. You have my word."

"This is agreeable. Your word is good, Eva Destruction." He leaned back and closed his eyes. "Please tell firing squad should be late morning. I need beauty sleep."

Eva pressed the doorbell and Eva waited. The owners had bought a novelty doorbell that played movie themes. This one was *Jaws*. Ominous as it was fitting. Normally Eva would barge right in regardless of how dressed or otherwise the owners were. But not today.

The door creaked open to reveal a sunken-eyed Paul with an instant-coffee-weak smile.

"It would have been really cool," Eva started, "if when you opened the door there was some dude playing the cello."

She gave Paul a peck on the cheek.

"Last week we had the theme from *Indiana Jones*." His voice was less jovial than normal. "I wanted to set up a giant rock ball to roll down the stairs. My beloved said it was impractical and, in her words, a death trap that would kill us all."

"She's such a stickler for the rules—no fun at all."

"That's what I said. But I'm pretty sure I've got her over the line for lightsaber duels next week, though."

"Outstanding."

Paul shut the door behind her and they headed up the narrow hallway. Before they reached the lounge, Eva turned to Paul.

"How you doing?"

"Fine. Fine."

She grabbed his arm. "No. How are you doing?"

He sucked air through his nose and exhaled while mulling the question over. "To be honest, I've had better days, Evie. I apologise for my actions earlier, they were most inappropriate given the current state of affairs."

"Don't you fucking dare," Eva said in a harsh whisper. "You never have to apologise to me. Ever." She ran her hand along his upper arm. "I understand more than anyone what you went through today, and even I can't begin to imagine the shit that went through your brain. Don't you dare apologise for being human, especially not to me."

Taken aback by her earnestness, Paul righted himself and nodded. "I was surprised by my reaction, to be honest. I thought I'd dealt with those demons long ago. Obviously not. I've booked in to see the shrink the day after tomorrow. I have some things to work through, clearly. Hope you don't think less of me."

"Dude, shut the fuck up. People go to the doctor all the time, but for some reason there's a stigma about going for a mental check-up or to address something specific."

Paul accepted the statement with a wink. "I do like the way you tell a person who has admitted they have psychological issues, who happens to be your boss, that they should shut the fuck up. But I'll accept the rest."

"I'm always here when you need, you know that, you big stupid twat."

Before Paul walked another step, Eva stopped him once more. "I don't think it was Boris who... your father. He didn't, you know. He gave the order for his people to go weapons hot, but he says he didn't pull the trigger."

Paul's face was neutral. "And you believe him?"

"This is espionage, mate. Nobody knows who to believe."

Rather than reply, Paul nodded and continued the trek towards the lounge. Taking her usual position in the kitchen, Nancy juggled steaming pots and sizzling frying pans.

"What's for dinner?" Eva asked.

"Either haloumi nuggets with tomato chilli jam and polenta chips or, alternatively, takeaway pizza, if this little bastard doesn't brown." Nancy poked a frying pan with a wooden spoon.

"Sound delicious," Eva said.

"It better be. Got the recipe from the cookbook you gave me for Christmas."

"I meant the pizza."

"Feck off," Nancy said with a chortle.

She wiped her hands on her apron and gave her friend a hearty hug.

"Eww!" Eva shrieked. "Did you just cover me in placenta?"

"Polenta."

"Same, same." Eva held up a bottle. "I bought wine."

"You wouldn't have gotten this far if you hadn't." Nancy flashed her a sneaky smile.

While Eva poured them each a glass of wine she glanced in Paul's direction. She could tell he was only partially engaged in the conversation. That was hardly surprising, given the revelations of the day. It was Eva's way to leap in feet-first and bring up what-ever was on her mind. Especially with her two best friends. But it wasn't that simple now.

They were all playing a role of some sort. Nancy knew Eva's

secret about being a spy, but was apparently keeping it from Paul... who was Eva's boss. Paul was hiding his pain from his wife for exactly the same reason: he couldn't tell the person he loved more than life itself what he did for a living. And there was Eva, stuck in the middle, unable to talk plainly to the two people she trusted most in the world. It was maddening.

Too many secrets. Too many agendas. Maybe Boris was right. If her career was no longer fun, it was time to get out. But that was a decision for another time. She had the architects of a new Cold War to bring down first. After dinner.

Paul retired early. Making the excuse of oncoming man flu, he made his way upstairs feigning the sniffles. He was always a terrible actor. Eva had to seriously wonder how he'd ever managed to keep his secret from his wife for so long.

Before then, whenever Nancy left to grab something from the kitchen Eva checked on her friend. He continually claimed to be fine, but she only half believed him. He wasn't a player, so his assertion of being okay was believable—to an extent. There was little doubt he'd work through his troubles, but it would take time.

She wished there was a way to alert Nancy to Paul's inner demons. How the hell do you tell your best friend to support her husband when you can't tell her why?

"Another?" Nancy waved a bottle.

It was the best red "wyne" by the litre Wales produced. If they still had their eyesight in the morning it would be a minor miracle. Eva nodded, and Nancy filled her glass to the brim.

Eva took a sip and made a sour face. "How're you doing after the little run-in we had?"

Nancy let out a derisive laugh. "You call that little?"

Eva thought for a moment. "Actually, hate to say it Nance, but after what I've seen, yeah, that was little."

"Feckin' hell. That explains all the bruises and shite you come in with." She sloshed the bottle towards Eva. "You enjoy it?"

"Most of the time, yeah. I'm bloody good at it, too. Most of the time. I've made mistakes, people have been hurt, but on the whole there's a fucktonne more positives than negatives in my ledger."

With a sage nod, Nancy topped up her own glass. "That partner of yours…"

"Bishop."

"Hmm, yes, Bishop. You two a thing? Is he another secret?"

"No. Well, yes, but no."

"See? Now you sound like a proper spy."

Eva poked her tongue out. It was probably black by now. "I mean, when he turned up that night we were being shot at, there wasn't anything going on between us. But when we were in… when we were on a recent mission, things kind of happened. He's not the kind of bloke I thought I'd end up with, but I can't stop thinking about him. It's… I still have to work it out."

Nancy avoided Eva's eyes as she put down the bottle. "I've met him before. Took me ages to remember where from, but I knew I knew him from somewhere."

Eva hoped Nancy couldn't see the panic in her eyes. "Oh, really? I'm sure he has one of those faces…"

"Clive," Nancy cut in. "That's what he was introduced as. Clive. Does that walking GQ shoot look like a feckin' Clive to you?"

"I really don't…"

"It's okay, love." Nancy patted Eva's hand. "I remembered when my beloved introduced me to 'Clive'." She said the name with an over-heaped serving of sarcasm. "Said he was from work. Worked in legal procurement or some bullshit." She gulped half her glass. "As if a man who looks like that works as a Treasury pencil pusher."

"Oh."

Nancy gave Eva a sympathetic expression. "Don't worry, lovie. I've known for many years Paulie didn't work for Treasury. I figured that meant he either worked somewhere secretive, like the Secret Service, or he was a stripper."

The two women stared at one another evenly.

Nancy cocked one eyebrow. "So MI6 it was."

The two burst out laughing. Poor Paul.

"But never in a million years did I think *you* were a spy." Nancy took a moment to take a sip, trying to appear casual. "You and Paul work together?"

Having known her best friend intimately for years, Eva knew Nancy wasn't fishing because she thought there was anything untoward between her and Paul. She genuinely wanted to know.

"Nance, I can't…"

In response, Nancy held up her hand. "Yeah, sorry, shouldn't have asked. The old hubby and I are long overdue for a chat. He's lucky I love the stupid bastard."

"He really is."

"Yeah," Nancy said, furrowing her brow. She held up her wine and the two clinked their glasses together. "He bloody well is!"

"So, what about you? This Bishop bloke. Actually, what's his real name?"

The blank expression on Eva's face must have been visible from the moon. There may as well have been tumbleweeds rolling out her ears.

"Uhhh."

"Eva? You know his name, right?"

Eva blinked several times. "Shit!" She waved her hand at Nancy. "Charles. Charles Bishop. Sorry, I always call him Bishop."

Eyes narrowed to slits, Nancy stared into Eva's very soul. "Right. So, deep emotional connection then?"

Overcome with a sense of trepidation, Eva second guessed herself yet again. Why wasn't she rushing headlong into Bishop's arms? She'd promised herself she'd be more careful after her last few disastrous relationships, but did her consternation have another source? Was her subconscious aware of something she wasn't? Should she reconsider diving into a relationship with Bishop? Was she asking herself too many questions? Should she ask one more? Eva decided to ask one more question, and she already knew the answer. Yes, she should definitely have more wine.

Before she could gulp down her wine, her phone vibrated in her pocket. Taking it out, she glanced at the name and then answered.

"Good evening, Charles." Her voice was dripping in syrup.

Nancy rolled her eyes.

Eva went on. "What can I do for you, Charles?" She elongated the last word. "So nice to hear from you, Charles."

"Jesus, I don't know if you've ever called me that."

"I'm trying it out. What's up?"

"You want some good news?"

"Nickelback have died in a fiery bus crash?"

"I said good news, not spectacular news. This one's slightly more personal. We have Alexie and Bourke, they're both in Frankfurt. Well, they were."

"Were? That doesn't help us much. I can tell you where they were too. Fuck, I can tell you what I had for lunch, but it's not entirely helpful."

"Snippy much?" Bishop laughed. It was a very nice laugh. "It *does* help us knowing they were in Frankfurt when they both boarded a plane to Berlin. And you want to know the best bit?"

"The plane exploded during take-off?"

"Almost. Durov is scheduled to give a talk at the Reichstag in Berlin the day after tomorrow."

"Holy motherfucking shitkittens."

"My thoughts exactly. All three are going to be in the same city at the same time. If you're right about Durov's lineage, there's going to be a family reunion."

"Normally I hate family gatherings, but I'm willing to make an exception just this once."

"You in?" His grin practically beamed down the phone.

Eva stood, waved to Nancy and picked up her handbag. "I'm already out the door."

# CHAPTER SIXTEEN

---

Eva should have been on a plane by now. Except she wasn't. She was in Paddington. Which was pretty much as far away from Berlin as you could get. At least conceptually. The situation was made worse because it was because of someone she had thoroughly determined she never wanted to see again.

Paul had gotten it into his head that Eva should visit Harry. The logic was solid enough, but that hadn't prevented Eva from conceiving new and inventive ways to flip Paul the bird from different parts of his office. The double-barrelled middle-finger flick from her shoulder holsters was her favourite.

So far the MI6-conducted interviews had produced nothing but Harry's stony silence. Well, there was one phrase he repeated again and again: "Bring me Eva Destruction."

Eva hadn't read the transcripts, there was no need. She knew how stubborn he could be. Paul had tasked her to politely ask Harry to give them anything that could help them nab Alexie, Bourke or Durov. Or, ideally, all three at once. With all three in custody she could finish early and go to the pub.

The Paddington safe house wasn't a house at all. It was a coin laundry. When Eva had first been told this, she'd been surprised, but it made more sense in the taxi on the way over. A laundrette in a well-to-do suburb would attract customers day and night. Although "MI6-safe coin laundry" didn't have the same cachet.

The laundry was utterly unremarkable and nondescript. She shouldn't have expected any different. It was unlikely that MI6 would paint it bright pink and place a neon sign on the roof saying, "Top Secret Spy Safe House Here!" For one, they'd receive a tetchy letter from the council.

Walking in, the bell above the door *tinged*. It was midday, so there were several customers milling about, and washers and drying droned in the background. Three of the five customers were a little bulkier than the rest, their posture in their grey suits a little straighter, their haircuts sharper. She assumed they were MI6 guards. What a fun assignment that must be. Literally watching washing spin around all day. Poor buggers.

The two remaining customers were an elderly gent scowling at his smartphone and a guy in the corner with a beanie, his back to her. Eva strode through the laundry until she reached the far end, where a hunched old woman sat making piles of coins.

"Eva Destruction, I believe you're expecting me?"

She really hoped she had the right laundry.

The elderly woman jerked her head behind her and to the left. In a voice stained with decades of cigarettes, she said, "Last door on the right."

There was an electronic buzz and the door silently opened. Slowly making her way down the long, thin corridor, Eva mentally prepared for the oncoming encounter. Normally you could leave an ex far behind. Apart from the occasional vengeful thought or accidental Facebook sighting, you should be able to leave them in the past, where they belonged. But not Harry Bloody Lancing. He had a way of reappearing like a weed. Or syphilis.

The corridor was dimly lit. All seven doors were open, except two. The door at the end of the hall on the right was one of the closed ones. Behind it lay an uncomfortable discussion. Eva sighed. Better to get it over and done with. She had a plane to catch.

Eva assumed there was no point in knocking; they knew she was coming. Opening the door, she was surprised to find the room completely dark. This wasn't the fluorescent-lit stark white interrogation room she had envisaged.

"Uhh, hello? Did someone forget to pay the electricity bill?"

From behind, a violent push propelled her into the room. As she stumbled in and collided with the floor, the door slammed shut. The only light came from the sliver of a crack beneath the door. The sound of footsteps bounded away from the scene.

Stumbling towards the door, Eva fumbled for the handle. Locked.

"Cock-slapping chunder-twats."

Flicking the light switch garnered no illumination. Reaching into her pocket, Eva extracted her phone and switched on the torch function. It was an interrogation room alright. At least, it used to be. Now the interrogation table was piled with three prone bodies, resembling a grotesque crypt. Each of the men had holes where their chests used to be. A pool of blood dripped onto the floor.

Eva frantically checked each to make sure Harry wasn't one of the dead. He wasn't. Going by their bulk and matching suits, these were MI6 guards. Redundantly, Eva checked for pulses. None. They were all still warm. Fresh kills.

Where had the person who had shoved her come from? It must have been the other unopened door. She would have chastised herself for not checking, but why would she? This was meant to be a secure MI6 safe house.

There was another reason she needed the light of her phone. Eva extracted her pistol and aimed for the handle. Three precise bullets later, the door swung open, flooding the room with light.

Carefully, she entered the corridor, weapon at the ready. There was no discernible sound, but that couldn't be relied on. Losing precious moments, Eva quickly swept all the rooms, revealing nothing. Finally, she opened the door to the laundry. Recoiling behind a brick wall, she awaited an onslaught of bullets.

None came.

Braving the breach, she dove through, ready to place a bullet between the eyes of any adversary.

There were none.

The old lady who had buzzed her through was gone. All but one of the customers had disappeared. Only the old guy scowling at his phone remained.

"Where did they go?" Eva asked breathlessly.

The old guy glanced up, confused. "What? Who?" He saw Eva's gun and shrank back, terrified.

Who could blame him? He'd come to do his dirty laundry, not get in the middle of a gunfight.

Ignoring the man, Eva cursed herself and retraced her steps in her mind. She must have missed them when she came in, but how? *Fudge monkeys.* The three grey-suited guys milling about when she came in. They weren't MI6 at all. They must have come out of the back room, having murdered the guards.

But where was Harry?

Beanie guy!

The bloke in the corner with his back to her when she came in. His frame could have been Harry, for sure. She'd missed foiling their plan by seconds. That meant she still had a chance. Eva burst through the door and ran outside. Scanning the scene, all she saw was an empty Paddington suburban street. There was no sign of the men.

Which way to go? There were two choices: left or right. 50/50 chance.

"Sod it."

Eva turned left and ran. She chose not to tuck the pistol away. At any moment one of the bastards who had slain the guards could fire on her. It made sense to have her gun at the ready. If that offended the delicate sensibilities of Paddington's elite, so be it.

Rounding the corner of Bathurst Street, Eva stopped short. A white SUV pulled up and three grey-suited men piled in. In front of them was Mr Beanie guy.

Before she could call out, the closest of the grey suits pivoted towards her and took aim. She went to raise her gun, but his was already pointed at Eva's head. Eva was too slow to react. She'd been outdrawn.

As the grey-suited man pulled the trigger, Mr Beanie pushed himself off the car door and into the gunman. The bump threw the man's aim off and the bullet sailed into the sky. For the third time in as many minutes, Eva nose-dived to the ground. Rolling, she took cover behind a shiny Subaru.

The shoving and jostling of Beanie guy seemed to suggest he wasn't being taken voluntarily. Also, Eva had seen his face. Harry Lancing had shoved the grey-suited man so he wouldn't hurt her. He still cared. He was still protecting her.

Bullets ricocheted off the bodywork of the Subaru. She wasn't completely safe. There were three armed men about to escape in a car. Time for Eva to even the odds.

Rolling until she was flat on the ground, Eva peered under the car. She saw the SUV's wheels and the feet of the grey-suited men, who were most likely waiting for Eva to poke her head out so they could put a bullet in it. She'd give them no such advantage.

Taking her time, Eva lined up her targets and steadied her breath. She'd have one chance, and a slim one at that. Exhaling slowly, she pulled the trigger.

The ankles of the first man detonated in a burst of blood and bone. The second turned, but his feet remained fixed in one spot. His error. Like the first, his ankles exploded, rendering the target useless and writhing in pain. The third had time to react, and leapt onto the running board of the SUV. Harry had jumped in after the first bullets. Smart boy.

Next, Eva targeted the tyres. Thankfully they weren't bullet-proof. With a *hiss* the three tyres she could see deflated, and the SUV slumped. Amid the screams of the two downed attackers, a car door slammed, followed by running footsteps. Eva couldn't get a clear view, but had to assume the grey suit was making a run for it, with Harry in tow.

Rolling from beneath the Subaru, Eva had no time to dust herself off. She took a step forward, wary of the writhing attackers on the ground. She'd decimated their ankles, but they could still fire a gun, although one glimpse told her that was optimistic at best. As they cradled their ruined limbs they keened pitifully. No threats there. Eva ran on.

The gunshot startled her. Halting once more, she retreated to safety behind a parked car. Scanning, she searched for where the sound had come from. A man in a white shirt and a ponytail positioned himself behind the engine block of the SUV.

*Dammit.* She'd forgotten the driver.

Waiting for the driver to pause, Eva extending her firing arm and took her time. He stood to take another shot, and she squeezed the trigger. The driver's shoulder exploded and he staggered backwards. His white shirt was rapidly turning red. Striding towards him, gun dead ahead, Eva saw the fear in his eyes. With the instinct of a cornered animal, he tossed the gun away with his functioning arm, rightfully determining that otherwise, the hunter would make the killing blow. He crumpled to the ground, threat neutralised.

Eva ran.

Why hadn't they killed her at the safe house like they did the others? There was only one explanation. Harry god damn Lancing. He appeared to have played an unwilling part in his own escape, but Eva would bet her virginity Harry had said he'd refuse to cooperate if any harm came to her. He really did care.

Harry had just saved her twice. The gun poked into Harry's back told her he wasn't a willing participant. Who wanted to extract Harry from MI6's grasp? Durov and Alexie must be in desperate need of Harry's services. Desperate is exactly the word for anyone mad enough to kill MI6 agents in the middle of London. Eva ran on.

It didn't take long before she caught sight of the two men. In normal circumstances, the delay would have meant Eva had lost them, but forcing someone to flee at gunpoint was never going to be high speed. Captives had a way of being uncooperative. Eva knew that would go double for Harry Lancing. Not only was he obstinate, he was no stranger to firearms, and wasn't easily intimidated. She almost felt sorry for his captor. Almost.

The two jogged through the north entrance to Hyde Park. Eva made ground with every bound. If they stayed on the main path, she'd be in striking distance within seconds. Unfortunately, it wasn't a simple matter of letting loose a few rounds. Hyde Park was a well-frequented public park full of tourists. Best to avoid firefights if possible.

The park was beautiful. The lake on Eva's right was full of ducks, geese and swans. On the right were lovely gardens, dotted with clumps of people taking in the pleasant surrounds.

When one of Mr Grey Suit's frequent glances behind caught Eva's advance, he shoved Harry off the path. A group of twentysomethings lay on the grass, several pushbikes scattered about them. Mr Grey Suit virtually threw Harry towards a bike and brandished the pistol so there would be no "excuse me sir, you seem to have accidentally picked up an incorrect bicycle" discussions. Every member of the group held up their hands and backed away.

As Harry and Mr Grey Suit pedalled away, Eva sprinted up to the same group and pointed at a bike. "Do you guys mind if I—"

On seeing the pistol in Eva's hand, a young man said in a high-pitched tone, "Take it!"

"Cheers."

Eva threw a leg over and pedalled, doing her best to remember how the hell you rode a bike. Swerving around a waddling duck, she tucked her gun into the back of her jeans. The handlebars wobbled as she struggled to take out her phone. There was only one person she needed to contact.

Waiting for the call to connect, she kept her eye on her prey. They were well ahead, but still visible. He finally answered the phone.

"Bishop!"

"You seem out of breath," he said casually. "Did you call me up to breathe heavily? If so, I need you to know I approve."

"Shut up, you smarmy twat. I'm in a high-speed pursuit. Okay, medium. Fine, I'm in a leisurely paced pursuit."

"Have you been drinking with Nancy again?"

Eva quickly explained her predicament.

"I'm on it. Sending backup agents to your position to secure the safehouse and assailants. And Eva," he paused, "go get 'em, gorgeous."

Eva would have swooned if she was given to such things. "Will do, sweet cheeks."

She hung up and considered what she'd just called Bishop. She may have to shoot herself. But only after she had caught the bad guys. *Sweet cheeks?!* Why not call him Schmoopy and be done with it? She'd slap herself in the face if she wasn't trying to keep her balance.

She pedalled faster.

Up ahead, her quarry slowed. Eva's guess was they were as used to riding bikes as she was. The problem was, they were steadily closing in on the exit. As soon as they hit the streets, Eva's line of sight would be reduced to nil. No matter how fast she rode, she couldn't catch them in time.

Nearing the Kensington Road exit, the two men dismounted and tossed their bikes aside. Eva's brief moment of exhilaration was dashed when a white SUV skidded to a halt before them. Harry was shoved into the back seat, with Mr Grey Suit close behind.

The SUV sped off, cutting off cars as it hurtled down the road and away from Eva. Soon it was lost in the river of flowing London traffic.

Eva skidded to a halt and wheezed out a panting gasp.

Harry Lancing had escaped. Again.

～

"When do I burst through the window?" Eva asked eagerly.

"You don't."

Berlin Station Chief Chandler was far from impressed. It was doubtful he could even see impressed from where he was sitting. It probably wasn't even in the same time zone.

They stood in the deserted Operations control room at the Berlin Station. Empty coffee cups were strewn about the room, remnants of a planning session completed before Eva's arrival. It was frustrating that she'd jumped on a plane so quickly only to be hamstrung when they arrived.

"Okay, cool. I'll kick down the door, then?" Eva pointed to the blueprint projected on the boardroom wall. "Bit boring, though."

"Nobody will be kicking in doors."

Chandler appeared close to losing his patience. Eva was baiting him to see exactly how close he was.

"The air vent?" she asked.

Chandler may have actually growled. "No."

Eva planted her hands on her hips. "Well, you're sure as shit going to have a hard time getting a giant cake in the hotel room for me to pop out of."

Baiting Chandler was too easy. From the moment Eva and Bishop had appeared at the Berlin Station he'd done his best to undermine her. Unsure if it was a sexist thing or if he was just an all-round arsehole, Eva did what she did best in these situations: infuriate her opposition.

Eva herself was infuriated. MI6 had tracked Durov, Alexie and Amanda Bourke to the Ritz-Carlton in Berlin. Within a minute of arriving, Eva knew Chandler was resistant to taking any proactive action. Or any action at all, it seemed.

The German Chancellor had made some ill-advised remarks signifying a change in stance and a newfound love of Russia. Eva had to wonder if it was somehow connected to the security breach. Did Durov have dirt on the Chancellor, or on Germany as a whole? Many Germans were unhappy about the dynamic shift. Editorials appeared lambasting Durov's address before the entire German parliament.

It seemed Germany and Russia were slipping into bed with one another. Parts of Berlin, particularly in the East, were about to rebel. Anarchists had taken to the streets. Impromptu demonstrations were breaking out. There was talk of an imposed curfew. The city was a powder keg. Eva was sure Durov held the match.

Eva wondered how much of Chandler's reluctance was related

to the state of the city. Berlin was on a knife edge. No wonder Chandler was jittery—the whole city was.

Eva also had the impression MI6 was in conflict with itself. On one hand, they wanted to apprehend those responsible for the attacks and deaths on their government and others. On the other, if it all went tits up and Durov came to power, they would have made the situation exponentially worse. That worried Eva. Internal conflict could cause indecision. Indecision got people killed.

There had been no sign of Harry. What part he was going to play in all this, she didn't know. It was too much to expect that she was rid of him. Eva had to wait until he imposed himself into her life yet again.

"Might I remind you, Ms Destruction, while you're lead on this assignment, in case anyone has news to the contrary, this is still my city. I run the Ops. I say how and when we take down the targets." He tugged his vest. "I would have thought the Kremlin incident would have taught you due caution."

Seeing that Eva was about to launch into a tirade at the officious bureaucrat, Bishop placed his hand gently over hers. In an instant, her righteous anger subsided and she was becalmed. She sighed. Keep on mission.

Between clenched teeth, she asked, "So... you suggest we... wait?"

"Yes, we wait." He nodded as if that was the end of the discussion. "It is the consensus of the strategic division to observe and take no provocative action. We're unsure as to their intent, so we have them all under surveillance. They're not going anywhere. We can move if we must, but for now, we wait."

If Eva clenched her teeth any harder they'd shatter. "Of course." She was about to add, "Are we waiting for the rapture too, you rotting arse bint bender?", but after taking a sideways glance at Bishop, chose not to. She really was maturing.

When Chandler turned his back on her, Eva gave him the finger. Bishop covered his smirk with his hand. Slightly maturing.

Bishop had flown with her to Berlin. Their delayed arrival at the briefing was due to the reports Eva had to fill out in London. All the details from Harry's escape, the description of the attackers, and her discovery of the slain MI6 guards. The attackers Eva had shot had been extracted before MI6 arrived on site. Another logistics nightmare after yet another firefight in central London. The press was spinning it as a new drug war. Eva wasn't sure if MI6 had stoked the story or not.

Even if they'd made the briefing, she doubted she could have dissuaded Chandler's cautious strategy. Given Durov's elevated world status, Eva could appreciate his tactics. That didn't mean she agreed with them.

"We may never have all targets in one place again." Eva tried to keep the pleading tone from her voice.

"You don't know that," Chandler said flatly.

"But what if this is our only chance?" Eva asked.

"What if it's not?" Chandler spat back with much more ferocity than the question warranted.

Chandler waved his hand around, part apology, part frustration, the weight of the situation apparent on his slouched shoulders. "We have every operative in Western Europe at our disposal. The targets are under more observation than a lab rat. We have this in hand."

Taking a moment to steady herself and rid her voice of any emotion, Eva leaned forward. "You have only one thing in your hand, and it's not the situation."

As he blustered for a response, Eva silenced him with a raised palm.

"These targets aren't like any you've ever dealt with before. They're trained in every espionage and anti-espionage trick you have. They're not only twelve chess moves ahead of you, they've already finished that game and have moved on to the next. These people have no time for your caution. They have no time for your tactical assessments. They're smarter, more cunning and more utterly ruthless than you could possibly imagine. So, while you sit here on your lily-white arse, remember that you're going to go down in the annals of history as the man who got it completely and utterly wrong. You're Chamberlain shouting 'Peace in our time', or Franz Ferdinand's driver going, 'You know what, let's drive with the top down today, yeah?'"

Chandler's face grew red. Just as he was about to launch into a tirade of his own, Eva pivoted on the spot and walked out, Bishop at her heel.

From behind, Chandler shouted, "I forbid you to engage the targets. Consider that an order, Destruction. You hear me?"

Eva and Bishop made their way down the short hall to the elevator. Getting in, Eva slammed her thumb against the ground floor button. As she did, a flustered Chandler marched towards them, apparently not finished. Eva hit the "close door" button. The doors slid shut.

"Did you hear him?" Bishop asked as the elevator descended.

"Oh, I heard him."

"And are you going to listen?"

Taking out her pistol, Eva checked she had a full magazine. "What do you think?"

Slapping the mag base in place, she turned to Bishop and winked.

"I feared as much." Bishop checked his own pistol. "Are we about to do something incredibly stupid?"

The elevator pinged and she leaned across to give Bishop a kiss on the cheek. Striding towards the exit, Eva cast a glance back at him. "Have you met me?"

# CHAPTER SEVENTEEN

Another luxury hotel, another stakeout. Eva wished one of her foes would hang out in a trailer park, just once. Although she supposed the five-star restaurant across from the Ritz-Carlton was acceptable. Finishing off the last of her black truffle panna cotta, she could see that the waiters were growing impatient. As she'd feared, her story of an Interpol investigation and promise of a sizable tip had only secured the window table for so long.

There was also the issue of what they would actually do if Durov, Alexie or Bourke showed up. This stakeout wasn't sanctioned by MI6, and it was highly unlikely any of the targets would give themselves up willingly. These were some of the most dangerous people on the planet—ruthless, cunning and resourceful. They wouldn't come quietly no matter how nicely you asked.

Added to that, there was only Eva and Bishop. Sure, the hotel was under observation, but that meant little when the dog was defanged. She had no doubt Bourke, Alexie and probably Durov would kill, given a fraction of a second's chance. Possibly quicker.

Waiters hovered nearby, ready to swoop in and clear the table, eager to make way for the expectant patrons at the bar. Eva wasn't ready for that yet. She had other ideas.

Realising they finally had time to themselves, Eva thought it was as good a time as any to talk to Bishop about something other than missions, assassins and world domination. That didn't mean she took an eye off the hotel across the street, though.

"I don't even know where you were born," she said, as if they'd already been discussing the topic.

"Where I was... Are we on a date?" Bishop smirked. "I thought we were saving the world."

"We can do both." Eva cocked an eyebrow.

Bishop pursed his lips and his eyes twinkled in amusement. "Glasgow. I was born in Glasgow."

"You're Scottish?!"

"No," he said firmly. "I was born in Glasgow, my dad was stationed there. Mother moved back to Yorkshire when they split up."

"Your folks are divorced, then?"

"Happily, their subsequent partners were good for them. Dad and Angela are still together, mum and Douglas were very happy until she passed away five years ago."

"Your mum passed away? I'm sorry." Eva stabbed the white tablecloth with the end of her spoon. "It's like I hardly know you."

"Eva, I don't know where this is coming from..."

"We don't really know each other that well." Eva kept her focus on the Ritz. "Not intimately. Not the way people who are about to commit to what... We should know each other better, is all I'm saying. We spend all this time together, but I don't know you. Not at all."

"I think we do."

With a curled lip, Eva took her eyes off their target long enough to throw him a sceptical look.

"We really do, Eva. Fine, you didn't know where I was born, but so what? I know the face you make when you think you're going to die, and when you make up your mind that isn't going to happen—it's the most determined face on the planet. Some couples spend a lifetime together without knowing anything like that. People in the most pedestrian and short-lived relationships know where each other were born. That doesn't make them a great couple, it makes them mundane. Do you want to be like everyone else? That doesn't sound like Eva Destruction to me. To know the someone's true self, how they react when they're happy, in danger or bored, to know their very soul, that's unique. It's not something to dismiss—you embrace it with all you have."

Eva folded her arms, not yet convinced. "You have a silver tongue."

"You have no idea."

"I'd like to." Before her mind wandered to just how cunning his tongue could be, Eva tried to refocus on the topic at hand. "And you're a sexist."

"No, I'm a flirt. There's a difference."

"Oh, way better."

"Only with you."

Eva let loose a derisive snort. "I've seen you flirt with women dozens of times."

"Lately?" Bishop put his elbow on the table and rested his chin on his fist challengingly.

He had her there. He also hadn't made any recent mention of conquests. She couldn't even remember the last time she'd seen him glance at another woman. He was more enlightened than when they'd first met, mostly thanks to her. He'd actually listened to what she'd said. That was something, wasn't it?

"Who's to say that won't change and you'll fall back to your old ways?"

"This is seeming less like a date and more of a job interview."

There was no reply.

Taking Eva's stony silence as his cue to talk, Bishop said, "Who's to say we won't die tomorrow? Or get invaded by aliens? Or I get an infected foot from cutting my toenails and die from gangrene?"

"Pretty sure that's not how gangrene works."

"Or any of a million other things we can't predict. Here's what I don't have to predict, here's something I know. I love you, Eva. I have for a very long time. From the first moment I met you I knew you were unique to this world."

Unable to respond with the "L" word—not yet at least, not until this mission was done—Eva focused on the other part of his statement.

"I thought you were a twat when I met you."

"I was. Because you hadn't made me a better person yet. And I didn't change to make you like me, I changed because you were right. You made me better because that's what you do. You make things better." Leaning in, Bishop took her hand. "Eva, you need to stop analysing this, us. We're not intelligence data to be assessed, categorised and filed away neatly. Human feelings are far more complex. Can I guarantee we'll live happily ever after? Of course not, especially given what we do for a living. What I can guarantee is that you'll have all of me, my heart, everything. If this doesn't work out, it won't be because I didn't give my all. If you can say the same, then we owe it to ourselves to try. We both deserve happiness. We deserve one another."

Was he right? Was she overthinking the whole thing? Eva stared into his hopeful eyes.

*Geronimo.*

She leaned over and kissed him hard on the lips.

All in.

Bishop clicked his fingers and called out, "Cheque please!"

Eva didn't even try to hide her laugh. Were they really doing this? Plunging into the unknown, together?

With a glance across the road, she finally accepted that their little jaunt to spy on Durov and his parents had been, at best, over-enthusiastic. At worst, a threat to the whole operation. Maybe she and Bishop could find something a little more stimulating to do with their evening.

In retrospect, Eva realised, there was no way their prey would merely wander out to be seen by the world.

Then Durov wandered out to be seen by the world.

He wasn't alone. A small gaggle of press engulfed him as he exited the hotel and strode towards the waiting limousine. Pausing theatrically, as if an afterthought, he seemed to deliver some sort of statement, perhaps setting the scene for his speech the following day.

The two spies didn't hesitate. Bishop threw a wad of bills on the table and they bounded across the road to the small gathering. Durov was pontificating in German to the weary-eyed journalists present. If Eva was to guess, she'd say he was talking about the protests that were breaking out, and assuring the press that he held all Germans in the highest regard, or something equally bullshit.

Sidling up to the six journalists and two cameramen, Bishop and Eva knew to be on guard. They knew the man was far more dangerous than his genial public persona suggested.

The tiniest jerk of Durov's head told Eva he'd seen her, but chosen not to acknowledge her presence. After winding down his off-the-cuff pre-prepared statement, he nodded at the journalists and tried to escape Eva by heading straight to the limousine. The trouble was, he bounced off the solid figure of Bishop, who he'd failed to notice.

"Terribly sorry, old chap." Bishop didn't move to assist him.

As Durov staggered, Eva shouted, "Say hi to your mum for me."

Durov's head snapped around like a whip.

"What?" He positively spat the word.

Several members of the press twisted their bodies, following the exchange. If they were half-decent journalists they would know that Durov was supposed to be an orphan.

"Just being nice and asking you to say hi to your mum." Eva cast her hand towards the hotel's upper floors. "She's been away from home for so long, I thought—"

"That's enough," Durov sputtered, before recovering his affable façade. "I have no idea what you're talking about, young lady, but I'm late for dinner…"

"Sure, sure." Eva's smile was as painted-on as a clown's. "Must be my mistake." Eva pulled out a notepad. "You have time to answer some questions for *Cockhandler Monthly* magazine?" On seeing the blank glares from the press, she added, "It's an agricultural magazine. I have subsidy questions."

The journalists looked sceptical. One of Durov's bodyguards, face like the side of a steel mill, leaned forward menacingly and in an American accent hissed, "Let me take her for a ride, boss."

Durov seemed to consider the idea for a moment before darting his eyes towards the press. In a low growl he said, "She's not the one you're after this weekend."

The heavy nodded and took a step back. His eyes bored into Eva.

Perhaps weighing up press embarrassment and curiosity, Durov jerked his head to the side. Eva followed him to a vacant area in front of the hotel. Bishop hovered near the journalists, a steel trap ready to spring. The heavy split his attention between Eva and Bishop.

Durov and Eva glared at one another. She wasn't about to flinch first.

"It's your dime, as the Americans say." Durov's voice was carved from ice.

Most likely expecting her to scream, or attack him, Eva did the opposite. She smiled. A big, beaming smile.

Leaning in, she said, "Your mum wins the international hide-and-seek championship."

Durov snorted. "Took you long enough. You know this changes nothing?"

There it was. Confirmation. Eva's crazy theory wasn't as far-fetched as she'd first thought.

With a slight cough, Bishop pulled a wallet from his pocket. He extracted a five-pound note and handed it to Eva, then gave her a slight nod and stepped back. There was no hiding the amusement in her eyes. That changed when she turned back to Durov.

"You're officially the worst family since the Mansons. Or the Osmonds. Or the Hansons. Shit. Okay, you're at least the fourth worst family ever."

Durov sighed. "Still working on your humour, I see?"

"Still working on the megalomania, I see?"

With one eye on the press, ensuring he couldn't be overheard, Durov said, "One does not call it megalomania if one succeeds. Then it is called world building. It's called being a visionary. It's called…"

"Cry-wanking?"

Durov tried to appear bored, but Eva detected a flinch. That one hit him. "Could you be more droll?"

"I don't know. Could you be more of a douchebag?"

A heavy sigh signalled the expiry of Durov's patience. "Is that all you have?"

"Nope. I just wanted you," Eva rammed her finger into his lapel, "to know that we're not going away. You haven't gotten away with shit, you constipated wank rag turd fondler."

Sniffing, Durov waved a dismissive hand. "If you had anything we wouldn't be talking right now, woman. So now you've told me you have nothing, you can go. Time to crawl back under your rock. Off you go."

Pivoting on the spot, he marched towards the waiting limousine and got in. As it drove off, Eva turned and approached the gaggle of press, and was met with a wall of confusion.

One of the journalists furrowed his brow. In heavily accented English, he asked, "What was that about?"

"The Presidential presumptive loves a cock. I wanted to know how much."

Realising the discussion was over, the press dispersed, leaving Eva and Bishop alone in front of the gaudy hotel.

"What did that achieve?" Bishop asked. "Besides showing our hand?"

"Our hand was pants, anyway, dude. Twos and eights. He's got a royal flush, we were never going to win the pot, no matter how we bluffed."

"So we go all in and… can we stop the poker analogy? I'm getting a headache. If we couldn't win, why confront him?"

Eva didn't immediately answer. "What's the first thing someone who's rattled would do?"

"Call their partner."

Eva waved her phone at him and beamed. At first Bishop crinkled his forehead in confusion, then broke into a grin.

"You planted a cobbler on him, didn't you? You cheeky little vixen."

A cobbler was a new piece of MI6 tech. A tiny tracking device, the size of pinhead, it could track your prey and listen in to their conversations, as well as identifying all phone numbers and IPs to and from their devices.

When Eva had poked Durov, she'd planted one on him. Her phone screen already told her it was accumulating data. She'd vowed to go the offensive and that's exactly what she'd done.

Although she wasn't a doctor, Eva was reasonably certain Chandler was having an aneurism. The Berlin Station Chief flailed his arms about with a face redder than an Irish girl who'd been sunbaking.

Sitting next to the flailing Station Chief, Paul tilted his head, half amused, half annoyed. Eva wasn't sure which parts were directed at her and which at Chandler. Knowing full well she'd need support when she informed Chandler about the planted tracker, she'd advised Paul ahead of time. He'd jumped on the next plane. Paul had already planned on coming anyway. This just sped things up.

"I want her sanctioned and recalled immediately!" Chandler thumped the conference table to emphasise his point.

Paul didn't immediately respond, but took his time, taking a sip of tea. Finally placing his cup back on the saucer, he raised his head and asked, "Was she successful?"

"This isn't about success, it's about the chain of command. It's about—"

"MI6 isn't about success?" Paul cut in. "Bloody hell, good to know. I can stop putting in all this overtime then." Over his shoulder to no one, he raised his voice. "You can all go home, people, we don't have to succeed at anything anymore. Take the rest of the week off."

Paul stared at the man before him incredulously.

Flustered, Chandler flapped his lips several times. "I didn't mean, I, ah, look, it's not about being successful in this instance, it's about following the right course of action."

"If it's more important to be right, someone better tell my wife, because she'll be the Prime Minister tomorrow."

Eva stifled a laugh, as no one in the room seemed to find Paul's comment as amusing as she did. Beside her, Bishop gave the tiniest of smirks. It was unfortunate in the rush to alert the right teams about the cobbler, she and Bishop didn't get to have their time together. Eva felt no regret about her decision to be with Bishop, which was telling in itself. Now that she was completely on board, she was keen to leap in feet first. And more than a little frustrated that they hadn't. Very frustrated, in fact.

Chandler appeared ready to burst, but rightfully recognised that the incorrect choice of words would be career ending.

"Fine."

"There's a good lad." Paul smiled at the man, who was ten years his senior. "Now, please offer operative Destruction all pertinent resources and assign operational staff at her disposal. This is a K5 priority, so will bypass oversight. Are we on the same page, Chandler?"

His lips were so thin they were practically non-existent. "Understood, sir."

"Outstanding." Paul turned his attention to Eva. "What have you got for me?"

For the next few minutes Eva detailed the information they had obtained from the cobbler. After their run-in, Durov had phoned two numbers. The second was known—his campaign manager back in Russia, who he spoke to for two minutes. The other was unfamiliar. The number had been traced back to a handset sold in a convenience store in Frankfurt. The link to Alexie or Bourke was strong. Especially given that, several minutes later, the same phone was tracked within half a kilometre of the Ritz-Carlton Berlin.

Now they had a line on Durov and either Alexie or Bourke. Finally, things were looking up. Eva knew the spy game sufficiently well to know it wouldn't be enough. They were dealing with three of the most devious minds on the planet. One lucky break didn't mean they were any closer to bringing them to justice.

But it was a start.

Clapping her hands together, Eva said, "Right. Let's get this shit sorted. When do we execute the plan?"

All eyes turned to Chandler. His bottom lip trembled slightly. "Bourke, we have no issue with bringing in. There's no statute of limitations on treason. The Germans will allow us to extract her, no questions asked."

"*Allow?*" Eva asked in disbelief. "Since when does MI6 ask permission for rendition?"

Chandler ignored her and went on. "Likewise, Barinov. We have evidence, circumstantial or otherwise, to make a case regarding the embassy bombings and attacks on MI6." There was a hesitant pause. He avoided eye contact with Eva. "But Durov is another matter entirely."

About to launch into a creatively swear-ridden tirade, Eva waited. She knew Bishop would want her to constrain her comments so she didn't antagonise Chandler. She'd already beaten him down once, now she needed him on side. She needed his people and their knowledge of the city. Was she learning tact? Past Eva would be shaking her head in disgust right about now.

She took a moment to choose her words. "But being the son of two of the most dangerous spies…"

"If the crimes of one's parents were grounds for arresting people, half the House of Lords would be locked up."

He was right. Unfortunately. If the assassination of the Russian President in the Kremlin wasn't enough, the kidnapping of the likely next Head of State was definitely grounds for World War III.

They needed evidence against Durov. What they had was insufficient to hold up in The Hague. Hell, a paper scarecrow would hold up better.

Hearing no argument to the contrary, Chandler went on. "Make no mistake, this is a delicate mission. We need to be nowhere near Durov or his people when this goes down. We need it to be completely clear of political blowback. That's going to be tough. If we can't separate Durov from Barinov or Bourke, I won't authorise action." Chandler turned to Paul. "Take my Station if you must, but I'm standing by that."

Poking his teacup, Paul nodded. "Fair enough. I'll support your stance." He turned to Eva. "We need to isolate Bourke and/or Barinov. Do you have any ideas on how to do that, Evie?"

In answer, she slowly raised one eyebrow.

Simultaneously, Paul and Bishop said, "Uh oh."

Eyeing the two men, Chandler asked, "What? What am I missing?"

"That face." Bishop nodded towards Eva. "That face means she's got a wicked scheme in mind. Basically, if you're the bad guy and she makes that face, you better run the other way, because Eva Destruction's about to fuck you up."

# CHAPTER EIGHTEEN

Eva wondered if the trench coat was too much, but figured if she couldn't wear one while performing nefarious spy work on a drizzly Berlin afternoon, she'd never wear one at all. Gendarmenmarkt Square was mostly deserted, given the weather. Puddles lined the plaza, and the darkened grey sky hung ominously low. The background thrum of the city did little to dissuade Eva from the feeling that she was completely alone, about to face one of the most ruthless human beings alive.

Well, completely alone except for the dozen-odd MI6 personnel who were either nearby or viewing the scene through the scope of a sniper rifle.

Using the phone number obtained by the cobbler, Eva sent a message to the unknown number Durov had called immediately after their run-in. She'd studied the syntax and brevity from previous messages. Short, sharp, with a lack of any affection. Eva had used the same tone in her urgent request for a meeting. Any replies would be rerouted to her phone. There weren't any.

Earlier in the morning, Durov was seen heading off to prepare for his address at the Reichstag. As requested, MI6 were making sure he was well clear of events about to unfold. Whatever they may be. Eva didn't know if she was about to meet Alexie, Bourke or the Queen of Denmark. She was kind of hoping for Dave Grohl, but that was more of a personal preference.

Gendarmenmarkt Square was surrounded by old churches and the Konzerthaus concert hall. At its centre was a monument to Friedrich Schiller. Try as she might, Eva had never warmed to his poetry or plays. Too flowery and self-indulgent for her taste. Although one line from Wilhelm Tell came to mind: "A tyrant's power has a limit." Maybe it was an omen. Maybe Eva read too much.

She sat at a small café at the outskirts of the square, nursing a Krombacher beer. The message had asked for the recipient to meet at this exact time. With every tick of the clock on the nearby tower, Eva became more convinced the exercise was folly. Shivering against the cold, she pulled her trench coat tighter. Only the beer and the overhead heater prevented her from freezing to death.

Across the cobblestone square, a lone figure strode towards the café. Without a formal announcement, definitely without fanfare, Amanda Bourke walked in. Her hair was grey, her coat dated. She carried herself like a dithering old woman. Eva wasn't fooled. Bourke's eyes betrayed her. Sharp as a diamond cutter, they assessed the area within seconds, lingering on possible exit points, potential weapons and who or what was a threat. She was searching for Durov, but if there she felt concern at not seeing him, she didn't show it. It took a brief moment before she spotted Eva. A curious grin crossed her wrinkled mouth. She tilted her head in amused disbelief before approaching Eva's table.

To her credit, she didn't run. She must have known she was cornered. Eva had to hand it to her, the woman's face showed no hint of fear. Elegantly, she glided over, pulled out a chair and sat casually. Her demeanour was pleasant, even though she must have known her decades of freedom were at an end.

"Guten tag, Frau Devastation."

"G'day, how's it hangin'?"

"My, you really are Australian, aren't you?"

Choosing not to reply, Eva let the silence stretch as they assessed one another. Besides her eyes, Bourke was most unremarkable up close. A perfect spy. She never would have been considered pretty, but some may have considered her intriguing. The way she evaluated Eva made her feel like she was being X-rayed, dissected and analysed inside and out. It was intimidating.

Given the way Bourke had successfully disappeared without a trace and what she had orchestrated since, Eva wouldn't have expected any different. Having said that, one of the most experienced and dangerous spies on the planet had just fallen for the most rudimentary trick in the book. Believing the text message without question was a rookie mistake. If they made it past the next thirty seconds without a gun fight, Eva would ask Bourke if she was embarrassed about it.

After a bored sigh, Bourke said, "I suppose this is where you chastise me about treason and whatnot and send in the troops?"

"I thought we could have a chat first."

"Did you now? How marvellous."

There was a callousness to her words, telegraphing her anxiety. Her spy skills had slipped to let out such weakness. She was aware of the circus that awaited her return to England.

"I guess my biggest question is, why? Why groom your son for such a power play when you could have just retired as a couple of old spies? Why become active after all these years?"

The slightest flutter of amusement crossed Bourke's face, then disappeared just as quickly.

"How long have you been a spy, my dear?"

It was a ridiculous question. Both women knew Bourke already had the answer. There was also no denying Durov's lineage, both she and Durov had confirmed Eva's wild theory as fact.

"Two years."

A tut. "Two years and look what you've achieved. Bagged the big one." She held up her arms as if showcasing herself as a prize on "The Price is Right". "My, they'll probably give you a medal of some sort. Do they still give medals? I trust they do. How splendid for you."

"Hey, don't take it out on me. I didn't fall for the spy equivalent of, 'Hey, look over there!'".

Bourke leaned back in her chair. "You think you're special?" She waved her hand dismissively at Eva. "Edgy trollop in a man's game? You're nothing exceptional, Eva Destruction, just another pink cog in the white man's machine. Don't think you're anything more than what you are to them, a pair of tits with legs. They'll toss you out as soon as they start to droop, be sure of that. They might package it up in a PC wrapping, but little has actually changed in this line of work."

Keeping her face neutral, Eva said, "The head of MI6 begs to differ."

Bourke snorted. "She can beg all she wants, I'm not coming back to the mother country."

"It sounds like you're under the misapprehension that you have a choice."

Bourke hefted an eyebrow. "Maybe we can strike a deal?"

Eva shrugged. "What do you have to bargain with?"

Taking her time, Bourke slowly leaned forward. "How about Horatio Lancing?" Cherishing the reaction on Eva's face, she leaned back and tilted her head. "See? There," she said, poking a wrinkled finger at Eva, "the crack in your façade. You're no spy. You should have anticipated that move, but you didn't. Even worse, you let me know it. Never give away your tells, girl." She shook her head. "You need to go back to your coffee shop, my dear. This isn't for you."

Ignoring the bait, Eva stuck to the matter at hand. "Why would we trade one for the other? You're right here. You're not going anywhere."

"Who am I? A forgotten old hag, hardly front-page fodder. But your ex? The biggest story of the last decade? My, what a headline grabber. A real feather in MI6s cap, wouldn't you say?"

"Nobody knows he's even missing. As far as the world knows, he simply disappeared. A modern-day Amelia Earhart."

"Really?" Her mouth opened in fake shock. "You might want to check on that. Coincidentally, it seems the news just broke. He's been spotted in Europe. Frankfurt, to be exact. You see, a few journalists have been sitting on the story, waiting for the right time to tell the world."

There was no need for Eva to check, Bishop confirmed as much in her earpiece.

"You told them?"

Bourke reached over and took a sip of Eva's beer. "Just before our little meeting. You wouldn't want MI6 to miss him *again*, would you? My, imagine what would happen if you didn't take up the offer? One wouldn't be surprised to find him dead in a ditch somewhere."

There it was. Swap her for Harry, or he dies. The idea horrified Eva, but she was determined to stay on mission.

Did Bourke know she was heading into a trap? Why would she wantonly release information about Harry? Now Eva had her ex's life in her hands. The wrong reply would spell his death.

For a minute or two Eva had allowed herself the self-satisfaction of believing she'd one-upped the spy veteran. Now it seemed to be the other way around.

"He still pines for you, you know." Bourke placed the beer on Eva's side of the table. "Pathetic, really. Here he is, once the world's most powerful man, brought down by a mere slip of a girl. He's jailed, humiliated, and yet can't get over his adolescent infatuation with you. It would be laughable if it wasn't so pitiful. You really did a number on him didn't you, girl?"

The woman was trying to throw her off balance. Bourke had seen a chink in her armour and was trying hard to exploit it. Eva was doing her best to hold her focus. She no longer had feelings for Harry, but she certainly didn't want him to come to any harm.

"He's right here in Berlin," Bourke went on. "I just need to make a phone call and he'll be here within minutes." A renewed sense of self-satisfaction had come over her. "Ask your superiors. They'll understand the sense in this. Go on, ask them. I'll wait."

"There's no need."

Both women turned to see Paul standing beside them. Eva hadn't noticed him approach. Either she was slipping, or Paul was becoming stealthier in his old age.

"Ladies," he said as he took a seat at the table.

Bourke extended a delicate hand. "I don't believe we've had the pleasure."

Glaring at the offered hand, Paul made no move to shake it. It was withdrawn.

"I assume you're some lackey from '6?" Bourke said evenly.

"Correct." Paul motioned to the waiter, pointed to Eva's beer and held up three fingers. He went on. "An MI6 lackey, like my father before me."

Amused, Bourke tilted her head. "Your father?"

"Mmmm," he said, nodding. "I believe you worked with him." Paul issued one of his famous pauses. "Steven Cavendish."

Eva held her breath. All she could think of was the moment in the Vauxhall Cross boardroom when Paul had been ready to tear off Boris's limbs and beat him to death with them.

There was a parting of Bourke's lips, and the slightest of gasps escaped, almost inaudible. Tiny movements emphasised her shock.

Eva leaned across the table. "Never give away your tells, girl."

Bourke sneered at her. For the first time she seemed vulnerable, but the moment passed, and her stony disguise returned.

"There's no need to deny it," Paul said. "Boris Nikolayev told us all about it."

It was a lie. Boris had told them nothing.

He went on. "Even if you have Lancing to bargain with, there's no way we'd let a treasonous murderer escape. So while we're all here in these pleasant surrounds, I'd be intrigued to hear your take on events."

Why wasn't Paul hauling her in? Surely this would be best conducted on home soil. Perhaps he couldn't wait that long for the truth.

There was a pause while the beers were served. Once the waiter had left, Bourke took the time to savour hers. She must have known it was likely her last.

"I didn't kill your father."

"Did I say you did?" Paul replied evenly.

Bourke scowled. "But I wish I had."

Her tactic was to go on the offensive. The shock had worn off. To his credit, Paul gave no reaction. After a moment, he did something Eva didn't expect. He smiled. He'd been prepared for the verbal attack and countered it. Eva had much to learn.

Bourke slammed the beer on the table. "Your father was incompetent, like the rest of them, and that's why he died. I hope the saying is true, like father like son."

Customers at the other tables were noticing the exchange now. They did their best to pretend they weren't listening.

"I want to hear it from your own mouth." Paul leaned forward. "Who killed my father?"

"Like I said, it wasn't me. I had the opportunity to rid the world of the worthless human being, but I can't say I had the pleasure."

"So it was Alexie Barinov or Boris Nikolayev, then?"

The laugh was like a knife. "Nikolayev was as useless as the other side. He wanted me, you know? Was devastated when he found out about Alexie and I. we thought he'd ruin everything by doing something rash, but he was blindly faithful to Mother Russia, bless him." She took a swig of her beer. She was no stranger to drink. "It was so many years ago." She eyed Paul. "I suppose you're entitled to some sort of truth after all these years." She shrugged. "Alexie always protected me, far more than the English ever did. That was the moment I knew my husband would do anything for me. He still would."

There it was.

While his face remained emotionless, Eva could read the relief in her friend. Paul finally had his closure. After a lifetime, he finally knew who his father's killer was.

Bourke took a sip of her beer. "This is a fine beer. There are some things the Germans do best. Make cars, make war and make beer." She jutted her chin towards Paul. "What happens now, Hightower?"

The two spoke as if a major life-changing revelation hadn't just been made. The consummate professional, Paul was all business. Underneath, Eva was sure her friend was grappling with what had been revealed. On the surface, however, he was a representative of His Majesty's Government and carried himself with the decorum his position mandated.

For a while Eva tuned out. Was there a way to save Harry? Was he truly in danger? Something still wasn't sitting right. Why would Bourke drop the news about Harry's disappearance as a bargaining chip? Surely the best course of action would be to not get caught in the first place? Then there would be no need to trade Harry for her. No, something else was definitely at play.

"Why distract from Durov?"

The statement cut across a diatribe Bourke was issuing.

"What, Evie?" Paul was flustered by the non sequitur.

"The news, about Harry," she said. "It's not about trading her for him, that's just wank-stain waffles. She backwards engineered it as a desperate Hail Mary. She's bullshitting us, Paul."

"I'm right here," Bourke said, annoyed.

"There's absolutely no way Durov or Alexie would hand Harry over," Eva went on. "Not with what he'd helped them with, what he knows…"

"Why grab him from the safe house and not kill him then?" Paul asked. "If they wanted him gone, that's the time to do it. Not have a bike race across Hyde Park."

It was a good point. Then again, they hadn't extracted him for his technology, they already had it. What did they need Harry for? What was Eva missing?

Eva tapped the table with her finger. Everything Bourke, Durov and Alexie had done was grand. Bombings, assassination, cyber attacks, they were all about statements. All-encompassing. Head-line grabbing. How did Harry fit into it? And why?

A phrase jumped into Eva's mind. The one Durov had muttered to his bodyguard outside the Ritz. "She's not the one you're after this weekend."

Eva's gaze burned into Bourke. An idea struck her like an arrow. She knew what they were planning. Bourke really was an evil witch. Eva peered at her, eyes blazing.

"I don't know how they're going to spin it," Eva said to Paul, not taking her eyes off Bourke, "but they never wanted Harry back to help them." She sneered. "They're far more murderous."

With a tight little laugh, Bourke threw her hand towards Eva flippantly.

"Durov's speech, it's a statement to the world," Eva said. "His moment on the world stage, right? Why would they need Harry?"

"My thoughts exactly," Paul said. "Why would they—"

Eva cut in, "Because they're all about grand moments. Memorable, world shaping. A speech is nice and all, but what would it be missing? Gravitas. It wouldn't be history making, extraordinary, unforgettable."

"You've lost me, Evie."

She turned back to Bourke. "You're going to try and bolster his popularity, aren't you? Give him a banner on the news websites. You're going to do a Barinov Special."

Eva recalled what Boris had told her back at MI6 the last time she'd seen him. "An attempted coup or assassination can be as effective as a real one."

Assessing every crease in Bourke's face, Eva saw a flicker. The old woman tried to mask it with another dismissive laugh. There was, however, the slightest desperation in it. The laugh came too quickly, was too forced. She may as well have written a confession on a napkin.

"They're going to use Harry, Paul." Eva kept her eyes on the defector. "Somehow, before the speech or during, they're going to frame Harry for trying to assassinate Durov. I'm sure they'll put a clever spin on it. Probably along the lines of 'if the world's most diabolical dude hates our political dude, he must be alright', or something. I don't know. It was Alexie's forte back in the day. Stage a political assassination or a coup d'état and bolster your guy. They're going for the double win. Remove the man who knows who they are and what they're doing and grab Durov head-lines for surviving an attack. Imagine the editorials: 'Despite the assassination attempt, Durov took to the stage and wowed the crowd'. He'll fucking win in a landslide." Eva could tell by Paul's face he didn't quite get it. "They're going to assassinate Harry. And they're going to do it publicly."

# CHAPTER NINETEEN

"The Barinov Special is a wild theory, Eva," Bishop said as the black sedan sped through the Berlin streets.

"Yeah, you're right. I totally don't have a history of wild theories panning out."

Eva held up a picture of Bourke that she'd taken on her phone. The old spy's hands were bound and she was bookmarked by heavily armed operatives. Eva was considering having it framed.

"Point made." His eyes twinkled in the early evening light. "Speaking of, what are you going to spend your fiver on?"

"Not sure yet," Eva replied. "I've heard Cabbage Patch Kids are on their way back, I might blow the lot on them. Could be worth a fortune one day."

"Perhaps you could take me to dinner with your future windfall."

"Nah," Eva said, crinkling her nose teasingly. "I'll probably reinvest it."

"Cheapskate." He laughed throatily.

They exchanged cutesy smirks. Eva would have punched herself in the face at the schmoopyness if she wasn't so smitten. But there was a lot to do before she could fall into Bishop's arms like she wanted. Her happy mood fell away when she remembered who they were speeding towards.

As they drove, they passed at least half a dozen small protests. People chanted slogans and carried signs protesting against Durov's presence and the sudden close ties between the two nations. Perhaps the Germans had developed a sixth sense for when there was a megalomaniac dictator in their midst. The whole city seemed on edge, as if everyone in Berlin knew something was about to happen, but no one was sure what.

Taking her mind off the millions of Berliners, Eva focused on one person. Could they save Harry in time? She willed the car to go faster. She was surprised by how much she cared. It was an odd sensation to be sitting next to the man who was soon to become her lover, rushing to save the life of her ex. She definitely needed to book in to see a therapist when this was over.

Bourke had been unceremoniously hauled off by burly MI6 types. Eva could have sworn it was the same team who had extracted Harry in Hong Kong, but it probably wasn't. All the paramilitary types were starting to blend into one. She needed spend some time around less brawny individuals. When all this was said and done, she'd go to a yoga retreat. After the therapist.

As Bourke was being taken away she'd said over her shoulder, "This changes nothing, you know? Events will unfold with or without me. They are already in motion, you can't stop them."

She may very well have been right, but Eva and Bishop had a history of ruining the party for the bad guys. If Alexie was still capable of pulling off a Barinov Special it would all but cement Durov's presidency. Surviving an assassination attempt would see him emerge stronger. It would strengthen his support and put him on the world stage. Eva wasn't going to give up any time soon.

The driver said they were five minutes away from the Reichstag. They had no idea what to expect. Eva tried to think how you would frame someone for an assassination. Harry was no fool. He wouldn't blindly follow orders. Eva knew firsthand how stubborn he could be. Would they set him up in a sniper's nest and somehow have him discovered? Unlikely. Guns weren't his thing.

He wouldn't lie down looking through a sniper scope for the fun of it.

*Think.*

Inside the venue would be tricky. First, there would be extensive security checks for any weapons. There was the added complication that in a crowd that size, whoever was controlling Harry could lose command in an instant. Too many variables, too many barriers to success.

*Think.*

Outside. There would be more turmoil, especially if the protesters were still active. More opportunities. That's where she'd do it.

"Where is Durov coming in?" Eva asked Bishop, who was huddled over his laptop. "Is there a VIP entrance or is there a red-carpet kind of set-up?"

"Protocol steward advised he's coming up the front steps. Always good for a man of the people act."

"Will the press be there?"

Bishop laughed his manly laugh. "No idea. But he'll be wearing pink lacy underwear and his favourite make-out song is anything by S Club 7."

Squinting at Bishop, Eva said, "So that's an unknown on the press, then?"

"Affirmative."

The two watched the scenery speed by for a minute.

Eva shook her head. "S Club 7, really dude?"

"You question that over the pink underwear thing?"

"I have no problem with anyone's underwear choices, but I draw the fucking line at S Club 7."

"Good to know." Bishop started pressing buttons on his phone with a focused expression on his face.

"I swear to god if you play them on Spotify I will shoot you in the dick."

Bishop gently placed the phone back in his pocket and gave her a wink. She liked it when they played. It reminded her of simpler, less urgent times—not that they'd had many of those. She looked forward to more playing.

Glimpses of the Reichstag flashed through gaps between build-ings. It was an imposing structure. Burned down by the Nazis in 1933, it was ignored by Germans until reunification when East and West finally came together in one integrated Bundestag parliament in 1999. It seemed fitting that Durov had chosen a place of unifica-tion, something his parents had achieved decades before the rest of Europe, Eva thought wryly.

They passed the Brandenburg Gate, which was covered in scaf-folding, apparently being repaired. The monument representing the division between East and West had once seemed immovable, absolute. Then one day the world changed, and the wall fell. Eva was determined there would be no reason for another wall between East and West.

Still unsure what to expect, Bishop and Eva were winging it. It seemed to be their thing. They were lucky that it had worked so far. Unfortunately, luck had a way of running out. If they could just find a way to save Harry and get him back to where he belonged. Oh, and stop three megalomaniacs from tearing the world apart. That too.

Eva was a simple girl. She didn't ask for much.

"This is as far as I can take you," the driver said.

The car slowed as it pulled up to metal security bollards sticking out of the road. No doubt a precaution with all the protestors. A traffic cop directed vehicles away from where Durov was to address the Bundestag. Security was tight. The Germans seemed to be treating the speech like a state address. Durov hadn't even been elected yet, but they were regaling him with the privi-leges of office. In the shadow of a new Cold War, it seemed that countries were already taking sides. Or having their sides chosen for them.

Bishop and Eva climbed out of the vehicle and headed towards the grand steps of the Reichstag. The cold night air turned their breath to vapour. Their fake press credentials would be good enough to get them through the first layer of security ahead, but likely no further. The press usually didn't take kindly to being searched, but even they weren't immune to tighter security when entering the German parliament building.

If the staged attack wasn't outside, the spies would have to get inventive to move inside. That wasn't out of the question, but it added more complexity and would no doubt stretch the already tenuous grip Bishop had on her wild theory. Eva knew Bishop was only along for the ride because of her. The fact that it was to save her ex made the whole thing a confusing mélange of emotions and conflicting priorities. Maybe she needed that therapist sooner than she thought.

"There." Bishop nodded to the huddle of journalists, photographers and camera people.

The two moved together, eying every guard, cop, member of the press and member of the general public. They showed their badges and mingled with the press, searching for anything out of the ordinary, a posture suggesting anything other than the boredom of a routine assignment.

Other MI6 assets were rushing into support positions, but it would take time. It was unlikely that they'd be in place by the time Durov entered the Reichstag. It was up to the two of them. And only one wanted to be there.

A murmur in the crowd told them something was happening. A shift in stances, cameras hoisted onto shoulders. Durov was coming. Touching the earpiece, Bishop gave Eva a slight shake of his head. No additional MI6 teams were in position.

Eva's attention was drawn to a murmur of French cursing to the rear of the press gang. It was quiet, but directed at the genealogy of the target's mother, and implied bestiality. She turned to see an annoyed cameraman plug a cable into his camera while shaking his head and staring intently at unknown targets. Eva followed the stare.

Through bobbing heads, Eva tracked whoever had accidentally unplugged the cameraman's cable. Her breath hitched when she saw two figures closely intertwined, walking towards the cordoned-off area. They were headed exactly where the press would engage Durov when he exited his vehicle.

Eva fought to get a glimpse of their faces. Like everyone else, they wore heavy coats and scarves. One head of hair was grey, directly behind was a foppish head of hair that could absolutely be Harry's. More journalists moaned or gave mumbled international curses as the two jostled their way towards the front of the pack.

The objections doubled down as Eva tried to follow the same path. Elbows and deliberately unmoving torsos were less inclined to let anyone else through after Eva's target had barged forward. There was no time for polite "excuse me's". Sharp jabs and pressure-point knee kicks to thighs cancelled any resistance she encountered. Krav Maga did have its uses.

One journalist with a lanyard stating he was from the *New York Times* let out a whining shriek as she delivered a swift jab to the ribs. As Eva issued an insincere apology, the grey-haired figure she'd been pursuing glanced around sharply. Alexie's eyes went wide with panic when he saw her, and he began glancing frantically in all directions, as if expecting the SAS to rappel down the Reichstag.

Harry's startled expression told a different story. One of relief. He beamed like a lighthouse. He'd always had the nicest smile, even if today it was beneath the most ridiculous fake moustache Eva had ever seen. It kind of made sense. The journalists around them hadn't seemed to notice the modern-day Jimmy Hoffa who stood among them. Any one of them could have had the scoop of the year if they'd whipped off that ridiculous fake moustache. None did.

With panicked glances in every direction, Alexie hunted for an escape. He knew he'd been made. If Eva Destruction was in his face, something had gone drastically wrong. Fear smeared across his features he grappled with Harry, as if trying to fling him over the barrier. To his credit, Harry fought back. As a billionaire, he'd received security training from the best in the world.

Realising Harry wasn't going to give in easily, Alexie pushed him away and leapt over the security barricade. Police shouted and rushed towards him, hands darting to their weapons. Agitated orders were issued in German.

"Eva!" Bishop shouted, his hands on the barrier.

He was asking if he should jump the barrier and pursue Alexie, and likely be gunned down by police. He would, too. If Eva asked him to leap into the very jaws of hell he would. For her. She shook her head. *Not now.*

Two police forged ahead of the pack and roughly accosted Alexie before he'd progressed two metres. After a brief pat-down they shoved him heavily towards a waiting police car and escorted him away. The other police backed away, eyeing the press corps for any more trouble. MI6 didn't have Alexie, but at least he was out of play for the time being.

As Eva watched the three figures approach the police car, something struck her as odd. There was something unhurried about their movements, relaxed. Alexie didn't seem upset about being caught. Quite the opposite, in fact. As he got into the back seat he turned to Eva, an amused sneer creasing his weathered lips, and blew her a kiss.

Alexie wasn't being arrested. He was escaping.

The two cops, if they even were cops, were working for Alexie. Of course he wouldn't have left it to chance. He'd always have an out.

*Tea-bagging scrotum puncher.*

She turned her attention to Harry, who grinned at her like the village idiot.

"You saved me." He had a whole litter of puppy dogs in his eyes. "I've been at gunpoint since I —"

Eva cut him off. "Are you armed?"

He baulked. "No, of course not, why would I be..."

Without asking permission, Eva frisked Harry. He didn't protest. In the left inside pocket of his coat, there was the distinct outline of a snub-nosed pistol. She made sure not to pull it out, but guided Harry's hand so he could feel it too. He gasped.

"Not armed, hey?"

"That's not... Jesus."

Using both their bodies to shield the gun from view, she

removed it from his jacket and slipped it into her own. She could smell that it had been recently fired.

Watching the gun transfer, Harry's eyes were wide, his breathing panicked.

Whispering so only Harry could hear, she said, "Don't make a big fuss. Just fly casual, Chewie."

She assumed Alexie had an exact replica of the gun on him. If it were her, Eva would have made sure the gun barrel signatures were as close as possible to match ballistics on the bullets. Damn, the man was good.

Through the crowd, Bishop sidled up to them. He continually scanned for more threats while doing an excellent job of ignoring Harry.

Harry's eyes narrowed. "Well, isn't this awkward?" Receiving no reply, he went on. "Thank you for saving me. I didn't know what was going on. Why they sprang me, brought me here. The... what you found tells me they didn't have my best interests at heart." He paused and touched Eva's face. "But you did. You still care."

In a flash, Bishop snatched Harry's hand and yanked it downward. "You touch her again I'll snap off every finger on your pretty little hand."

Harry groaned at Bishop. "Oh, poor little schoolboy with his unrequited love." His gaze darted between them both as Harry assessed their faces, then his lips parted with the slightest of gasps. "Perhaps not so unrequited."

It was as if Eva could see his heart shattering before her eyes. In an instant, Harry's face fell from cocky bliss to abject disillusionment. Whatever deluded hopes he had clung to were dashed completely.

"Entschuldigen."

A Berlin cop was addressing Harry. Two other officers flanked him.

"Entschuldigen Sie bitte." The cop raised his voice, trying to remain calm.

They must have seen Alexie wrestle with Harry and wanted to

find out his part in the fracas. Were they part of Alexie's plan, or regular cops who'd noticed something amiss in the press corps?

Eva assessed her options. She couldn't fight her way out. The cops were innocent, they weren't part of this, and neither were the journalists. Not only that, but if she caused a fuss, she'd be hauled in too. She was armed, plus she'd taken the gun from Harry. MI6 would spring her, but it would take time, something they didn't have.

They'd come all this way to save Harry only to have him taken from them. The fake moustache would last all of ten seconds—within hours everyone would know who he really was. The infamously missing Horatio Lancing would be missing no more.

Durov's car was rolling to a stop. Eva had an instant to decide. If Harry went with the cops, he'd be safe. Harry glared at her frantically for help. She eyed Durov's car. Eva had to choose.

She nodded at Harry, telling him to go with the cops. Her former lover's face fell, his descent from elation complete. But he complied. The cops gingerly escorted him around the barrier, there was no urgency to their movements.

Watching him led away, Eva felt a pang of regret. *Why do you care so much, bitch?* she asked herself. It was a damn good question.

"Go with them," she said to Bishop. "Make sure they're legit."

Bishop nodded and tapped his ear. He'd be listening. More importantly, he'd come running if she needed him.

There was no time to dwell on it. Durov's car pulled up at the base of the grand stairs. The press were instantly more alert. Flashbulbs popped. Cameras rolled. Journalists preened.

It was the first time Eva had ever seen Durov nervous. Of course he was. It wasn't every day you expected someone to shoot bullets at you. Even when you knew they were meant to miss, it was probably still brown trouser time.

With a plastered-on smile, Durov nervously waved to the crowd and walked towards the stairs in an arc that would take him conveniently near the pack of journalists. He winced, expecting shots that would never come. With each step his anxiety morphed into confusion. His jumpy disposition turned into annoyance.

Surveying the crowd, Durov must have been searching for his father. He didn't see him. He saw Eva. She waved.

When he was within earshot, the journalists began firing questions in English and Russian. He waved at them amiably and walked on, ignoring the queries.

Raising her voice above the others, Eva shouted, "Ethel Tabernacle from *Human Taxidermy Monthly*, a question if I may…"

Durov did his best to ignore Eva until she shouted, "Did you hear they have found the long-lost MI6 spy Amanda Bourke?"

That made him flinch. Indecision clouded his expression. Curiosity getting the better of him, he edged towards Eva, looking as if he'd been slapped across the face. He was no spy. Still trying to understand his father's absence, now Eva was telling him his mother had been captured. His expression was of someone lost in uncertainty.

Recovering slightly, he said, "What does this have to do with me?"

He really must have been stunned. Any politician worth his salt would have avoided the question, or worded it in such a way that they weren't part of the reply. Using the word "me" in there created a link. One Eva was more than happy to exploit.

"Well, she defected to your country and has apparently been living there until she was captured an hour ago. By the British. I was wondering what your reaction was."

Durov gulped. It seemed every journalist was holding their breath. This routine assignment had turned into a story that would push the assassination of the President off the front page.

Feigning a blasé attitude, Durov said, "Indifference."

Eva nodded journalistically, if that was even a word. "I see. Can I quote you on that?"

Giving her a thin-lipped sneer, Durov said, "Certainly."

Eva leaned her head towards the politician. "She says hi."

Gritting his teeth, Durov leaned over and in a barely audible voice said, "You're playing a dangerous game with forces you can't possibly defeat."

Eva smiled and whispered, "I have something you don't."

"A penis?"

Eva baulked and let out a laugh. "Did you… did you just try to insult me by saying you don't have a dick? You're really rattled, dude. You want to try again?" Eva inhaled calmly. "Wait, ready? Okay. I have something you don't." She pointed at him as if to say, *your turn.*

Durov sneered. "A short time to live?"

"There you go! Good job you." She patted him on the shoulder and his bodyguards flinched. "I knew you could do it." Lowering her voice to a whisper, Eva said, "What I have is all the evidence to bring you down." She had nothing of the sort, but he wasn't to know. "And the architect of your rise to power." Extracting her phone, Eva held it up, displaying in high definition the picture she'd taken of Bourke. "That's enough to end you, and you know it. Meet me in four hours, Checkpoint Charlie. Bring Alexie, I'll bring your mum. Come alone. We have a way to end this amicably."

A bodyguard tapped Durov on the shoulder. He'd spent too much time in one place. He had a speech to deliver—the German parliament was waiting. Before striding off, Durov gave Eva the slightest of nods.

Resuming his amicable public persona, Durov waved to the crowd, who responded with a mix of boos and half-hearted cheers. He mounted the stairs, showing his pearly whites for the cameras. As Eva watched him perform for the world she wondered how many people noticed the slouch in his shoulders, the strain in his neck. She'd rattled him. Until that moment, he'd probably never faced much opposition. He no doubt regretted making an enemy of Eva Destruction.

Without a word, Eva made her way through the crowd of journalists. A few asked her about her source on Amanda Bourke, but she kept walking. When she was finally clear of the press, Bishop met her.

"They took him in a squad car. We face scanned the cops, they're legit. The Ops team are trailing the vehicle, it's headed straight for the nearest police station. Seems to check out."

Trying not to show the relief she felt, Eva nodded. The conflict was confusing. Before her was the man she wanted to dive head-first into a relationship with, and they were discussing the safety of her ex-lover. If so much wasn't at stake it would be laughable.

Bishop tilted his head inquisitively. "End this amicably?"

Eva shrugged. "Sounded good, didn't it?"

"It did. What did it mean?"

"Absolutely no idea, but we have four hours to figure something out."

"They'll know it's a trap, Eva. They're a lot of things, but stupid isn't one of them. If they turn up at all, they're going to come in all guns blazing. There's no way this ends without bloodshed."

She sighed. "I know." Eva pulled out her phone. "But either way, it ends tonight."

# CHAPTER TWENTY

Tensions were high. So was Chandler's blood pressure. Eva had christened the colour of the Chief's face as "just about to burst" red. If it got any worse they'd need to cordon off the bulges at the sides of his temples as a traffic hazard.

The conference room had been transformed into a weapons store. A handful of agents loaded a multitude of firearms, readying themselves for the meet at Checkpoint Charlie. There should have been more. Once again, Eva was reminded of MI6's reluctance to go all in on this mission. The number of agents assembled would have a hard time apprehending a little old lady and her shopping. But they had to work with what they had. Every single man and woman in the room had their game faces on. It was a high-risk mission. They knew what was at stake.

There was no way Alexie would turn up alone and unarmed. It was highly likely he wouldn't turn up at all. But there was a small possibility. Alexie must have known the meet was the only chance of getting his wife back before she was flown out of the city. Once back in the UK, Bourke would be untouchable, even to him. He had a tiny window of opportunity, and he may well take it.

The few agents present armed themselves, checked weapons

and verified orders. The plan was simple enough: cover all possible routes in and out with the few assets they had. A sniper was ready to fire if there was trouble. If Alexie did turn up, the team at Checkpoint Charlie was to attempt to apprehend him peacefully, however unlikely that would be.

Chandler's other order still stood: Durov was to be kept out of it unless absolutely necessary. What "necessary" actually meant was open for interpretation, which Eva fully intended to exploit if given half a chance.

The task of arresting Alexie fell to Eva, Bishop and Paul. It was the latter member who had Eva nervous, but she chose not to mention her concerns. Paul wasn't a field agent. Never had been. His insistence on being on the ground made Eva anxious. His emotional investment was too high. Bourke had all but admitted it was Alexie who had killed Paul's father. Eva had always known Paul to be a consummate professional, but she recalled the primal anger he'd directed at Boris. This situation was delicate enough without Paul being a loose cannon. There was much to this plan that put Eva on edge.

"Next time give us more than a few hours," Chandler sneered as he scrutinised the local area map for the tenth time. "We've had to jump through flaming hoops to get the Germans to give us access to the tourist site. We've had to negotiate with apartment owners to get our sniper in place. It's been a nightmare." He shook his head to emphasise the point.

Eva holstered her fully loaded pistol. "You're welcome."

"I'm… what? I wasn't thanking you."

"Oh, sorry, I thought you were thanking me for bringing two of the most wanted spies in from the cold. My mistake."

Chandler sighed and held up a conciliatory hand. "As long as Durov stays out of the picture you'll not only get your thank you, but I'll buy you the most expensive champagne I can find."

"I'll accept that." Eva smiled. "Good deal."

To her surprise, Chandler responded with a smile of his own. "We better not fuck this up."

Eva gave him a nod. "My thoughts exactly."

On the other side of the conference table Bishop and Paul stood huddled over various weapons. Both were decked out in black, shoulder holsters strapped in place. Bishop wore his like a second skin, Paul like an ill-fitting dress-up.

Paul pointed at a Sig Sauer P226 and Bishop nodded. Eva's boss leaned down to pick up the weapon. Paul committed the cardinal sin of handling firearms: his finger was in the trigger guard. Before Eva could shout a warning, the pistol discharged. The shot was deafening in the confined space. Heavily armed agents picked up their own weapons, aiming them in all directions, wondering who the fuck was firing at them.

Thankfully, the bullet missed any personnel, although it blew out the screen Chandler had been perusing only moments before. The monitor sparked before going black. Bishop stared at Paul in shock.

Sheepishly, Paul gingerly placed the gun on the table. "Sorry, must be a hair-trigger."

Eva's anxiety about the mission wasn't going away any time soon.

The wind cut through Eva like a shiv in a prison shower. The Berlin night was freezing, but the sky was crystal clear. Shifting her weight from foot to foot, she attempted to circulate some heat through her body.

"Regretting going with the trench coat?" Bishop's eyes twinkled with amusement.

He stood beside her in his black turtleneck and thermal gear, strikingly similar to what he'd been wearing when they first met. Eva could virtually see the steam radiating off his warm body. Or it could just be Bishop being naturally hot. So hot.

They stood at Checkpoint Charlie, once the most iconic monument to the Cold War, now a holiday photo opportunity. Dozens had died trying to cross the barricade between East and West, but little remained of the schism the checkpoint had represented. Now it was nothing more than a wooden shack on a traffic island on a regular Berlin street. Of course, it was now situated next to a McDonald's, which had closed for the day hours before. It was late. Few cars passed, which only added to the eeriness.

Thankfully the pockets of protest they had encountered seemed to be nowhere nearby. The last thing they needed were random elements wandering into a firefight. Best to have quiet streets to alert them to any approaches.

Eva pursed her lips. "You have something against trench coats?"

"Not at all." Bishop shrugged. "I like imagining what you've got under there. But I have to confess, I'm not very imaginative. I've come up with nothing. Nothing at all."

Eva cast him a playful scowl. "I'm trying to keep my mind on the prize here."

"Oh, believe me, so am I." His eyebrows danced spiritedly.

"Down boy."

"If you two could find a room, or a bucket for me to throw up in, I would be most gracious."

Amanda Bourke stood with them, handcuffed to a handrail, her long coat more practical than Eva's stylish throwback. She had come along without complaint, but curiosity obviously bubbled below her cool surface. Unaware of the confrontation with Durov, the old spy must have assumed she was bait. She had the good sense not to ask.

"So what do I do if I require a lavatory break?" Bourke jangled her handcuffed hand. "Am I expected to soil myself or are you providing the aforementioned bucket?"

"I'm hoping we won't be here much longer." Eva checked her watch.

"He shan't come, you know." She said it in such a matter-of-fact manner Eva almost believed her. "It's simply impossible that he would fall for such an obvious ruse."

"I imagine you'll find out soon enough," Bishop said. "Eva Destruction has a way of redefining impossible on a regular basis."

Turning to Eva, Bourke said, "My, you have quite the fan club, don't you?" Acerbity dripped from every syllable.

Ignoring the bait, Eva walked around the corner of the small wooden hut. Bishop followed.

In a quiet voice, Eva whispered, "This is so risky, Bishop. It could slide into a shitshow in the blink of an eye. We don't have enough personnel. I've put everyone at risk, you included. People could die tonight."

Ignoring the ominous warning, Bishop beamed. "Every life has an end, Eva." He traced his finger along the belt of her coat. "That's what unites every living person. We all die."

"Uplifting. Thank you for totally turning my mood around."

"Shhh." He gave her a wink. "Everyone, every person that's ever lived, has had an end. A series of lasts. A last day. Last time they kissed a loved one goodbye. Last time they ate their favourite meal. Watched their favourite movie. Last time they had ice-cream."

"Cavemen had a last ice-cream?" Eva asked incredulously.

"Quiet now. If this is our last day, our last time, then I'm glad my last anything is with you. I want to be with you, Eva. Whether it's today, next week or fifty years from now, I want my last things to be with you."

More than anything in the world, Eva wanted to pull him in close and kiss him hard. That was another reason she wanted this whole thing to end tonight. He was standing right in front of her. There was, unfortunately, a distinct lack of inappropriate touching, given their fellow agents had eyes on them. She was thankful they hadn't turned on their mikes yet.

"Moving," Paul said in her earpiece, "but if we could turn our focus to the matter at hand?"

"Scrotum-licking cockthistle fondlers." Eva winced at what her boss had heard. "Sorry, Paul."

"You two are lucky I hadn't opened up to Ops yet. I usually hold off because of the Aussie's swearing."

Eva cast an apologetic expression into the night. "Sorry, Paul. Again."

"Never mind that, you have company. From the east, black Range Rover, travelling slow. This could be him. Switching you to Ops in thirty seconds, so mind your language."

"Yes, oh great sphincter sniffing clusterfuck herder."

An audible groan was her answer. The important things out of the way, Eva switched to back to serious mode. Alexie wouldn't come willingly, and he wouldn't come unprepared. As he'd shown many times, he thought six moves ahead and always had a back-up plan. He was unlike anyone Eva had faced before. She had to be ready for anything.

Eva was still worried about MI6's lack of commitment to the mission. There were too many conflicts to have a clear vision as to how it should go down. She just hoped that conflict didn't end up costing anyone their lives. There were far too few agents available for a mission this critical. They were understaffed and under committed. Not a great mix.

Bishop took up position on the other side of Bourke. She wasn't going anywhere without a fight. At the first glimpse of the Range Rover, Eva tensed. She forced herself to relax her stance. She needed to be fluid, to be responsive, to counter anything thrown at her. The one thing she knew not to expect was for the car to roll up and Alexie to get out and simply say hello.

The car rolled up and Alexie got out. He waved and said, "Hello."

Face neutral as she could manage, Eva gave a slight nod. "Been a while. When did we last catch up? Seems like ages."

Warily, Alexie approached, stepping through puddles of water. He wore a dark workman's coat. The random bulges in it could have been the make, or concealed weapons. In a forced jovial tone, Alexie said, "I believe it was MI6. Such a shame I did not make appointment. Sounds like I missed out on all the fun."

"Oh, that's right," Eva said, clicking her fingers as if recalling the memory. "That was before we thought you were dead and you killed a whole mess of agents and whatnot, yeah?"

Exhaling a tired breath, Alexie raised his eyebrows, as if

already bored with the conversation. He turned to Bourke. "My love. I trust you are well?"

In return she beamed warmly. "Darling."

They appeared to genuinely love each other, even after all these years. In different circumstances it would not only be remarkable, but admirable. But these weren't different circumstances.

Eva knew Alexie wasn't there to surrender. "What happens now?"

In the distance there was a low rumble. It sounded like thunder, but it echoed too long, had more elements to it. Eva shut it out.

Alexie smiled. It was as warm as glacial ice. "I take my wife home."

"Really?" Eva knew better than to laugh. The bastard always ensured he had a better poker hand.

The phone in Eva's pocket vibrated. She took a quick glance and typed a response.

"I am sorry, am I not interesting enough for you?" Alexie asked.

Ignoring the old spy, Eva forwarded the message on. Waiting for Bishop to glance her way, she gave him a sharp nod. He returned the gesture and walked away. Confused, Alexie watched Bishop go, but chose not to ask.

The low rumbling turned into a much louder roar. It seemed to be approaching from the south—too far away to be seen. Eva's stomach felt queasy, as if she'd just swallowed a big spoonful of dread. It no longer sounded like thunder. It seemed more human than that.

Echoing footsteps from behind made Eva turn. Across the rain-soaked street, Paul approached. He must have wanted to take Bishop's place, to give Eva support. It didn't fill her with relief.

"What's the rumble?" she asked.

"We're not sure." Paul's stare bored into Alexie. "It's outside our net, we'll have eyes on it in a moment."

Alexie shrugged, as if to say, *what would I know?*

Again, Eva was reminded of how undermanned they were.

Normally they would have whisked Alexie and Bourke away before now, but they couldn't. Not yet.

Bourke lifted a hand but it came to a sudden halt, restrained by the handcuff. She chose to ignore it and politely said, "Darling, this is the offspring of Steven Cavendish."

"Really?" Alexie said pleasantly. "Good spy, your father."

"He was useless as the rest of them," Bourke spat. "Not worth a fraction of you, my darling."

"No, no," Alexie said soothingly to his wife, "you are too harsh, I think. He was very loyal spy." He bobbed his head towards Paul. "I remember him mentioning you as he died. If I recall correctly," he said, rubbing his chin, "he said he had child as he begged for his life while bleeding out in the snow."

Eva's hand reached for her gun instinctively, in part to cover Alexie, but also so she could shoot Paul in the leg if he went crazy.

Face etched from granite, Paul merely answered, "No."

Eva was unsure if Paul's response was a refusal to take the bait or a rejection of Alexie's version of events. Regardless, she didn't take her eyes off her friend. She needn't have worried. Paul appeared to have been prepared for the taunt and remained as calm as a Buddhist monk.

"Charming," Eva said in Alexie's direction.

Paul's head twitched. At first Eva thought it was following on from his conversation with Alexie, but then he held his finger to his ear.

"What kind of not good?"

He must have had a direct link to Control. While Paul talked, Eva turned her attention to Alexie.

"You would be wise to let us go." Alexie looked up the road, as if expecting rescue to come. "I think you would not like my darling in your country. None of you would be safe, I think."

"Sure. But we'll take you as a set, you bastard. Your megalomania has caused the deaths of many. Time for your scheming to end."

The statement seemed to amuse Alexie no end. "She thinks I am architect," he said to his wife. Leaning in, he motioned Eva closer. She stayed put. "I am not behind these things. I am cog, you are big feminist, da? Lady can do all the things? You have no idea what she," he poked a finger towards his wife proudly, "is capable of. She will burn your country to ground if she wants. I will give her match. You want to know what power is. There, that is power. You? You are nothing. She is alpha and omega. She is brains behind all things, and that is why you will all soon be dead."

"Darling, you're embarrassing me." Bourke may have blushed.

With a nod, Alexie regained his composure. "But this is, as they say, neither there nor here." In a slow movement, Alexie glided his hand towards his jacket pocket. Hand on pistol, Eva tilted her head warningly.

"I only reaching for cellular phone," Alexie said with a leer. "I have thing to share, da?"

Eva gave a sharp dip of her head. Her eyes seared hot. Alexie knew if he tried anything it would be his last mistake.

Sidling up to Eva, Paul's face was filled with worry. In a hushed tone he said, "We have to be gone within two minutes. The situation's becoming… complicated. Time to get our skates on."

Not hearing Paul, Alexie continued. Extracting his phone, he gave it a swipe, then held it up to Eva. On the bright screen was a photo of Horatio Lancing standing in front of a TV that was showing footage of Durov's speech at the Reichstag. They'd somehow sprung him from the Berlin Police.

Bourke strained her neck to see the photo. "Oh, very good, my love. Well played."

"Thank you, dumpling. I think this is surprise to…"

His voice trailed off. The cause was Eva's expression. There was no shock or fear, as he had expected. In fact, just the opposite. A broad grin stretched across her face.

Shaking off his surprise, Alexie went on with what appeared to be a pre-prepared statement. "I know you both still love each other, you and this Lancing. You'll do anything to get him back. We can trade my wife for world's most wanted man. I have him to exchange for my darling at moment's notice."

"Everything in that statement is so blatantly wrong it's pretty laughable, dude."

For the first time, Alexie's confidence faltered. This wasn't going down as he'd planned. He knew something was amiss, but seemed unable to figure out what.

"You... you still love him, of course. He has told me great many—"

"Lies. He's told you a great many lies, Alexie." Eva shook her head. "At least from my perspective."

"But you will trade him for—"

"I said you were wrong, didn't I?" Eva leaned in. Conspiratorially, she asked, "Want to find out how wrong?"

Panic crept into the corner of his eyes. By now he had expected Eva to be cowering, begging. That wasn't happening. Bourke saw it too. She searched for salvation, but none would come.

Wet footsteps drew near. Bishop walked behind the two figures. Before him was a shamefaced Durov, replete in tuxedo and tails, a striking contrast to his father's workman's coat. Beside Durov was Harry. Bishop propelled a reluctant Durov forward with a poke from his gun.

Alexie's spun around. "What have you done?"

Learning from the masters, Eva had thought several moves ahead. She knew if Alexie was to come, he wouldn't do so without insurance. The most likely card to play was Harry. Bourke had tried as much when she was cornered. Eva had no idea how Alexie would do it, but if recent weeks were anything to go by, she knew he could achieve much from the shadows. Eva had organised for Harry to be supplied with a phone, making sure he knew it was from her.

The message Eva had received minutes before was from Harry. He was around the corner—he even named the store the car was parked in front of. She'd sent Bishop to retrieve him. The fact that he was with Durov was a bonus. The Presidential Presumptive had obviously not put up a fight, Bishop had a way of being persuasive, especially with gun in hand. With all the key players in one place, the next few minutes would decide the fate of the world.

Alexie's ace turned out to be a three. His hand was poor, no amount of bluffing would make it otherwise. He'd been outplayed.

"Evie," Paul said with urgency, "well played, but we really need to go."

Eva ignored Paul. She was enjoying her moment. "The one thing you never do is give Harry Lancing a phone. You of all people know that." Eva recalled her realisation in Hong Kong. "Nothing is more dangerous than Horatio Lancing with an internet connection."

Bishop shoved Durov forward and he thumped into the wooden shack. Harry beamed at Eva like always. Even though he was bouncing from one captor to the next, he still seemed pleased to see her. Bishop gave her a knowing wink, impressed that Eva's little plan had unfolded as well as it had. Durov's face was a mish-mash of anger at being manhandled and embarrassment at being captured so easily, especially in front of his parents.

Chandler wouldn't be happy, but with both Alexie and Bourke in custody, Durov's little empire would crumble. The political fallout would be minimal—evidence to tie him to events would cascade like sweets from a piñata.

The distant din became less distant. More portentous.

Alexie sneered at Harry. "Why would you do that? We were partners."

With a chuckle, Harry said, "And then you tried to frame me for the assassination of a Presidential candidate. You'll forgive me if I'm not overcome with a sense of camaraderie."

Recalling their conversation in London about the Russian Alexander the Great, Eva said, "No matter how good you are, someone is always there to stab you in the ribs, Alexie."

The old KGB agent fumed. Her moment of gloating over, Eva was about to call in the extraction team when the deafening sound manifested as an angry crowd that tore around the corner. A smattering of signs condemned globalisation and Germany's cosying up to Russia. The protesters wore bandanas over their faces and carried bricks and metal poles, seemingly rummaged from building sites. A peaceful protest it wasn't.

Ignoring the immense rumble from the mob, Alexie didn't turn. Instead of alarmed, he seemed more relaxed.

"That's what I've been trying to say, Evie," Paul said, alarm in his voice. "The Berlin police have been overrun and are regrouping. The mob is here far quicker than I was advised. We have to go."

This wasn't a demonstration, it was a diversion.

The crowd surged towards them. Hundreds of protesters screamed and chanted. Their path direct, they smashed windows in a stampede towards their position. A few at their lead urged the screaming mass towards Checkpoint Charlie, no doubt on Alexie's orders.

"You need to get him out of here," Alexie said to Eva, tilting his head at Durov.

There was a slight waver in his voice. Perhaps he wasn't as in control as she'd assumed. It was possible the mob was more unruly than he'd anticipated.

Coldly, she asked, "Why would I do that?"

"These people, they do not like... he is the next President of the Russian Federation. You need to protect him. He should not be here. He is more important than," he waved his hand at the small group, "all this."

Durov was never meant to be here. Alexie had miscalculated. He'd organised a protest, but never meant for his son to be engulfed in the tsunami about to swamp them.

It wasn't only Durov, they all needed to get out. The crowd, as if spurred on by an order, ran towards them. The screaming intensified. A car burst into flames, to the cheers of the crowd surrounding it. It was out of control.

Both Paul and Eva tapped their earpieces and called in extraction. But it was too late, the mob was closing the gap too quickly. Makeshift weapons danced in the hands of the fearsome mob as they ran.

Alexie pulled at his wife's handcuffs. "Unlock her, please."

Genuine concern was stamped across his haggard face. The elderly spy had asked for both his son and wife to be spared. He actually did care. It was ironic that he pleaded for them to be saved from his own monstrous creation. There would be no extraction in time. They would be engulfed by the mob.

"You bought this on yourself, Alexie," Eva said, pulling out her gun. "This anarchy you've brought, it's your fault. I think there's a life lesson in this for you. That's the thing about anarchists, they don't follow the rules."

Paul and Bishop followed Eva's lead and took out their pistols. Paul urgently issued orders into his lapel while Bishop pushed Harry, Durov and Bourke into a tight huddle at the apex of the wooden hut. Bourke was at the front, because she was still hand-cuffed to the rail.

Alexie hung nearby, not willing to leave his loved ones. "They were meant to be peaceful, they were meant to be…"

He stopped babbling when the surging crowd was within fifty metres. They were like a rabid dog, but with more teeth.

Inhaling a shaky lungful of air, Eva stepped forward, towards the mob.

Alexie's eyes went wide. "What are you… Are you mad?"

Bishop mirrored his concern. "Eva, don't."

With a grimace, she said, "Come on, this isn't even in the top five dumbest things I've ever done."

She turned and held her head high. Gun by her side, Eva marched towards the encroaching mob. They refused to slow. As if revved up by some mass hysteria, they came.

Raising her pistol, Eva fired three shots into the air. That got their attention. Eva lowered her firearm and aimed it at them. It took only a few moments before the crowd surged to a halt. The street wasn't wide, so the bottleneck held back the majority.

As loudly as she could manage, Eva bellowed, "Halt! Zerstreuen!" There, Eva's German failed. "Er, go home to, ah, Fuckoff Strasse, you douchecanoes."

Too late, Eva saw a rock thrown from the rear of the crowd. It connected with her shoulder, forcing her to stumble back a couple of steps.

"Great fucking shot, whoever that was. Now—"

A second rock connected with the side of her head and knocked her off her feet. As she hit the ground with a thud, the world tilted and went black.

When Eva pried her eyes open she was lying on the ground. Everything happened at once, and in slow motion.

A surge behind the halted crowd thrust a new mass of protesters forward. Following Eva's lead, Bishop and Paul fired into the air. The majority of the throng prudently ceased their advance and kept well away from the armed men. A large number, however, chose to run on—perhaps in response to the challenge, as some sort of social commentary, or because in the collective fervour they hadn't heard the gunshots. Whatever the reason, a few dozen came screaming towards Checkpoint Charlie.

The air was filled with the stench of flares, the stink of burning cars. Visibility was down due to the choking smoke. Some of the rabble turned as the front windows of the McDonald's were smashed, and the crowd cheered. Wisely, those who kept moving forward gave the woman with a firearm a wide berth. Some ran on, past the tourist attraction, scrambling towards some unknown goal.

Others slowed their pace and assessed the odd collection of humans huddled together in front of the old shack.

Shaking loose from Paul's grip, Durov positioned himself in a protective stance in front of his mother. Some masked members of the mob assessed Durov, from shiny shoes to expensive haircut. They may have known who he was, or perhaps his manner of dress garnered their attention. Durov's tails juxtaposed starkly with their tatty jeans.

Behind him, Paul quietly said, "Don't."

Assuming the confidence of a politician on stage, Durov raised his palms. Calmly, he called out, "Leute, bitte! Hör mir zu."

The piece of masonry was the size of a large fist. It struck Durov square in the centre of his forehead. Instantly, Bishop and Paul fired more warning shots into the air.

In front of Checkpoint Charlie, Durov's limp form fell forward.

It was as if his soul had been ripped from his body. No movement, no breathing. He was dead before he hit the ground.

The youth who had thrown the rock suddenly burst into an explosion of bone and brain, their head the target of a sniper's bullet. Screams radiated from everywhere.

Now there was complete pandemonium. Protesters ran in all directions. Shouts and cries seemed to come from everywhere. People scrambled over one another to get away from the area. Their panic incited more panic. Every time Eva attempted to stand, she was knocked down.

Alexie dove to cradle his son's lifeless husk. Bourke wailed, and wrenched at the handcuffs, tearing at her restraints like a caged animal. Her anguished cries came from the very depths of her soul. She couldn't reach her son.

Harry hung back, bemused by the fracas before him. Bishop and Paul covered them all.

Eva staggered forward, blood dripping from her forehead. Tears streamed down Alexie's face. He and his wife had watched seen their son killed in the most senseless of ways. He had wanted a diversion. Instead, he'd invited a mob. It had cost him his son's life.

The couple who had manipulated the entire world had been taken down by something they couldn't control. Human nature. Durov was dead because of it.

Reaching into his pocket, Alexie pulled out a pistol. With so much smoke in the air and panicked civilians everywhere, the snipers were unlikely to have a clean shot.

Standing before Eva was a man with a gun in his hand and nothing left to lose.

# CHAPTER TWENTY-ONE

With a sneer of pure malevolent evil, Alexie raised the gun and pointed it at Eva's head.

But before he could take the shot, a hoodie-clad youth ran between him and Eva. Without a moment's hesitation, Alexie shot the youth in the face. The screaming doubled, and so did the panic. In the mass hysteria, more of the mob ran between and around Alexie and Eva.

Into her mic, Eva screamed, "Take the shot. Take the shot!"

"We can't... we can't get a clean... There's too much smoke," the sniper's disembodied voice said. "And there's too many civs running into the fucking line of fire!"

Apparently uninterested, or unable to take a shot at Eva, Alexie turned 180 degrees and fired at the small group at Checkpoint Charlie. Harry ducked for cover as the first bullets hit. Paul and Bishop did the same. More shots quickly followed.

The scattershot rounds chipped wood and kept heads low. Before Paul and Bishop could return fire, Alexie was engulfed by the crowd. It was almost David Copperfield-esque. One instant he was there, the next he was gone.

Chaos reigned.

When Eva finally managed to fight her way through the crowd, her teammates were picking themselves off the ground, guns pointed to either side of the checkpoint.

Eva had to yell to be heard. "Where the fuck is Bourke?"

They all stared at the single dangling handcuff still clipped to the centre of the railing. The chain had been shot off. Alexie hadn't been firing wildly. He'd been helping his wife escape.

All three members of the MI6 team scanned the crowd. The bedlam around them made it extremely difficult to stay focused on any one person, let alone find two in the madness.

"We'll split up. Bishop, you and Paul head that way. I'll take Harry and head left. I want updates every two minutes. Go."

There was no debate. The team selection was the only logical choice. Eva would have preferred to team up with Bishop, but pairing Paul and Harry was a bad idea. Not only did they have a past, but Paul's greenness in the field would be a liability. He needed an experienced agent with him. There was also no way she could send her ex and her future lover off together—They'd be at each other's throats within seconds. Plus, it was kind of creepy.

Eva pushed Harry forward. Gun raised, she searched the crowd for any grey hair. They were in there somewhere.

"Do I get a gun?" Harry asked.

"No," Eva said, humour dancing in her words. He already knew the answer was coming. "But I'll tell you what, I'll do my best to not shoot you myself."

"Come on," Harry said. "You know I'm not going to shoot you. You need the coverage."

He was right. Given the pandemonium around them, someone had to have her back. Harry had been through all the security training and knew how to handle a firearm with respect. "Alright, fine."

Pulling out her second pistol, she ejected the clip, checked the rounds, slapped it back in place and released the slide guard. She handed Harry the loaded weapon.

"You know that's sexy as hell, right?"

Eva ignored him and walked on. More and more protesters

flooded around them. Some were panicked, still believing they were part of a protest. Others were there for the destruction and anarchy.

Harry clung to Eva's back as she forced her way through the crowd. "This is all my fault, you know? Durov, Alexie and Amanda having gotten this far. They used me, it's my fault. I should end it."

"How do you plan on doing that?"

"I get up there." He nodded to the roof of Checkpoint Charlie. "And lure them in. Then you catch them by doing your spy thing. Be a, you know, a spy."

"Why would you do that? Risk your life like that?"

"What do I have to live for?" Harry's face was completely devoid of humour. "Do you have any idea what it's like to have the woman you love with all your heart stare back at you with such hatred, such contempt?"

Eva stopped walking and stared at Harry. "I don't hate you, Harry. I never could. I may as well stop breathing."

For an instant, there was a fragment of hope in his eyes.

"But I don't love you," she added. "I did. Oh my god, with every atom of my body, I did. But I'm not that person anymore." Eva ran her hand along his arm. "Do I hate you? No. Am I in love with you? No, Harry, I'm not."

"Oh." His heart seemed to shatter all over again.

She gave him a sad smile. "And before you ask, I can't let you escape."

"Then arrest me."

"I can't do that either. Jails mean nothing to you."

"Then what?"

She shrugged. "We'll figure it out. Come on. Bad guys to catch first."

They wandered through the crazed crowd. Eva was unsure if they could find Bourke or Alexie in this madness. Her gamble may well have cost them their chance to catch two old spies, as well as the life of a tyrannical politician. She had to wonder if it was worth it.

"Freeze!"

Eva and Harry turned, and so did half the crowd. On the other side of Checkpoint Charlie, Paul pointed a shaking gun at Alexie's chest. Eva rushed towards the confrontation, but protesters darted between them.

*Where the fuck is Bishop?*

Even though he had the advantage, Paul didn't fire. Noticing his hesitation, Alexie raised his gun own and calmly pulled the trigger.

Nothing happened.

More clicking. Nothing. Alexie was out of bullets. Frantically, he reached into his pocket for a new clip and expelled the spent one. Eva ran towards them but couldn't get a clean shot.

"Put the weapon down!" Paul shouted. "I *will* shoot!"

Alexie ignored him and slapped in a new clip. the whole time he was reloading, Paul could have fired but didn't. His gun stayed aimed at Alexie, and shook, but he didn't fire. The murderer of his father stood before him, but Paul had frozen. After a lifetime of hatred, of being denied a parent, of seeking vengeance, Paul was unable to pull the trigger. Whether it was fear, lack of training or the reality of actually taking a life, Eva didn't know. Paul's hand continued to tremble.

Alexie pulled back the slide to chamber a round. Finger on the trigger, he sneered.

The gunshot shocked Eva into stopping her advance mid-stride. The sound sent a fresh wave of panic through the mob. She was jostled left and right and pushed off balance.

The body lay on the ground, a tiny bullet hole directly between the eyes. It was the perfect shot. Deadly.

Next to Paul, two metres away, Bishop stood with gun in hand. Smoke escaped from the barrel.

"Sorry," Bishop turned to Paul. "Must be a hair-trigger."

Alexie Barinov lay motionless on the Berlin street, a pool of blood spreading from the back of his lifeless head.

The scream was so loud they all turned, even Paul in his dazed state. Amanda Bourke stared at her husband's corpse in disbelief.

She must have seen the shot and watched the man she adored fall to the ground, limp and lifeless. Disbelief slapped across her distraught face.

Stepping forward, Harry stood beside her. His eyes moist, he too gazed down at Alexie Barinov's prone body.

"Oh, Amanda, I'm so…"

Still stunned, she turned to Harry. Her face hardened in an instant. Her actions were swift and precise as she disarmed Harry and held the gun to his head, using his body as a shield.

Without issuing a warning, she fired randomly at the three MI6 agents. Staggering backwards, she yanked Harry by his collar, her shots relentless.

Bishop doubled over with a pained grunt. Eva took a bullet to the left arm and spun around. Paul returned fire, but the shots went wide.

Amanda Bourke and Harry were engulfed by the crowd.

"Medic! Man down!" Eva screamed. "Repeat, man down!"

She had no idea if their team would find them in the mayhem. Terrified, she crawled desperately towards Bishop, who didn't move. She ignored the searing pain in her arm. Paul stood defensively above him, gun sweeping the crowd.

When she reached Bishop, Eva let out an agonising wail. She tore open his jacket. His black turtleneck darkened even more, his face pale. He'd been shot in the belly and the blood flowed in all directions. His hand on the wound wasn't doing anything to stop the blood spurting through his fingers.

"Medic!" she screamed desperately, tears streaming down her face. "Get me a fucking medic!" Her voice broke.

"Hey." Bishop coughed painfully. "Hey, it's okay. I'll be okay, Eva."

"You're a terrible fucking liar."

"See?" He inhaled deeply. "Missed the lungs, my heart's still ticking. Think it missed all the important bits. Looks worse than it is."

"I'm not leaving you. No fucking way, you bastard."

Bishop gave her a weak smirk. He grew paler by the second.

"I'll be fine. Paul's got me." He nodded in the direction Bourke had run. "You go. You'll never have another chance. Go save him. Go get her. Finish the mission. End this."

He was right. She glanced at Paul. His eyes were wide. There was no way she could send him after Bourke.

Eva slid her hand across his cheek. "I love you, you sexist son of a bitch."

"I love you too, you feminist know it all."

Leaning down, Eva gave Bishop a kiss, then stood on unsteady feet.

"You need to have that fixed up." Paul dipped his head at her shoulder.

"Later," she said.

Taking her first step, Eva's legs faltered and she staggered. The world tilted slightly, but she remained upright. Forging ahead, she checked her weapon and strode towards the street where Bourke had disappeared with Harry.

With her son dead, her lover gone, Bourke's vengeance would be swift and terrible. She would stop at nothing and be utterly ruthless.

Eva pursued her prey. She raced after the architect of it all.

It would end tonight.

After only a few minutes, the crowd thinned. Genuine protesters had fled. Without the cover of the mob, the troublemakers soon did the same. Most headed back in the direction they'd come from, in the south. Eva's path north was thankfully relatively clear of protesters. The night was cold and still, and the streets grew more silent with every step.

Not trying to conceal her pistol, Eva limped towards where Bourke should have been. Her head throbbed, and her left arm was next to useless. But she walked on. Now was no time for rest. She had somebody to save, and vengeance to extract.

Using every mind trick she knew, Eva tried to keep the image of a bleeding Bishop from her mind. Regret at not staying wouldn't help her capture Bourke. It would only aid her prey. She couldn't allow that.

Doubling her pace, Eva jogged on. Every part of her body screamed in protest. She ignored them all.

Several blocks later, she saw two huddled figures ahead, lurching forwards. One woman, one man. Eva broke into a run. Assessing their speed and direction, she split off down a side street to overtake the pair. Lungs screaming for relief, Eva ran like her life depended on it.

Rounding the corner, Eva crossed a large open space. Once she reached the other side, she heaved in huge lungfuls of air. She fought to control her breathing, knowing if there was a firefight, she'd need a steady hand. Leaning against some scaffolding, she covered the corner with her pistol, waiting for the couple to walk into range at any second.

Distracted for an instant, Eva realised where she was. She stood at the base of the Brandenburg Gate. The whole structure was covered in scaffolding. It was laughably fitting that Eva was to face Bourke at what was the focal point of the Berlin Wall, the divide between East and West.

Slow footfalls announced the arrival of two figures. Eva tensed, then relaxed into her firing stance.

As the pair came into view, Eva yelled, "That's far enough, Bourke."

Seeing the gun pointed at her head, the traitor knew there was no time to raise her own weapon. Harry was positioned in front of her. Eva had no clean line of fire.

Bourke scowled. "How did you find me?"

"You don't listen, do you?" Eva motioned her gun towards Harry. "He has a phone, remember? We were tracking him on it."

Harry shrugged at Bourke. "It's not like I was going to tell you."

"Agh!" Bourke pushed Harry to the side and shot from the hip. Her shots were wild and unfocused, but they sent Eva scurrying behind the scaffold.

With one blast, Bourke shot out the padlock for the gate labelled "Aufzug". *Elevator.*

Wrenching the gate open, she shoved Harry forward and slammed the gate behind her. There was the whirring sound of an external building elevator in use.

Eva gazed up at the poles that made up the scaffolding. The Brandenburg Gate was tall, but not ridiculously so. Twenty-five metres, maybe.

She climbed.

Ignoring the searing pain, Eva forced herself to use her left arm. The pain was unbelievable as the wound tore from within, but she couldn't stop. Too much was at stake.

There would be no reasoning with Bourke. She was inconsolable at the loss of her son, then the love of her life had also been killed before her eyes. She really did love the old bastard. Amanda Bourke was grief-stricken and irrational. The woman must have been operating on autopilot—long-dormant survival instincts were driving her now. How long would that last? Soon she would realise all she'd lost, and how little she had to live for. She truly would have nothing left to lose.

Eva climbed.

Heaving herself onto the top of the scaffolding, Eva rolled onto the green copper roof. After a brief glimpse of the cobblestones far below, she rose on unsteady feet. Bourke and Harry stood before the Quadriga sculpture of the horse-drawn chariot at the apex of the gate. Bourke had her gun aimed at the elevator shaft. She hadn't noticed Eva's ascent.

Bourke's manic panting was too loud. It masked Eva's footfalls. She was looking in the wrong direction.

Eva extended her hand and put her gun to Bourke's temple. "It's over."

Bourke turned, shock smacked across her face. She sighed in defeat. Dropping the gun, she stepped back and held up her hands.

Harry shook himself free of his captor. "I seem to require a lot of saving lately."

In spite of recent events, Eva spared him a joyless smile. "I guess we swapped, and you turned into the Bond girl in the end."

Harry tilted his head. "Is that what you think? You were never a Bond girl, Eva. You were far more than that. You were my everything."

"Oh, for fuck's sake." Bourke kicked Harry forward, sending him toppling into Eva, then she picked up the pistol and fired. The bullet hit Eva's gun and it flew from her hand. It sailed over the side and smashed onto the hard cobblestones below.

In a fraction of a second the tables had turned.

Eva held up her hands, one bloody and hurting like hell. Bourke paced, rubbing the grip of the pistol against her temple.

"What do you do to these poor idiots, woman?" She howled. "You turn hardened men into snivelling sycophants. I'd be impressed if I wasn't so sickened."

Eva went to rise, but Bourke stepped towards Harry, wrapped her arm around his neck and held the gun to his head.

She let out a bitter laugh. "It's funny, you know? In the space of just a few minutes I'll have wiped out all your lovers."

"Darlin'," Eva said evenly, not wanting to make any sudden moves, "you're going to need more than a few minutes for that. There's quite a number. We better order pizza."

"Shut up!" Bourke screamed.

She was becoming more unhinged as the seconds ticked by. She backed away to the edge of the roof, dragging Harry with her. She was heading for the elevator, but was smart enough to put as much space between herself and Eva as she could. Bitter wind swirled around her.

"It's fitting, you know?" Bourke scoffed. "I take out the two men you loved, just like you did mine. That's *fair*, isn't it? Eye for an eye and all that bullshit. You cost me everything, little girl." She ground the barrel into Harry's temple. "It's only fair I repay the debt."

Scanning the roof, Eva searched for anything she could use. Any distraction, any weapon. There was nothing. She was out of options.

"Eva." Harry spoke softly, with Zen-like calm. "You once asked me how much I loved you, what I would do for you." Harry looked down, eyes heavy. "At the time, I didn't know how to reply."

Desperation in her voice, Eva said, "Harry, don't. Please."

"I finally have an answer, Eva. I love you this much."

Using his legs, Harry propelled himself backwards, into Amanda Bourke. She let out a grunt, and her foothold faltered. The force of Harry's shove was too much for her slight frame. They both careened over the edge.

"No!" Eva scrambled to the lip of the roof.

The roar of the wind was all Eva could hear. It buffeted her, flinging her hair across her face.

Frantically she peered over the edge. Far below, two bodies lay sprawled on the ground, their figures at grotesque, unnatural angles.

Screams erupted from passers-by who ran to their aid. They needn't have bothered.

Horatio Lancing and Amanda Bourke were dead.

# CHAPTER TWENTY-TWO

Eva watched from the boardroom window as a smattering of boats slowly navigate their way down the Thames. Adjusting the sling around her arm, Eva sipped her coffee. It was the same room where, years before, she'd first been offered a job at MI6. The day she found out Paul didn't work for Treasury. The day her life changed forever. The day she'd agreed to help catch Horatio Lancing.

That day she'd set herself on a course that would lead to her to the top of the Brandenburg Gate. To Harry's death.

A week later, she still hadn't come to terms with it. She meant what she'd said. She had loved Harry, but she was no longer in love with him. That didn't mean his death hadn't affected her. It had—far more than she would have expected. The man who was once everything to her, her entire life, was gone.

Devastating as it was, Harry's death did serve a purpose. All the damage he'd wrought by siding with Bourke, Alexie and Durov had been partially undone by his final action. The new Cold War had thawed. Without mad men and women pulling levers, tensions had eased, if only a little.

It would take time for Eva to get over Harry's death, but she'd try. He'd pulled Eva into his orbit and his actions had led to her becoming a spy, but now he was dead. Now Eva could forge her own destiny without the dark spectre of Harry Lancing hovering over her. She'd make it a worthy one.

The fallout from Durov's death was minimal. Dozens of witnesses had attested to a random act of violence at the hand of an unruly mob. The deaths of the youth who'd thrown the fatal rock and the one Alexie had shot were put down to mob madness. Certain groups cried for further investigation into the Presidential candidate's death, but without Durov's blackmail supplying wind to his political sails, the seas were soon becalmed.

Amanda Bourke's death scored headlines momentarily before being brushed aside by news of an impending royal birth. With no one to interview about her sudden reappearance, then death, the defection story soon retreated to conspiracy sites and Reddit chat boards.

As far as the public were concerned, Harry was still missing. He would forever remain so. Like his fellow Australian, Harold Holt, the world would never know the fate of the infamous Horatio Lancing.

There were no news articles lamenting the passing of Alexie Barinov.

Thankfully, no one had connected the deaths and recent events into one story. As far as the public knew, they were all unrelated events, each lasting one news cycle before the world moved on to the next.

"Penny for your thoughts?"

Bishop stood unsteadily in the doorway. He held himself up with a cane. The bandages around his ribs were visible through his tight-fitting t-shirt.

"That's a bit cheap, isn't it?" Eva asked with a grin. "Pretty sure my thoughts would be worth a smidge more than that. Like, ten pennies, at least."

"Look," Bishop hobbled in, "I'm prepared to go as high as fifteen."

"Fifteen, eh?" Eva let out a whistle. "You must really want them, hey?"

They kissed tenderly, conscious of each other's injuries. They didn't want to be too rough. Yet.

They both sat, waiting for Paul. They didn't have to wait long.

"Well, if it isn't the walking wounded!" he said, in what Eva saw as forced joviality.

Paul had also had many wounds to address in the past week, though his weren't nearly as physical. The shame at his failure to kill Alexie was slowly easing.

Not one to pussyfoot around, Eva had accosted him on the flight back to London. She'd reminded Paul that he wasn't a field agent, and that taking a life isn't like it's made out to be on TV. It's not bang, reload and move on. The act of killing stains a soul forever. She was glad her friend had been spared that pain. He wasn't a killer, he shouldn't be burdened with that for the rest of his days.

What he did have, though, was closure. The burden he had carried for years, the mystery of his father's death, was finally solved. Not only that, the perpetrator had been held accountable for his crimes.

That reminded Eva of a loose thread. "Paul, what's going to happen to Boris?"

Paul frowned. "As he wasn't, ah, responsible for the, hmm, things we thought he was responsible for, we've offered him permanent residency. His Majesty's government will provide him with a nice little house in a nice little village and a nice little pension to spend as he pleases. We wouldn't have got as far as we did without him."

"Great to hear." Eva was pleased to have some good news.

"Well, at least someone gets the thanks of the government," Bishop said with a tinge of sarcasm.

"Ah." Paul raised a finger. "That reminds me, I have something for you both."

Reaching into his pocket, Paul extracted an envelope and slid it across the table. Opening it, Eva gasped and leapt from her chair. She rounded the table and kissed Paul on the cheek.

"What did I miss?" Bishop asked.

Eva did a little dance, as best she could with one arm in a sling. Extracting the thick paper, she held it up to Bishop.

"Two plane tickets to the Maldives."

"I think you've earned it." The joy on Paul's face was obvious. "You two deserve some happiness. I called you in for this little chat to let you know that you're all done. No more briefings. Four week's leave is all yours. Make the most of it, we'll have a lot for you when you come back, believe me."

"Yes boss," Eva said with a sloppy salute.

Paul rolled his eyes and kissed the top of Eva's head. He gave a Bishop a firm handshake and left. They grinned at one another across the boardroom table.

"My, Mr Bishop, whatever will we do with four weeks in the Maldives?"

"I can think of a few dozen things." With his trademark dazzling eyes on her, he added, "I'm going to treat you like a shin in the dark."

Eva laughed. "What?"

"I'm going to bang you on every piece of furniture in the hotel room."

Eva swaggered over and sat on his lap. "I look forward to it."

"You should."

He had such a cheeky smile, Eva couldn't help but return it. "We have some planning to do."

"Pretty certain I just gave you the plan," Bishop said.

She rolled her eyes. "This is the plan to get us to your very good plan."

Bishop gave her a wink. "Where should we go?"

"I know just the place."

Sitting in Eva's coffee shop, the two pored over brochures for the

Maldives. With coffee cups strewn across the table, Eva and Bishop sat huddled in each other's arms, flipping through travel catalogues and making notes.

"You know," Eva began, "we'll have weeks together, with no mission to discuss. You okay with that?"

"I can't wait." Bishop's face told her he meant every syllable.

"I want to get to know you, Charles. The real you." She poked him in the arm. "I want to know everything. Where you came from, your history. Everything. I want to know all your dirty secrets."

"Are you sure?" Bishop asked warily. "It's quite a ride."

"I'm sure." Eva snuggled into him. "We have time." She enjoyed the smell of him. Very masculine. Very him. "What kind of secrets do you have? Tell me something about the real you."

"Well," Bishop sighed hesitantly. "Bishop's not even my real name."

"What?"

## THE END

# KISS MY ASSASSIN

**You've never met a spy like this before!**

When the Turkish ambassador crashes his car in central London, it launches an unforeseeable series of catastrophic events—and a naked body.

MI6 spy Charles Bishop flies headfirst into intrigue, gun battles and assassinations. He's on the hunt for a mysterious and powerful arms-dealing organisation named Kali—and they have him squarely in their sights.

Along the way he falls for a mysterious woman who may just be the death of him.

Fast-paced, with whip-smart dialogue and twists at every turn, *Kiss my Assassin* is the very definition of unputdownable.

# COMING JULY 2019

To be the first to find out when the new Bishop novels will arrive, and to get free stuff (who doesn't like free stuff?), sign up for my VIP Book Club at:

https://davesinclair.com.au/newsletter/

# ACKNOWLEDGMENTS

It was a little sad closing off this chapter of Eva! It was always my intention to complete Harry's tale and bring some closure to certain parts of Eva's story. Is this the end? I highly doubt it! As you saw, a new Bishop series is coming and I'm already having way too much fun bringing that to life.

This book came together so easily. It almost wrote itself. Well, not really, I helped a...bit. But getting my crazy ideas down was made so much easier with the phenomenal help and support I receive every day.

First and foremost, Kristi, who has boundless encouragement and support it makes me thankful so many times a day it's ridiculous. Monkey heart unicorn.

Then there is the crazy G-Mob, all great writers and completely crazy individuals. Craig, Justin, Luke, Nathan, Steve, Amanda and Amanda have provided support, assistance, insight and laughter when I need it most. Plus they know how to make a mean Old Fashioned. Go read their stuff! http://genremob.com

Thanks to my beta team, including Steve & Gerard. Thanks for making me doublethink setting the whole thing on the moon. You guys are smart. Thanks to Nathan who formats my pages to make me look almost professional.

A big thank you to my editor Vanessa Lanaway. Not only does she make my words goodererer, she actually looks forward to reading more Eva adventures. Crazy person.

As always, the biggest of big hugs to my two awesome and amazing daughters, Quinn and Esther. I'm doing my best to ensure they grow up as fearless as Eva, because the world needs more sweary heroes.

Thank you also goes to my VIP Book Club team who receive my exclusive newsletter. There's a mention in this book of Mark Field – he won a competition in the newsletter to be murdered in this very book. I mean, who doesn't want to be murdered in a book?

Finally, thank you to the reader. I love hearing from you, and don't be shy dropping a review, it is greatly appreciated. Thank you and here's to many more adventures!

Cheers!

To find out more, you can stalk me at all these semi-reputable places:

https://davesinclair.com.au
https://twitter.com/thedavesinclair
https://facebook.com/DaveSinclairAuthor

This edition first published 2018